Sister Girls

Sister Girls

ANGEL M. HUNTER

Hunter

Sister Girls

By Angel M. Hunter

Urban Books
6 Vanderbilt Parkway
Dix Hills, NY 11746

ISBN 0-7394-5426-9

*This is a work of fiction. Any references or similarities
to actual events, real people, living, or dead, or to real
locals are intended to give the novel a sense of reality.
Any similarity in other names, characters, places, and
incidents is entirely coincidental.*

Gift
|||||
MJ

i 13780025

Acknowledgements

God, My Father... I thank You for assisting me in putting these words on paper and walking by my side when I've needed You. I thank You for my sister girls and my brothers in spirit, who have supported me in struggles near and from a distance. I thank You for Your grace and mercy.

Sister Girls is dedicated to my late grandmother, "Nanny" Marian LaJean Watson.

I've decided to pass her words of wisdom on to my readers.

For the ladies, sisters, friends and women:
Don't hesitate to state
what's on your mind or what's in your heart.
Speak with pride and assurance,
and like a lady, always depart.
Whatever situation you find yourself in,
whether with a loved one, enemy, lover or friend,
hold your head high and never doubt.
When the going gets tough, there's always an out.
We've all made mistakes, just know when to move on.
Each day is a new beginning, a way of being reborn.
Keep a sharp pair of boots, a nice suit,
a hat and some sexy shoes.
Take care of your body, your skin, your hygiene;
frequent a spa or two.
Know your boundaries; ask for what you want,
and if you've got that special charm, it's okay to flaunt,
just don't offend.
If you question someone's motive,
ask them their purpose,
but keep yours in mind.
Listen to these words of wisdom,
they will carry you through time.

I send my love to Tony Irby (I'll be your groupie, baby) and my son Anthony, "my biggest supporter."

My Appreciation goes out to....
Carl Weber for his belief in my work.
Roy Glenn for his words of wisdom.
Martha Weber for her guidance.

Please Feel Free To Email Me At msangelhunter@aol.com And Visit My Website At www.essenceofselfcenter.org Or www.angelmhunter.com

CRYSTAL

Dressed in red leather pants and a leather vest that fit like a second skin, with red stiletto boots, hair pulled back so far that it tugged on her eyes, Crystal paced back and forth ten steps. Every now and then she'd look to her left, smirk and turn to her right, where in the center of a small round table sat a gun. Filled with rage, anger, hurt and betrayal, the only thing on Crystal's mind was revenge.

The room was pitch black, except for the flickering flames from the candles placed sporadically in the room. Finally making a decision, Crystal went toward the gun. She appeared to be in a trance. Picking up the gun gently as if it were a newborn, she ran her fingers up and down the metal, caressing it. She looked to her left and aimed.

There sat a man shaking, with sweat pouring down his face. His hands were tied behind his back and his feet tied to each leg on the chair that barely contained him.

"I'm sorry. I'm so sorry. Don't do this," he pleaded with tears running down his face.

Instead of responding, Crystal smiled and pulled the trigger.

Billie's bark startled Crystal out of her nightmare. Glancing at the clock on her nightstand, she saw that it was not quite 5:00 a.m. She also noticed the empty half- pint bottle of vodka.

"Ugh," she moaned and drew the blankets over her head. "Just one more hour and a Tylenol, that's all I need."

Billie barked again.

"All right, all right." She threw the blanket off, stumbled out of the bed, lifted her arms in the air and stretched. She must have tossed and turned all night. Crystal could hear the cracks and creaks of her cramped muscles and tired bones.

Placing her hands on her hips, she glared at Billie. "What do you want from me?"

Billie peered up at her with his pleading eyes and Crystal frowned. "Don't give me that look. I'm still tired."

Dragging her body across the newly installed plush cream-colored carpet and down the stairs, Billie lapping behind her, she went into the kitchen, pulled the dog food from under the sink and poured some into his dish. Looking at Billie, she told him, "When you're done, let yourself out."

She headed back up the steps and went into the bathroom. Hopping across the cold tiled floor to the little rug in front of the sink, she looked in the mirror and was not happy with what she saw staring back. Not only were her eyes bloodshot, she could have sworn she saw more lines around them today than yesterday. She leaned forward and took a closer look. Now she was positive that she did.

Crystal shook her head in the mirror. She had fallen asleep in her clothes once again. She pulled her shirt over her head, looked at her size 34B breasts and wished they were a C cup. She unzipped her jeans and pulled them down along with her panties. Standing back, she examined her size 6 figure. The pounds were just falling off.

Crystal didn't know whether to be pleased or concerned. Not even a month ago she was an athletic size 8. She wasn't trying to lose any weight. Crystal used to work out a minimum of four times a week. It recently trickled down to once a week and that was from guilt.

She ran her non-manicured hands through her dreadlocks, which fell between the center of her back and her waist. She pulled them on top of her head and tied them into a knot. Turning her back to the mirror, she reached into her shower and turned it on as hot as she could stand it then climbed in.

"Mmmm." Crystal stood directly under the shower head. The steam from the water relaxed her. She closed her eyes, threw her head back and dropped her shoulders, letting the heat and pressure take her away. She stood like that until she felt the water turning cool. Opening her eyes, she reached for her loofah and vanilla scented bath gel, trying to scrub away her feelings of doubt, fear and anxiety.

People looking from the outside in would have no idea that she felt this way. Her life seemed perfect. She was 31, single, had no kids, attractive, in shape, a partner in a law firm, owned a home in the suburbs and drove a white Lexus SUV. She was the shit. But the material things that meant everything to most people meant nothing to Crystal. Owning a home, driving an expensive vehicle, all those things that were admired by others didn't make her feel any more complete. Just as quick as she bought them, she knew she could lose them. She yearned for something solid, maybe even some*one* solid. Something was missing in her life, and it was getting harder every day to maintain the front. Shit, she wasn't as strong as she appeared to be. It was all an act. She had to convince herself with the sips of liquor she took day in and day out that she'd get through another day.

She wanted to pull herself out of the mental rut she was in.

How? How can I do that? she asked herself. *Maybe I need a change—a change of scenery, and a change of pace. A change within.*

Making a change was easier said than done. To Crystal, her life was lacking. Each day unfolded like the one before it, and she was growing tired of doing the same thing day in and day out—work, home, work, home. She was tired of seeing the same faces, hearing the same voices. Most of all, she was tired of being lonely.

She thought of all these things as she chose her outfit; a long, black fitted sweater dress and duster with boots. Crystal took one last look in the mirror and sighed. Opening her Louis Vuitton purse, she pulled out her M.A.C. lipgloss and applied it. Smacking her lips together, she pulled out her slightly tinted prescription glasses and placed them over her eyes.

"Yeah, that's better." She was ready to start her day.

She walked down the stairs and called for Billie. When he didn't come barking, she wondered where he was. Before she could open the front door and yell out for him, he came charging in.

Crystal bent down and patted his head. "That's my baby. Mommy's sorry for snapping at you this morning."

Billie looked up at her like he understood.

Crystal grabbed her briefcase, which was near the front door and stepped out into a slight breeze. Breathing in the scent of fall, she looked down the street at the kids on the sidewalk. It was the first day of school and there was an energy in the air. Damn, she remembered those days when she didn't have a care in the world. When she had no bills, nor did she have a business to run.

Gem, Carlson and Shaw, Attorneys at Law, was located in the downtown area of Riverhead, New Jersey. Located on the fifth floor of one the few high rises in the area, the business where Crystal was partner took up the entire floor. It included a reception area, a walk-in closet used for storage and four suites. Each attorney occupied one suite for use as an office The fourth suite was for meetings. There were also two bathrooms, one with a shower and one without.

Crystal Gem had two partners, Susan Carlson and Elsie Shaw. They were quite a team. Crystal was the business minded one, making sure every detail was in place, testimonies were tight and paperwork was up to date. Susan was the take no prisoners, tell it like it is, no holds barred attorney, and Elsie was the laid back one, the hand holder.

Crystal and Susan coming together was a godsend. They went to the same high school, where they befriended one another. They lost contact once they went to college, then ran into one another at a class reunion neither wanted to attend. After talking for over an hour, they discovered they were in the same profession, both working for firms where not only did they feel unappreciated but partnership wasn't likely.

"Have you thought about going out on your own?" Crystal asked Susan.

"Of course, but I don't think it's something I could do alone."

"Well, why don't we get together and see what we can come up with, see if our work ethics are the same and perhaps . . ."

She didn't have to finish her thought. Susan was thinking the same thing. After talking that night and meeting several times over the next few months, they decided to start their own firm, but not before contacting a headhunter to find a third person. They knew they wanted an all-female firm. Finding the right woman was the mission at hand. They met with several and grew discouraged because either the interviewees came in with chips on their shoulders, expecting to take over, had foul personalities or didn't have the funds to put up for partnership. Everyone was required to invest the same amount of money and be willing to comfortably take a loss during the first couple of years if that's what became necessary. Finding such a person turned out to be quite the challenge.

Right when they were considering giving up on their search, in walked Elsie. They were taken with her laid-back attitude and her confidence, and the fact that she was attractive and didn't play it up also helped. Most importantly she had the money to put up. After meeting with her a couple of times, they drew up contracts and became partners.

Gem, Carlson and Shaw was now in its third year of business and semi-successful, making enough profit to cover overhead and have a little extra left over.

Pulling into the parking lot, Crystal reached in the back of her car for her briefcase then headed for the elevator. From the corner of her eye, she saw Lange Houston heading her way. His firm was two floors up from hers. Lange was a criminal attorney, and she'd seen him in action quite a few times. Each case he'd won. She was in awe, not only with his looks—tall, at least 6 feet 4 inches tall with a creamy caramel complexion, wide shoulders and broad back—but also with his charisma. He displayed a confident attitude that bordered on arrogance.

Crystal wanted this man, but knew he was off limits. He was married—happily, she believed. Each time she ran into him and his wife, they were holding hands. Was it real or was it a front? She wondered. If the opportunity ever arose, she wasn't sure what she would do.

Quickening her pace, she made it to the elevator and tried to press the button to close the door. She didn't want to be alone with him.

Lange called out, "Hold the elevator!"

She looked up and saw him jogging toward her. In her mind he was naked, muscles bulging.

"Hey, lady," he said once he stepped on.

Lady. He always called her that. One day she would ask him why. For now all she could manage to mutter was "Hi."

She wondered what it was about him that made her freeze up. Stupid question. Heck, most of her sexual fantasies starred him, and if he was as good in the flesh as he was in her dreams . . . Have mercy!

"It is a little chilly in here," he commented, breaking into her thoughts.

"Chilly? What makes you say that?"

"You're standing with your arms crossed like you're cold."

Looking down, Crystal uncrossed her arms and laughed. "Isn't that something?"

The elevator reached her floor and she stepped off. Lange watched her every move.

Unbeknownst to Crystal, she was considered to be one of the most attractive women in the building. A few months earlier, Lange overheard some of the guys in the cafeteria discussing a bet. Who would get Crystal first? The men believed she was untouchable, off limits, and they were determined to break her down. Lange wanted to tell them they didn't stand a chance, but knew he had no say, being a married man and all.

Lange had been noticing Crystal a lot recently. He'd watched her in court and admired her from afar, more so than he wanted to admit. Maybe the fact that his marriage was falling apart contributed to it, maybe he was tired of his wife not being in the mood. Whatever it was, he knew it was unhealthy.

The elevator closed as he licked his lips.

As Crystal walked past the secretary's desk, she said, "Jewell, if I get any phone calls, take messages. I'll let you know when I'm available."

Trying to hide the gum that was in her mouth, Jewell mumbled, "Okay."

When Crystal stepped into her domain, she opened her blinds. Her office had a view of the streets, and when her day got hectic, she watched the people below and wondered what they were doing, where they were going, and if they needed an attorney.

Her office, like her home, was her haven. She spent a lot of time decorating it, personally picking the mahogany desk, the mahogany chair that fit every curve on her thinning body, and the hardwood floors that she spent too much money on.

She relaxed into her chair and thought about last night's dream, the same one she'd been having for over a week. What did it mean? It couldn't only be about revenge. There had to be more to it, but what? There were definitely a lot of people she wanted to get even with, that she would like to seek revenge on. There was one in particular, but that incident happened a long time ago. She thought she was past it. Obviously she wasn't.

Before Crystal could get lost in her thoughts, there was a knock at the door.

"Come in," she called out.

Jewell poked her head in. "There's an emergency meeting in the conference room in half an hour."

"Thanks."

Jewell closed the door and went back to her desk.

Twisting her locks as she walked out of her office, Crystal wondered what this meeting was about. They seemed to be having a lot of meetings with Susan asking what she should do about this or that client and how she should handle this or that case. This wasn't like Susan, who always had an answer for everything. Crystal had a feeling something was going on with her. Whatever it was, it was affecting her performance. She knew she would have to discuss this with her sooner or later. She just wasn't ready for the wrath of Susan.

SUSAN

Sitting behind her massive desk dressed in an Anne Klein A-line dress that hugged every curve on her shapely 150-pound figure, Susan wondered, *What am I doing and why am I doing this to myself?* She knew she needed to stop, but it was taking over, controlling her. She couldn't get through the day without at least one hit, and that one hit would turn into two, three and four. She knew cocaine was not only illegal, but her habit was affecting her decisions at work and in her personal life. She just couldn't get enough of it. It made her feel powerful, in control, like she could conquer the world.

Balling and unballing her hands as she paced the floor, Susan tried to convince herself that she was better than this. *I'm not an addict. I'm a skilled attorney who works hard to win cases. I pay my bills on time, I'm fairly attractive, wear designer clothes, and drive a white-on-white Mercedes SL 500. I'm not an addict.* The self-talk wasn't working. She found herself walking toward the door and checking to see that it was locked.

This is it, she told herself while heading back toward her desk. *After this week, I'm giving it up.* But she had told herself this same thing numerous times before. It didn't matter how many times she said it. She still craved the power of the first hit.

She walked over to her desk and glanced at her "To Do," "To File," and "Almost Done" piles. Susan reached underneath the desk and pulled out a secret drawer. She reached inside, hands shaking, for the mirror she kept in there with lines of cocaine. It was only a little after nine and she was itching for a hit. She had stayed up all night working on a case and was operating on three hours of sleep. You wouldn't be able to tell it from looking at her. Her shoulder length hair was pulled back into a neat bun, and not a hair was out of place. Her natural-looking makeup was applied to create the illusion of perfect skin, catlike eyes and soft lips. Too bad it was all an illusion.

She took a straw out of her purse as she thought about when this mess all started. It was in high school at the senior prom. Everyone was partying. Her cousin, Duvall, a known drug dealer, decided to throw an after prom party. He had the cash, the drugs and the know-how. Only a few were chosen to attend and she, being family and all, was on the top of the list.

Susan didn't know what she was getting into. Well, maybe she did know, but she wanted to be part of the crowd, at least once. People considered her different in high school. She was always looking out for the underdog, the new kid or the one the other students rejected. Not one to be played with, people stayed away from her. She had a reputation as someone who would fight anyone, boy or girl, and win.

Her willingness to fight had to do with her upbringing. She grew up on the bad side of town, around the corner from the Ave., where the gangs, drugs and fights occurred on a daily basis. She had to watch her back on the regular. Jealousy ran rampant in her part of town. Although mocha complected at a time when light skin was in, she was shapely, and this got her a lot of unwanted attention.

She could still remember the year that she started developing. It was over summer vacation. She was going to the eighth grade. When school resumed, a group of boys, led by JB Jones, decided to harass her on a daily basis. It was getting to be irritating and uncomfortable. All week they were following her around, teasing her and pinching her on the ass. Susan made up her mind that on Friday she would get them, one way or the other. Finally the day came and the school bell rang. Now was her chance. She stood by the locker of the ringleader.

"Move," JB barked.

"Move me." Susan stood her ground. She was going to fight him to the end, and not fairly either. She had a pocketknife in her pocket.

Not knowing this, he pushed her out of the way. After catching her balance, Susan caught him off guard and started hitting and kicking him. He tried throwing a few punches, but her arms and legs were flying. By now, students had surrounded them. Everything happened so quickly. How or when she cut him, she couldn't recall. The only thing she knew was that someone was pulling her off him, and from a distance she heard, "He's bleeding, he's bleeding." One of the nerds she protected whispered in her ear. "Give me the knife so I can get rid of it." She passed it to him and he walked off.

By the time the principal arrived, the crowd had disbursed. She was questioned about the knife wound and denied having a weapon. None of the other students turned her in. They believed JB had gotten what he deserved. As a result, they were both suspended.

No one really messed with Susan after that. Most kids stayed away from her for fear that she would go off on them. Everyone except Brandon Lewis. He was impressed and curious about this fine girl with the nerve to go up against one of the school bullies.

During their senior year, he gathered the courage, waited three weeks, sat at her lunch table, made small conversation and invited her to the prom. Surprised, she told him yes. At the prom, Susan let her guard down a little and had a good time, until he made it clear he thought they were going to have sex. Brandon started feeling on her in an aggressive manner. When she told him to stop, he kept on, telling her, "This is what all the kids do after the prom."

"Boy, I will break every bone in your hands if you don't take them off me."

From her tone, he knew she wasn't playing. He put her out the car at a place called The Point and told her to walk her ass home.

Susan didn't care, as long as she was safe. Home wasn't where she was going. She went to the party Duvall was giving.

When she arrived, everyone appeared to be having a good time. The music was blasting, people were dancing, cigarettes and weed were being passed around. She looked around the room and spotted her cousin with his hussy of the week. He glanced up and called her over.

"What's up cuz? Where's your date?" He looked over her shoulder.

"I sent his ass home. He thought he was going to get some pussy tonight, but I told him it wasn't happening here."

Duvall laughed. "Still saving it for the one, huh?"

"Why not?" Susan got defensive.

Duvall threw his hands up. "I ain't mad at ya. Hell, I'm proud of you, the way these girls are giving it up now."

Susan gave him a kiss on the cheek. "You would know."

After surveying the room and speaking to a few people, she decided to sit and observe the madness.

"Uh, uh, uh." Her cousin's partner Timothy sat down next to her. "Don't you look fine tonight."

Susan ignored him.

"So, you're going to ignore a brother? You need to loosen up. Why be so uptight?"

"I am not uptight," Susan protested.

"Yes, you are. Brothers be wanting to press up, but they're afraid."

"Of what?"

"Shall I break it down for you? Um, let me see . . . that evil look you always have, your attitude, and don't think I ain't hear about you stabbing that boy."

"I don't know what you're talking about."

"Yeah, okay."

"You want to know why I'm the way I am?" She turned to face him.

"Why?"

"Because of users like you and my cousin over there." She nodded her head in Duvall's direction. "Look at him. He has a different girl every week."

Timothy glanced over at Duvall. He had to hand it to him. He did have a way with the ladies. The honeys were always hanging around him, doing anything he asked, and he did mean anything.

"Wish it was you, don't you?" Susan teased.

"Nah, I'm right where I want to be, sitting next to the finest honey in the room."

"Yeah, right. Tell me another one."

Suddenly, Timothy got real serious. "You think I'm playing, don't you? Girl, I've been checking you out since you were fifteen, but your cousin wasn't trying to hear it."

Susan laughed. "What? Are you scared of him?"

"Scared? Nah, that's my boy. I respect him. He calls you his little prize—always bragging about you, about how you're all smart, still a virgin and about to go to college to be a lawyer and all."

"Get out. He told you all that?" She was embarrassed and pleased.

"I even had to get permission to come over here."

They both looked across the room. Duvall was looking their way. He held a drink in his hand, which he raised in their direction.

"What did he say?"

Mimicking Duvall, Timothy said, "What you asking me to talk to her for? She's eighteen now. She has a mind of her own."

"Yeah, I guess he figures there's only so much trouble I can get into now, since I'll be leaving soon for college."

"You're getting old, girl. You're getting old."

"Well, hell, you must be an old man. You're what, five years older than me?"

Laughing, Timothy pulled a dollar bill out of his pocket and unfolded it. Inside there was white powder. Susan wasn't dumb. She knew cocaine when she saw it. She also knew she should get up and leave him alone, but she was enjoying his company.

"I'll be back," Timothy announced.

"Where you going?" she wanted to know.

"To the bathroom."

"Why?" She waved her hand around the room. "Everybody else is doing it in the open. How do you know I don't want to try it?"

Timothy started folding the bill. "So your cousin can kill both of us?"

"I'm eighteen, remember?"

"I don't know." Everything in him was telling him no. He put the bill in his pocket.

"If I don't try it with you, I'll try it with someone else." Susan placed her hand on her hip to let him know she was serious.

"You're serious, aren't you?"

"As a heart attack."

Timothy looked to see if Duvall was still watching them.

Knowing what he was doing, Susan stood up and told him, "Come on."

"Where are we going?"

"To my car."

He followed her to the car. After making themselves comfortable, he pulled the bill out along with a straw and made some lines on the dashboard. "I don't know why I'm showing you this." He placed the straw on the first line and snorted it up his nose then passed the bill to her.

She copied what he'd done and immediately started rubbing her nose. "Oh my God," she said, putting her hand up to her chest.

"Are you okay?"

"That shit burns and my heart is racing."

"That'll happen the first time. Just relax."

They sat in the car for over an hour, getting high and getting acquainted. It was the beginning of their friendship/relationship.

Now here she sat, over ten years later, still doing her thing. She had quit a number of times only to resume the habit. Only a few people knew about this extracurricular activity, but they were professionals as well, and stood to lose just as much as she did.

She looked at her watch and took one more hit. She replaced her stash in its secret hiding place, grabbed some tissue and wiped her nose. She them pulled some files from her "To Do" pile and pressed the intercom button, telling Jewell, "Please let everyone know I'm ready to meet."

JEWELL

After she released the intercom button, Jewell turned her radio down a notch. They'd already gotten on her about playing it too loud. Shit, it was better than the elevator music they wanted to play. "This is a black law firm people, so let's act like it," Jewell wanted to say.

Another day, another dollar, but was it worth the aggravation? Some days, Jewell despised coming to this place. The days seemed endless. Watching the clock didn't help because each time she looked at it, only minutes had passed. It wasn't that her job was stressful or anything. Heck, she could deal with Crystal, because as long as her work was done in a timely manner, it was all good. Elsie was patient, always willing to answer questions if she didn't understand anything. But Susan, she was one female who was hard to get along with. Not a day went by when Jewell didn't want to curse her out and say, "Do it your damn self!"

The reason she allowed Susan to affect her this way was because she reminded Jewel of her mother. Her moms was always judging her. Nothing was ever good enough—her grades, her chores or her clothes. Her mom would yell things like, "You'll never amount to anything. All you're going to do

16

is have babies and be on welfare like your no-good, whoring friends."

Unable to take the verbal abuse any longer, Jewell moved out at the age of sixteen to live with her nineteen-year-old boyfriend, King. As predicted, she got pregnant, but she stayed in school. Eventually they broke up and she had to apply for welfare. Being smart, she used it for a free education and became a nurse's aid.

It wasn't long before she realized that wiping somebody's ass with her fifty-dollar nail tips on wasn't the move. After doing some research and talking with her social worker, Jewell decided to take some computer classes, become a secretary during the day and go to paralegal school at night. When she saw the position advertised at Gem, Carlson, and Shaw, she decided "what the heck" and applied.

Just because Jewell complained occasionally and watched the clock didn't mean she hated her job. She didn't. She was given the opportunity to learn hands-on, and not only did they pay her well, she received great medical benefits. No more Medicaid and going to the walk-in clinic with her son. She received one week paid vacation, had sick time and personal days. For the first time in Jewell's life, she felt worthy. She knew she had made the right decision.

School was going well. As a matter of fact, it was easier than she thought. She had convinced herself before starting that she was in above her head. She wasn't sure if she could handle the pressure of school, work, and parenting, but found she was able. Her son's father helped out, and she had an excellent babysitter. Actually, she would be using the babysitter tonight.

Jewell was going on a blind date set up by her best friend. A blind date was better than none. She hadn't been on one in a long time. She was looking forward to it. Therefore, this was one day she would not let Susan's stank attitude affect her.

Jewell took the gum out of her mouth, put it in some tissue, and threw it in the garbage can under her desk. She stood up, pulled down the hem of her mini-skirt, and went to make coffee in the conference room. They would be coming in any minute, and she didn't want any complaints. After she grabbed her Dictaphone and note pad, she started her day.

As Jewell placed the coffee cups, cream, sugar and Sweet and Low on the table, she recalled her interview for the position. Crystal, Susan, and Elsie interviewed her as a group, and she was nervous as hell. She sat with her hands crossed on her lap. Her legs shook and her voice quivered when answering questions. She could tell from the expression on Susan's face that she didn't want to hire her.

"Excuse me. I have to go to the ladies' room," she told them. What she needed to do was go in, throw some water on her face, and regroup. Before she stepped back into the room, she heard someone say her name. She stood near the door to listen to what was being said.

The first voice she heard was Susan's. "Simply put, I think she's ghetto. Look at what she's wearing. You do not come dressed for an interview like that. Her weave needs to be touched up, and her shoes are for the clubs, not for an office."

Jewell wanted to bust the door down, tell Susan to take a good look because her hair wasn't a weave, then she would knock her in the mouth. Instead she forced herself to wait and see what everyone said.

"That's true, but maybe she just doesn't know any better. She's young," Elsie said.

"That's not good enough," was Susan's reply.

Jewell looked down at her clothes. She didn't find anything wrong with her outfit. She wore black slacks and a body suit. Okay, maybe it was a little too tight, but damn, they were all women. On her feet were stiletto shoes, her best pair. Instead of beating Susan's ass, Jewell decided to leave, until she realized she couldn't because her Gucci knockoff was in the conference room.

"I think we should give her a chance," Jewell heard Crystal say. "Let's just finish interviewing her and see how it goes. Yes, she's a little rough around the edges, but it's obvious she's smart."

"I agree with Crystal," Elsie said.

"Well, if we hire her and she fucks up, it's on your heads," Susan let them know.

This was Jewell's cue to enter. The second she turned the knob, all conversation ceased.

Because Jewell knew that Crystal and Elsie had her back, she calmed down and handled the rest of the interview like a pro. When it was over, Jewell went into the ladies' room and stood in front of the mirror, wiping her eyes. She cried tears of relief. This was her first real interview, the one that she believed would make or break her spirits, and she knew she did a hell of a job.

Elsie walked in and asked if she was okay.

Might as well be honest, Jewell thought. *What do I have to lose?* "I'm just nervous. I really need this job."

"Are you interviewing anyplace else?" Elsie wanted to know.

"I am, but this would be so ideal. It's close to my son's school, and like I said in the interview, I'm going to school to become a paralegal. I've been on my own since I was sixteen, and that alone should show you that I'm smart and able to work well under pressure." Jewell was all set to plead her case.

Elsie put her hands up and said, "Listen, I have to get back to the group. Whether we hire you or not, I'm going to give you a couple of pieces of advice. Don't get offended, okay? I'm talking to you one sister to another."

"I won't get offended," Jewell assured her. She would appreciate whatever she was about to be told, because Jewell was on a mission to better herself.

"Well, for one, you need to dress more professionally. The bodysuit has to go. Actually a simple blouse and a skirt, pants

19

if that's your preference, would be better. Simple shoes, not stilettos, are more appropriate in a professional workplace. And when you walked through the door, you were chewing gum. Throw it out before you enter the building. Also make sure your hair is neat. Pull it back if you have to." Elsie grew quiet and waited for the blowup.

It didn't come, because Jewell wasn't upset. She appreciated the advice that was given. "Thanks."

Two days later, Jewell received a call from Elsie. "We'd like to offer you the position."

Of course, she accepted. That was over six months ago. She planned on staying with them for years to come.

ELSIE

Elsie leaned back in the reclining chair behind her oak desk. An arrangement of flowers sat in the corner, soft jazz played in the background, low enough to create a relaxed atmosphere. She was on the phone talking to her lover and playing checkers on the computer when Jewell buzzed and informed her that the meeting would be starting shortly.

"I have to get a haircut after work and then I'll be by." Elsie ran her left hand over her close-cropped bronze-colored cut, which accentuated her cheekbones and made her light brown eyes even more noticeable. She was striking, not only because of her looks, but because she stood over six feet tall. She was slender and comfortable in her body.

"Love you too," Elsie said into the phone before hanging up.

She stood, stretched her long legs, grabbed her briefcase, and headed down the hall. By the time she arrived at the conference room, everyone was sitting and making small talk.

"Elsie, your suit is nice," Crystal complimented, taking in the chocolate-colored single-breasted jacket and cuff pants with relaxed legs.

21

"Thanks." Elsie sat down, legs slightly open, and started playing with the small diamond hoops that hung from her ears. She always wore pants, never dresses or skirts, and definitely not tight clothing. The clothing she possessed was made for comfort. She could sit however she pleased and have room to move.

Susan looked over in her direction and nodded her greeting. "I thought we would go over our agenda for the upcoming month."

Elsie looked at her, wanting to say, *"How about we not?"* She didn't. Instead, she just nodded to keep the peace as they started a two-hour discussion on cases pending. A couple of times, Elsie found her attention slipping in and out of the meeting. She was thinking about her girlfriend, Summer, who wanted them to live together.

"I'm tired of feeling like a secret," Summer complained once again.

So, Elsie went against what she felt and promised her that she would move in. She regretted it the second she said it. It wasn't because she wanted to hide her female lover, but because she enjoyed her space. She liked not having to answer to anyone. She treasured her privacy.

Elsie had always been a private person. Her life was her life. She was not one to gossip and judge. She stayed to herself throughout high school and college. All major decisions she made alone. One of those decisions was starting a relationship with a woman.

She was in high school when she first realized that her hormones geared her toward her own. It frightened her so much that she started dating this guy named Troy, someone she knew was a dog.

The relationship and the lovemaking was a disaster. It did nothing for her. She didn't see fireworks nor did she feel any. All it felt like was something banging away at her insides. Instead of moaning, she cried during and afterwards. Troy thought it was because he was that good or because she loved him. She knew it was because she hated what she had just done, and she was not being true to herself.

Elsie stayed in denial and continued to see him. Each time they made love, she felt like a piece of her was lost. When she graduated from high school and left for college, she didn't try to contact him. She didn't want him to know where she was. She had grown tired of betraying herself.

It wasn't until Elsie went to college that she made the decision to be with women. Janay was her name, and she was not only Elsie's first female lover, but also her first true love. After college, they broke up then got back together years later, only to break up again two years ago.

Elsie met Janay on campus while participating in a fashion show. Elsie could have been a top model if she had chosen that path. She certainly had more than enough opportunity to do so. The offers came repeatedly. But not one to bring attention to herself, she turned the offers down.

Short on funds, Elsie decided to take part in a fashion show. One evening, she was at practice when in walked Janay. As soon as Elsie saw her, she knew. She knew she was attracted to her and it scared her. It frightened her to the point that it made her nauseous. She ran into the bathroom.

While Elsie threw up, Janay entered and stood behind her. "Are you okay?"

No, I'm not, Elsie thought. *I'm attracted to you in a big way and it's scaring the mess out of me.* Out loud she told her, "I ate something that didn't quite agree with me."

Janay pulled a bottle of Tums out of her purse and handed them to her. "I carry these everywhere I go."

Elsie accepted them and thanked her, She tried to stay calm during the rest of the evening, but it was damn near impossible. An hour before practice was over, Elsie heard Janay arguing on the phone. She was almost in tears. When she hung up, Elsie went over and asked her if everything was okay.

"No. My girlfriend just broke up with me."

Elsie thought she'd heard her wrong. "Did you just say your girlfriend?"

"Yeah."

"Oh." Elsie shifted on the heels of her shoes.

Janay looked Elsie up and down then asked her out for drinks. "I don't feel like going home and being by myself," she told her.

Elsie's mind was telling her to say no, but her curiosity convinced her to say yes. After a number of drinks, Janay drove Elsie home. Full of liquor and courage, Elsie invited her up. They must have been in the house all of five minutes before they embraced.

Elsie pulled away and told her, "I've never kissed a woman before."

"There's a first time for everything." Janay pulled Elsie to the couch and they shared a passionate kiss. It was the kind of kiss Elsie wanted to share with a man but was unable to, the kind of kiss that stirred something deep within her. It was a kiss that changed her life and would define her sexuality.

TIME TO GO

Sitting in that conference room for two hours was hell. Susan did most of the talking, which was nothing new. It took everything in Jewell's power not to nod off. Crystal looked like her mind was elsewhere, and Elsie was her normal quiet self. When they told her she could step out, Jewell almost sprinted. The day proceeded as usual—a whole lot of typing and a little bit of fun. The fun was only when Jewell had a chance to sneak on the phone and converse with her best friend, Kim.

Glancing up at the clock for the fifth time, Jewell saw closing time. If she left in the next few minutes, she would have time to get her hair flat-combed. She started clearing off her desk, but not before she glanced at the picture of her son, Tyson, and his father, King. She knew she needed to change it and put a recent picture in its place, but for sentimental reasons she just couldn't. Crystal and Susan were coming out of their offices. Noticing Jewell packing up, Crystal asked, "Is it that time already?"

"Yes, it is," Jewell said, thinking about her date.

Susan stepped forward, threw a file on Jewell's desk, and told her, "I need this typed up."

This was the kind of shit that pissed Jewell off. Susan always waited until the last minute to give her something to do. Susan and Crystal started to walk away when Jewell cleared her throat and announced, "I don't have time to do this."

Susan stopped in her tracks, turned around, and said, "Excuse me?"

"I don't have time to do this. It's time for me to leave."

"Is it your babysitter? You can't call and say you'll be a little late?"

"No, it's not my babysitter. I have plans for this evening that can't be disrupted."

Crystal just took it all in. She was curious as to how Jewell would handle Susan. She'd seen this confrontation coming for quite some time—Susan demanding her work get done first, Susan not acknowledging what an excellent job Jewell was doing, and Susan being bitchy was bound to start a fight.

"Don't you think your job is more important?" Susan asked.

Before Jewell could say a word, Elsie came out of her office. She was on the way to the bathroom but stopped short when she saw the tight faces on everyone. "What's going on here?" Elsie asked.

No one responded.

"Well?" Susan asked.

Now Jewell had three choices. One was to stay, and she definitely wasn't going to do that. The second choice was to go off and tell Susan that she was tired of being treated like she didn't matter. Choice three was to handle the matter professionally. She chose to go with the combination of two and three.

Well, here goes. Jewell started, "First of all, it bothers me that you always wait until the last minute to give me work to do. I'm here all day, and Crystal and Elsie utilize me during that time, but not you. It's always right before it's time for me to leave that you throw something on my desk."

"Well, you are the secretary, and it's your job."

"When I was first hired, I didn't make it a secret that I might need a little flexibility being a single mom and all. I don't mind staying late sometimes, but a little notice would be appreciated. I have a life outside of this office and a family, and I think you should take that into consideration. I've been here for almost a year and feel like I'm still trying to earn my stripes from you."

Susan placed her hands on her hips. "So, are you telling me you're not staying?"

"Yes, that's exactly what I'm saying," Jewell answered with confidence that she didn't feel. As badly as she needed this job, her integrity was more important. She was not about to lose her self-respect over it. She knew that speaking her mind might backfire, but so far neither Crystal nor Elsie gave her any inkling that they would fire her.

Susan fixed her face to tell Jewell that if she couldn't stay, she shouldn't bother coming back at all. Before she could get a word out, Crystal told Jewell, "Try to come in a little early tomorrow to get it done."

Smiling, Jewell said, "Thanks." She grabbed her briefcase and jacket from behind the chair and sprinted out the door.

Susan was furious. She turned toward Crystal and asked, "What the hell did you do that for?"

"I'll leave you two alone." Elsie walked away.

"You need to check your tone." Crystal didn't care how pissed Susan was. She too refused to be disrespected. Susan was her partner, not her boss.

"That was between me and Jewell. If I wanted her dismissed, I would have done so myself."

"Dismissed? Susan, you need a reality check." Crystal started to walk away.

"I think we should fire her. I'm one her bosses, and she straight out defied me."

Stopping in her tracks, Crystal faced Susan. "You know what I think? I think you need to take it down. I think you need to go home, take a bath, and relax before making a rash decision to fire someone because you're having a bad day. Don't think I haven't noticed how moody you've been lately. Taking it out on others is just plain wrong."

Susan couldn't say a word because she knew Crystal was right. She was having a bad day. Hell, she was having a bad month. She hadn't heard from her friend Timothy in quite some time. It was like he disappeared off the face of the earth. Not only was she worried about him, but she wasn't sleeping well either. She was on the edge and about to fall off.

"Maybe you're right," Susan confessed

Walking over to Susan, Crystal took her hand. "Do you want to talk about it?"

Susan moved her hand from under Crystal's. "No. I've got it under control."

Crystal was not convinced. "Are you sure?"

"I'm sure."

"You know I'm here for you. You can talk to me anytime. You do know that, don't you?"

"I know." Susan glanced at her watch. "Look, I've got phone calls to make."

Crystal tried to read Susan's face. It wasn't working. "All right. Just remember what I said."

They went their separate ways. Susan went to get high and Crystal went to take care of some personal business over the phone and online.

Crystal logged off the computer and sat back in her chair. She gazed out the window and thought about Susan's odd behavior. Even when paying her bills, she couldn't get Susan off her mind. As she stood up and stretched, she made the decision to stop by Susan's office to see what was up.

Crystal walked out of her office, past Jewell's empty chair, and tried to decide what she would say to Susan to get her to open up. As she approached Susan's closed door, she wondered if it was locked. Placing her hand on the doorknob and turning it, she saw that it was. She knocked. There was no reply. Crystal placed her ear to the door. She could hear some movement, so she knocked harder.

"Who is it?" Susan called out.

"It's Crystal."

Susan took a quick look in the mirror and made sure her nose was clean, then she opened the door. She wasn't surprised to find Crystal standing behind it. After all, she was usually the only one who came to her office unannounced. "What's up?" Susan greeted.

Crystal glanced around the room while entering. "Keeping your door locked now?"

"Just needed a little privacy," Susan responded, spotting a short straw on the floor. There was no way she could cover it up or bend down to pick it up without Crystal noticing.

"I just thought I'd see if you wanted to talk about what's bothering you," Crystal said.

"It's not anything I want to discuss right now."

"I'm just concerned. You seem so on edge lately."

Susan shrugged.

"So, that's how it is?" Crystal could tell she wasn't getting through to Susan.

"That's how it is."

"Susan . . . " Crystal wasn't ready to give up.

"Please," Susan interrupted. "I told you there's nothing to talk about."

Without another word, Crystal turned and left the room. She waited by the elevator. When the door opened, she was surprised to see Lange standing inside.

"So, we run into each other once again. How was your day?" he asked.

29

"Productive."

"Your locks are beautiful."

Crystal looked up at Lange. *Where the hell did that come from?* "Thanks."

"Crystal?" Lange started.

"Yes?"

"How about I walk you to your car?"

"Oh, that's okay." She didn't want to be alone with him in a garage.

"I really don't mind." He started to follow her.

They walked toward the garage in an awkward silence, both feeling the sparks flying between them.

"That's my car over there." Crystal pointed to the Lexus.

Lange followed and stood by the car as she opened the door and climbed in. She started her car and rolled down the window. "Thanks."

Shifting back and forth, Lange massaged his chin, leaned over and said, "Would you like to have lunch some time?"

"I don't know."

"As friends." It seemed to Crystal that his face was getting closer and closer. "We can get to know one another. Plus, I might need your advice on something."

Before Crystal could answer, Lange's lips were almost touching hers. The only thing that stopped a kiss was the ringing of his cell phone.

Lange jumped back and pressed the answer button. "Hello?"

Crystal mouthed, "I have to go," and pulled off.

On the way home, Crystal beat herself up mentally. *What the heck am I doing, almost kissing a married man? I know that shit is not kosher.* She tried to think of other things, but was unable. Her imagination started going to work overtime. She imagined Lange pushing her up against the elevator wall as he pressed the stop button, grabbed her hips and pulled her into him. His lips made their way to her throat.

"Are you sure you want to do this?" she asked him.

"Yes," he moaned while moving from her throat, to her chin to her mouth.

"Pull over." These words pulled Crystal out of her trance.

Crystal looked in her rearview mirror to see a police car tailing her with the lights flashing. "Shit!" Crystal had no idea what she was being stopped for. She pulled over and turned off her car. Her stomach was in knots. "Okay. Get it together," she said out loud. "You're an adult. Either you were speeding or you ran a light. All you're going to do is get a ticket—nothing more, nothing less."

"Your driver's license and registration card?" the plainclothes officer asked.

"Yes." Crystal reached into her glove compartment, avoiding the officer's eyes. *Only a ticket, only a ticket,* she reminded herself.

With shaky hands, she passed the officer her license and registration.

Looking at the ID then inside, the officer laughed. "Well, well, well, if it isn't Crystal Gem."

Finally, she took a good look at the officer and was shocked to see Roger Soloman, her high school sweetheart.

"We went to school together," he told her. "Well, actually, we dated."

"I remember," Crystal replied. She also remembered him breaking her heart.

"How have you been?" he asked

"Fine."

Roger waited for more.

When Crystal caught this, she asked him, "How have you been?"

"Life has treated me good. I'm a detective, as you can see."

An uncomfortable moment passed between them. "Why did you pull me over?" Crystal asked.

"You ran a red light."

Bringing her hands up to her chest, she was surprised. "I did?"

"Lucky for you, this is a slow time of the evening. What were you doing?"

Crystal couldn't think of a lie, so she was honest. "I really don't know."

Huffing, Roger handed her back her identification and said, "Listen, I'm going to let you go with a warning and," he reached inside his jacket pocket, "my card. Call me. Maybe we can get together and get reacquainted."

She took everything out of his hand and said, "Thanks."

"Be careful on these roads." Roger turned and headed back toward his car.

Crystal didn't even wait until he climbed in his vehicle. She started her car and headed toward the liquor store.

THE DATE

Erykah Badu was playing in the background and Jewell was dancing around her cluttered bedroom room. Her son, Tyson, sat on the floor watching her every move.

"Mommy, what are you doing?" he wanted to know.

"I'm dancing."

"What dance is that?"

"The Harlem Shake."

This made Tyson laugh. "That is not how you do the Harlem Shake."

Putting her hands on her hips, Jewell laughed and said, "Well then mister know-it-all, how about you show Mommy how to do it."

Shaking his head, Tyson said, "Nah, I don't feel like it."

Plopping down on her bed, Jewell patted the spot next to her and said, "What's up? How come you don't feel like dancing with your mother?"

"Because I want to know where you're going."

"I'm going out on a date."

"What's a date?"

"When a woman and man go out to dinner and a movie."

"So, when you and I go out to dinner, are we on a date?"

Jewell gently held his face in her hands. She kissed him on the cheek and said, "Yes, we are."

"Well, we haven't been on one in a long time, ever since you started working and stuff."

Jewell didn't have an answer for that because she knew he spoke the truth. Ever since she started working and going to school, there was less time left for her baby. She did feel guilty, but in order for them to get better things, move to a bigger place, she had to do what she had to do. She didn't want Tyson to want for anything.

"How about we go out on a date tomorrow?" She would take him to the Hibachi place. He loved that.

"I'd like that."

"Good, now go play in your room while Mommy picks out something to wear."

Opening her closet door, she stood there hoping an outfit would grab her. She didn't want to appear too sexy or too conservative; she wanted something in the middle.

"I need some new clothes," she said out loud.

Jewell pulled out three outfits: a black wrap dress, an olive green suede skirt set she'd recently purchased from Wilson's Leather, and a one-piece jean outfit that showed off her curves. As she was spreading them out on the bed, she heard the doorbell ring. Jewell glanced at the clock and knew it was the babysitter. "Tyson, let Ms. Tracy in!" she yelled.

Soon, she heard footsteps coming down the hall.

Tracy poked her head in the door. "Can I come in?"

"Sure. Maybe you can help me decide what to wear."

Tracy stepped in. Jewell was thankful to have such a nice girl as a babysitter. She had been Tyson's babysitter for the past two years and was always on time and dependable.

Looking at the clothes on the bed, Tracy asked, "So, where are you going?"

"Dinner and a movie." Damn, now that Jewell thought about it, what if she didn't like this guy? *Dinner and a movie,*

that's about three or four hours. That's a long ass time with
someone you don't know.

What if she didn't like him? That was a chance she had to take when she agreed to go on a blind date. Her girlfriend, Kim, who set it up, said he was extremely nice, well mannered and wealthy. Not that the money mattered much, but it was a plus.

Glancing at the clothes on the bed, Tracy told her, "Wear the skirt set. It'll show off your legs."

Jewell smiled because that was the outfit she was leaning toward. "Yeah, I think I will." She put the other items of clothing up in the closet. "I'm going to take a shower."

"I'll be in the living room with Tyson."

Jewell followed Tracy into the hallway and made a left into the bathroom. She pulled a shower cap out from beneath the sink and slipped it on her head. Poking her head out the bathroom door, she told Tracy to answer the phone if it rang.

Fifteen minutes later, as Jewell was putting the final touches on her makeup, Tracy knocked on her bedroom door.

"Come in." Jewell looked up to see Tracy smirking. "What's up?"

"Your date is here."

Jewell looked at her clock. "He's early."

Tracy didn't say a word. She just stood there with a big smile on her face.

"Why are you looking like that?"

"This is a blind date, right?"

This question caused Jewell's heart to skip a beat. "What, is he ugly?"

"No."

"Fat?"

"No."

Growing irritated, Jewell said, "You know what? Never mind. I'll come see for myself. Tell him I'll be out in five minutes."

35

Tracy turned and left the room. A couple of minutes later, Jewell went to meet her date. Standing in the middle of the living room was a white man.

I'm going to get Kim for this, Jewell thought. Walking up to him, Jewell said, "Hello, I'm Jewell."

He introduced himself as Evan as he reached out to shake her hand.

"Mommy, that's a white man," Tyson said.

"Tyson, watch your mouth."

Looking at Evan, Jewell apologized.

"That's okay," Evan assured her. Then after an awkward moment of silence, Evan continued, "You didn't know I was white, did you?"

"Actually, no." Jewell noticed that Tracy and Tyson were all in their conversation. "Can you two excuse us?"

Busted, they left the room.

"Is it a problem? If it is, I'll understand. We haven't left yet," Evan said.

Jewell had never dated a white man before. Never even thought about it. She couldn't wait to see Kim. This was why she wouldn't describe him. She just kept saying how nice he was. Jewell didn't have the heart to cancel with him standing there. Plus, she'd been looking forward to getting out of the house all day. She decided to go through with it.

"No, it's not a problem. Let me grab a jacket and we can go."

"Are you sure? I don't want you to be uncomfortable. "

"I'm positive, but I can only do dinner. My sitter has to leave kind of early."

"That's fine with me," he told her while he waited for her to retrieve her jacket.

When they stepped outside, Jewell was surprised to see a black Hummer with rims parked in front of the building. She

36

could feel her neighbors staring at them as he opened her door and waited for her to climb in.

Once he was in and they each had their seatbelts fastened, Jewell found herself staring at him. "Have you dated black women before?" she asked.

"Yes."

As he pulled off, Jewell asked, "Do you date mostly black women or white women?"

Evan looked over at her, surprised she was being so blunt. "Um, mostly black."

"Why?"

"Why?" No one had ever asked him that.

"Yeah, why?"

"I don't have a specific reason. This may sound corny and all, but I grew up around black people. Some of my best friends are black. My partner is black."

"Your partner?"

"Yes. I have an investment firm."

Jewell knew to be impressed.

"Plus, nothing beats being out with a beautiful woman like yourself."

Jewell smiled at the compliment. She knew she was a cutie, but didn't let her confidence turn into conceit. She was considered a redbone in the black community, and had what black folks called good hair—long, silky and straight. Because of this, people assumed they could take advantage and pick on her. In her neighborhood, the darker you were the tougher you were. She didn't understand how people equated the color of her skin with whether or not she could fight, but they did. That whole "if you're light-skinned, you're a punk" theory was not true in her case. She would put up her fists in a second. She was not one to back down, but because of her mixed heritage, people tried her anyway. Sometimes, she would sit back and think about it, take a look around at the other light-skinned girls and what she found was that they rarely befriended other people. It was like they were in a class by themselves. The darker sisters were tight, hung out together, fought together. They were a clique that she wanted to belong to but was unable.

Her mother was black and her father Spanish. He left shortly after she was born. Her mother never spoke of him. When Jewell would ask questions, her mother would tell her, "He's not here now, never was, so let's do him like he did us and pretend he never existed."

When she was younger, people would come up to her and say, "Girl, you look just like your father." She wondered if this was why her mother mistreated her, because she was a reminder of her father.

Looking at Evan, she wondered why she never dated a white man or a Spanish man, only black men. When she thought about it, she realized that the only white man she was attracted to was John Travolta, and she knew she didn't stand a chance with him. Come to think of it, Evan had that Travolta strut. He was also handsome; she had to admit it. Tall, olive skin tone, a buzz cut, dark hair, startling blue eyes, and to top it off, he had dimples.

Evan felt her staring at him and asked, "Is this your first time dating a white man?"

Jewell asked, "Is it that obvious?"

"Yeah, it is."

Together they laughed.

"So, where are you taking me?" Jewell wanted to know.

"Ms. Smith's. Have you been there before?"

She had not. It was out of her financial league. "No, but I heard the food was delicious and the décor was romantic." Deciding to tease him, she asked, "Are you looking for romance tonight?"

Surprised, Evan asked, "Are you teasing me?"

Laughing, Jewell told him, "Just a little."

Evan didn't reply. He just smiled as they arrived at the restaurant. "We're here."

The clientele in Ms. Smith's was mostly African-American and she was wondering how the people—forget the people—how *she* would handle being in a room full of Blacks with a white man. She wondered if she would be able to handle it.

As they pulled up to the valet parking lot, a gentleman opened her door. "Good evening, sister," he greeted as she climbed out.

He won't be calling me sister once he sees who my date is, Jewell thought.

Before the young man could get to his side, Evan was out of the truck. He handed the gentleman the keys. Noticing the color of Evan's hands, the young man looked up and mumbled under his breath, "Look at this shit."

Jewell knew Evan heard him because she saw him tense up just a bit. Leading him by the elbow, she said, "Come on. Let's go inside. I'm starving."

As they started to walk away, Evan stopped, turned around and said, "Excuse me," to the valet.

Before the valet could respond, Jewell took Evan's hand and pulled him along. "Come on. Let's go eat."

Evan heard the nervousness in her voice and decided not to pursue the issue.

Walking into the restaurant was like walking into a new world. Jewell had not been out in quite a while. The places she used to hang out at definitely weren't classy like this. There were mirrors everywhere and the room was dimly lit. The seats were close, giving the room an intimate feel, and candles were on every table. The cream and wine color scheme set the mood. There was a jazz band playing in the middle of the floor where couples were dancing or swaying. One couple appeared to be making love to the music.

"This is nice," Jewell managed to say while they were being led to their table. "This is real nice."

"I'm glad you like it."

As they were taking their seats, Jewell glanced around the room. When her eyes hit the door, she saw Elsie walk in with another female. Jewell noticed that they were holding hands, smiling and looking at one another intimately. The woman dropped Elsie's hand and wrapped it around her waist.

"So, that's it."

"So, that's what?" Evan followed Jewell's gaze.

Jewell didn't realize that she had spoken out loud. "Oh, nothing."

Elsie and her date, Summer, were being led to their table. It wasn't too far from Jewell and Evan. As they got closer, Elsie spotted Jewell and almost stopped in her tracks. Taking a deep breath and making the decision not to acknowledger her, Elsie kept her attention focused in another direction as she walked toward their table.

Elsie knew she was dead wrong for not speaking. She felt like a coward. After all, she and Jewell had to see each other five days a week.

"Is everything all right?" Summer sensed Elsie's preoccupation.

Elsie told her everything was fine, but it wasn't. She had tried so hard to keep her sexuality a secret.

"Are you sure?" Summer asked.

"Yeah, I'm sure," Elsie told her, knowing that was a lie. She would have liked to say "Let's go eat somewhere else," but what would have been the point? They were already spotted.

"What are you ordering?" Summer asked Elsie, pulling her out of her daze.

"You can order for me," Elsie said, standing up. "I'll be right back. I saw someone from the office."

When Elsie approached the table, Jewell was laughing at something Evan said. Against her better judgment, she was actually enjoying herself.

"I'm actually having a nice time," she told him.

"You sound surprised." Evan replied.

Before Jewell could respond, Elsie was standing at the table. "Hi, Jewell."

Jewell was surprised when she looked up and saw Elsie standing next to her table.

"Well, hello."

"It's good that you spoke up for yourself today." Elsie couldn't think of anything else to say.

"Thanks. I figured if things got out of hand, you and Crystal had my back." Jewell smiled, letting Elsie know it was in jest.

"Well," Elsie shifted, "enjoy your dinner."

"You too."

Jewell watched Elsie walk away.

"You two work together?" Evan asked.

"I'm so sorry." Jewell realized that she didn't introduce them. "That was so rude of me not to make introductions. She's one of the attorneys I work for."

"That's all right. Maybe I'll get another opportunity to meet her."

Jewell didn't respond. She knew that was his way of asking her out again.

THE PAST WILL HAUNT YOU

Crystal was sound asleep, sprawled across her bed when the phone rang. Popping up, she noticed that it was 10 p.m. She wondered who could be calling her at this hour. For a brief second, she was going to let the answering machine pick it up, but recalled that she'd turned it off.

"Hello," she snapped into the phone.

"Crystal Gem?" the voice on the other end asked.

From the tone, she knew it was the rape crisis center where she was a volunteer. "Yes, this is she." Crystal sat up.

"We need you at the hospital. Are you available?"

"Of course. Which hospital is it?"

"Park Memorial." The person on the other line proceeded to give her all the information she needed, such as the name of the victim, the age, any available information regarding the incident. After hanging up the phone, Crystal threw on a pair of jeans, a black T-shirt, her leather bomber jacket, socks and boots. She grabbled her ID and ran out the door.

Whenever Crystal was called in to comfort someone and help them through the exam, she recalled her own past. This time, she told herself she wasn't going to go there, so she drove with the radio on loud all the way to the hospital.

It seemed to take forever to get to the hospital when in reality it had only taken 10 minutes. Pulling into the parking lot, she took a quick look at her reflection in the rearview mirror.

"Okay, here goes," she said out loud.

She walked through the revolving door, past the people waiting impatiently to be seen. When she reached the front desk, she pulled out her ID and told them why she was there and who she was looking for. The nurse told her to go through the double doors, straight down the hall to room number six.

Crystal did as she was told. When she reached the door, it was closed. She tapped on the door. "May I come in?"

"Are you from the center?" a meek voice asked.

"Yes."

"Come in."

Crystal opened the door and on the bed sat a petite young lady with hazel eyes, wearing a hospital robe. She was looking at the floor.

"You must be Tina," Crystal said.

Looking up, Tina opened her mouth to say something then closed it. Her shoulders shook and she started to cry uncontrollably.

Crystal approached her slowly and held both of her hands. "It's okay, baby. Let it out. Do you want to tell me what happened?"

Tina looked at her and whispered, "He raped me."

"Who raped you?" *Get a name*, Crystal said to herself. The cops had not arrived yet, and in case Tina went into shock, at least she would have that much.

"Jake, Jake Newton." Tina said it so quietly that Crystal had to ask her to repeat it.

"Who did you say?" Crystal couldn't believe what she thought she'd heard.

"Jake Newton."

Unable to breathe, Crystal put her hand up to her chest. *Don't let it be. Please, don't let this be.* Jake Newton. That was the name of the man who raped her when she was fifteen. Crystal knew she should call someone else in at this point, yet she stood paralyzed. She had to know more.

"How old is he?" she asked.

"Nineteen," Tina murmured.

"How old are you?" Crystal needed to know if she was a minor. Her frame was so small, she couldn't tell.

"I'm eighteen."

Damn, she thought. *Could it be his son?* What if it was? Should she be this girl's counselor? Should she get involved? Was it unethical, a conflict of interest?

Sitting on the edge of the bed Crystal asked, "Tell me what happened."

Clearing her throat, Tina began. "I know him from school. We were at a party, I went into a room with him. Maybe I shouldn't have done that, but I really liked him. I thought all we would do is kiss. I didn't think he'd . . . I told him to stop. I tried to get him off me and everything. He just kept doing it." She looked up at Crystal and said, "I shouldn't have went in the room with him."

Crystal knew about self-blame and how a woman's mind could trick her into thinking it was her fault or she deserved what happened. "Don't blame yourself, sweetie. It's not your fault. You told him no and that's what's important. You told him to stop and he didn't."

There was a knock on the door. Crystal jumped off the bed and cracked the door open. It was the police and a physician. She let them in.

After all the questions were answered and the exam was done at almost 1 a.m., Crystal offered to take Tina home. They drove in silence. When they arrived in front of Tina's apartment complex, Crystal pulled out her card and told Tina to call her any time of the day or night if she needed to talk.

She watched as Tina went into the building. Still in shock, Crystal didn't feel like going home. She was almost certain this character who raped Tina was the son of her rapist. This was one hell of a coincidence. Needing to calm down a bit, Crystal decided to stop by The Oasis, a local bar, to have a drink.

"We close in an hour," the bartender informed her as she sat down.

"I know."

"What would you like?"

Before Crystal could get a word out of her mouth, a young-looking, jeans hanging off his ass, gold tooth in his mouth thug pulled up the chair next to Crystal and sat down.

"What's up, ma?"

Crystal gave him the "I don't feel like being bothered" look.

He didn't get it. "I said, what's up, ma?"

"Nothing."

"Let me buy you a drink." He pulled a wad of money out of his pocket.

Crystal was not impressed. "No, I can handle my own."

Placing the money back in his pocket, he looked her up and down. Before he could say something rude, the bartender told him, "Step off and leave the lady alone."

"Thanks," Crystal told him then ordered a shot of Hennessey. She gulped it and ordered another one.

Relaxing in her chair and gazing at the television that hung over the bar, she thought about the past. She thought about what led up to her becoming a volunteer at the rape crisis center. Even now, sixteen years later, she found herself wondering if there was something she could have done differently the day she was raped. After all, she did get in the car.

45

Crystal had been walking home from school, minding her own business, excited about the evening ahead. Her mother was allowing her to go to the roller skating rink that night. This alone was cause for celebration, because she was rarely allowed to go anywhere. Being an only child was a challenge. So much was expected of her.

As she walked in her glory, a car with three guys pulled over.

"Hey, sexy!" one of them yelled out the window.

Sexy. That was the last thing she thought she was, especially at that age, when her skin was breaking out and she barely had a shape. So, of course, Crystal turned to see who would be calling her sexy. It was Jake Newton, the most popular guy in school. Before she could stop herself, Crystal was walking toward the car.

"What's up?" she asked Jake, ignoring the others.

"You."

"Yeah, right." She turned to walk away.

Jake got out of the car. "Let's walk." He threw his arm around her. "So, what's up?"

"Why you want to know? You don't deal with girls like me." Crystal felt brave with his arm around her.

"What do you mean, girls like you?"

"You know—shy, quiet. I'm not what you would call popular, and I don't sleep around. I know your type."

"Maybe I'm turning over a new leaf."

"Yeah, right. Go turn it over somewhere else."

Jake started laughing. "Come on, girl. Let me give you a ride home."

Crystal knew her mother would be pissed if she rolled up in a car full of guys, so she decided to do the smart thing and say no.

"What? Are you scared?"

"Yeah, of my mother," she half-joked.

Jake smiled. "Oh, it's like that."

"Yes, it is. If I pulled up with a bunch of guys all hell would break loose."

"How about if you pulled up with one guy?"

Crystal stopped walking. "What? You're going to kick them out of the car?"

"Nah, I can't do that to my boys, but I am offering you a ride home tomorrow."

"In exchange for?"

"Why I gotta want something? Damn, give a brother a break."

"How about I let you know tomorrow in school?"

Laughing, he told her, "Okay, you do that."

He kissed her on the cheek and went on his way.

Crystal could not believe her luck. The most popular guy in school was checking her out and offering her a ride home. There was one problem. She already had a boyfriend. His name was Roger Soloman. How would she handle this situation?

"A ride home is innocent," she tried convincing herself.

That night she went to the skating rink and had the time of her life. When she arrived home, she couldn't get to bed early enough, anticipating the next day's events. She decided to accept the ride from Jake.

When Crystal woke up the next day, it was pouring outside and there was a slight chill. She wasn't going to let the weather put a damper on her day. Nothing was going to stop her from being in a good mood or getting a ride home from the most popular boy in school.

Crystal carefully picked out her clothes the night before, choosing a black mini-skirt and a black and white striped shirt. Normally she wore her hair in a braided style, but not today. She curled it.

"Why am I going through all this trouble?" she asked herself. "It's only a ride home."

When she arrived at school, the first person she looked for was Roger. She had decided to tell him that she was going to help Jake with a paper. Therefore, he would be giving her a ride home. Roger knew that she tutored people occasionally, so that was as good an excuse as any. As it turned out, there was no need. Roger didn't come to school. So, instead of feeling anxious, she could feel her anticipation building all day. When the final bell rang, she rushed out of the classroom door into the hall. There she lingered. "Maybe he won't show up," she told herself.

"Waiting for me?" Jake asked, tapping her playfully on the shoulder. "Come on." He tried to grab her hand, but she snatched it away.

"What, you don't want me to hold your hand?"

"I don't feel comfortable with it." She really didn't want anyone to see and tell Roger.

"You look nice," he told her while looking her up and down.

She was glad he noticed. He was not only the most popular boy in school, he was also the finest. He had light skin, wavy hair and light brown eyes.

They walked past several students amidst stares and whispers. Someone even had the audacity to yell out, "Uh, oh, miss goody two shoes is about to lose her virginity." Crystal rolled her eyes at the person and kept on walking.

Climbing into his car, Jake asked her, "Do you have a few minutes? I need to stop by my house."

"Sure, that's okay." She giggled nervously. *Get a grip*, she told herself.

Pulling off, Jake popped in a tape. "So, what's up with you and that Roger character?"

"We're friends," she lied.

"Word is, you're more than friends."

"What's that supposed to mean?" Crystal asked, thinking that Roger better not be going around saying they were having sex, because they weren't. She had too much respect for herself to give up her coochie to the first boy that asked. She didn't

48

want to be one of those girls that everyone whispered about in the hallways. She would have to find out what Roger was telling people.

When they reached Jake's house, he parked his car. Crystal wondered what his house looked like inside. She was given the opportunity to find out when he invited her in. "I promise I'll only be about ten minutes."

"Okay," she replied.

"Follow me," he said, going upstairs. She did.

They ended up in his room. She sat on the edge of his bed.

Jake searched his closet for something. He never told her what. "Damn, I can't find it."

He sat next to her. "So, tell me. Why are you letting me take you home when you have a man?"

"It's just a ride," Crystal said.

"Is that all it is?" Jake moved closer to her. "I know you like me."

"Yeah, and?" Crystal wasn't going to deny it. "Everyone likes you."

"Can I have a kiss?"

Kissing wasn't sex, so she said yes.

Next thing she knew, Jake was feeling her breasts. Crystal pushed his hands down, but he put them back up.

Pulling away, Crystal told him, "I think it's time for me to leave."

"Why? Are you scared?"

"As a matter of fact, yes."

Jake stood up and leaned over Crystal, making it hard for her to move. "So, you're scared of your mama and me? What else are you scared of?"

"Come on now, stop playing," she told him, trying to get past him.

"Who's playing?"

Crystal started to panic. She tried once again to get up. Jake pushed her back down and forced his tongue in her mouth.

"Jake, please." She tried to push him off her, but he was stronger and had her pinned down.

"What are you doing?" she cried out.

"Just go with the flow," he told her, putting one hand under her skirt.

Suddenly it hit her. He was going to rape her. *God, please don't let this be happening. Please.* Looking at Jake, she started to pleaded with tears rolling down her face, "Jake, please. Think about this. I'm asking you to stop. I'm begging you." She tried to push his hand away, but even with one hand under her skirt, he was stronger. "I'm a virgin. You can't do this to me. Please, please!"

She tried to move from under his grip, but it was like all her strength had dissipated "You're actually going to rape me?" she cried out, thinking if she used the word, it would snap him out of whatever zone he'd gone into.

He wasn't paying attention. He was busy trying to put his fingers inside her. Crystal started squirming, trying to move away from him, trying to push him off, but her little 110-pound frame was nothing compared to his. As he ripped off her panties, he was oblivious to the fact that she was crying and trying to fight him. Somehow he managed to get himself inside her.

The next thing she remembered was waking up with a cold rag on her face, skirt and panties off. Jake was sitting next to her. She looked around the room and at him, remembering what happened. She started punching him.

He put up his hands, blocking the blows, while declaring, "I'm sorry, I'm sorry."

Grabbing her skirt and panties, she covered herself up. She said nothing to him.

"I'll still take you home." He had the audacity to offer.

Hurriedly putting on her clothes, she yelled, "I hate you! I hate you! How could you do this to me? How could you rape me?"

"What are you talking about? I didn't rape you. You wanted it. You got all dressed up in that short-ass skirt, curled your hair and everything. What, you think I didn't notice?"

She couldn't believe the words that were coming out of his mouth. She ran down the steps and threw on her skirt and panties. Not looking back, she ran out the door.

When Crystal got outside, she looked around. She saw no one to help her. Crystal started to walk, glancing behind her more than once, in case Jake was following her. Thank God he didn't live too far from her.

Oh God, what am I going to tell my mother? Do I tell her the truth? Will she believe me? Will anyone believe me? Crystal wondered.

No matter what, the one thing Crystal was certain of was that she would tell someone. Jake would not get away with this. Unable to control her emotions any longer, Crystal sat down on the curb and put her head in her hands. She started to cry.

A car pulled up and stopped in front of her. "Are you okay?" It was Susan, a girl she went to school with. They spoke in passing sometimes.

"No," Crystal told her.

Susan reached across and opened the passenger door. "Get in."

Crystal did.

"Didn't I see you with Jake after school?" Susan asked.

"Yes."

"Did he do something to you?" Susan wasn't stupid. She'd heard stories about Jake and his friends, how they would make girls have sex with them or start rumors saying they all did her.

Nodding, Crystal started to hyperventilate. "I can't breathe," she managed to get out.

"Put your head between your legs," Susan said while rubbing her back. "What the hell happened?"

"He raped me." There, she had said it to another person. "Please just take me home."

When they pulled up to her house, Susan told her, "Don't let Jake get away with this. Jake and his boys think they can get away with anything just because they're popular. You have to stand up for yourself."

"I'm not," Crystal said as they walked through the door. Susan followed her inside.

Coming from the direction of the kitchen wearing sweatpants and a T-shirt, her mother yelled, "Where the hell have you been?"

"Mom," Crystal said, just above a whisper.

"I asked you a question," her mother said.

"Mom." Crystal started, but before she could get another word out, the tears started to fall.

"What the—What's wrong?" Mrs. Gem looked from Crystal to Susan and back to Crystal. "What the hell are you crying for?"

"I was raped." Crystal's voice trailed off.

Taken aback, Ms. Gem looked at Susan, "Who are you?"

"Um, I'm Susan, a classmate. I saw her crying on the sidewalk. I gave her a ride home."

"Please leave."

Susan looked at her like she was crazy.

"I asked you to please leave."

"But don't you want to call the cops?"

Mrs. Gem yelled, "Leave now!"

Sensing that Mrs. Gem was about to lose it, Susan turned to Crystal and told her, "If you need me, call me." She took a piece of paper and pen out of her purse and wrote her number.

No one said a word until they heard the door slam.

"Tell me what happened," Mrs. Gem demanded.

Crystal gave her a brief version.

When she was done, Mrs. Gem told Crystal to go upstairs and wash up.

"But Ma, we have to call the police, we have to report what happened."

"Just do what I said!"

"No," Crystal said, her heart pounding. She had never disobeyed her mother, but she didn't want to wash the evidence away.

"What did you say to me?" Her mother stepped close. Their faces were almost touching.

"I can't let him get away with this. We need to call the police." She waited for the smack. It never came.

"I'm going to take care of this without the police. Now, go upstairs and do as I said. Wash up, change clothes, and then we're going to this Jake character's house." Her mother walked over to the hallway closet and pulled out a gun.

Crystal was in shock. She didn't even know they had one.

"I said move! Now!"

Her mother sat in her bedroom as she showered and got dressed but didn't say a word. She had never seen her mother this way and it frightened her. After Crystal told her mother where Jake lived, they drove in complete silence. Crystal was afraid to say a word. They pulled up to Jake's house. There was a car was in the driveway.

"His parents are home," Crystal said, looking up at Jake's window.

Mrs. Gem got out the car. "Come on."

Crystal was scared. She didn't want to move. It felt like she was glued to her seat.

Looking back, her mother said sharply, "Come on! Get out of the car now!"

Crystal's heart was pounding through her chest. She wiped her sweaty hands on her skirt and looked at her mother's purse, which held the gun. What was she going to do? Would she kill him or just threaten him? Would she kill the whole family?

Crystal wondered how long they had a gun. She decided it was a good thing she didn't know about it because she might have come home and tried to use it on Jake.

Getting out of the car, Crystal trailed behind her mother, bracing herself for what was about to come. Mrs. Gem started banging on the door and pressing on the bell.

The door opened. "What the—" Jake stopped mid sentence when he saw who it was. He looked from Crystal to her mother and back to Crystal. Panic was on his face.

"Jake, honey, who is it?" A short woman with a little girl's face and petite body came from the back of the house and stood by Jake.

"Are you his mother?" Mrs. Gem pointed at Jake.

"Yes, I am. May I help you?"

"Your son raped my daughter!" Mrs. Gem got straight to the point.

Pushing the door wide open, Ms. Newton asked, "What are you talking about? Don't come to my house with a bunch of lies! Who the hell do you think you are? Please leave my house with your lies."

Mrs. Gem stood up close to Jake's face. Crystal didn't move. "Why don't you tell your mother how you raped my daughter?"

Jake's mother tried to stand between them. "I asked you to leave."

"Tell her," Mrs. Gem demanded.

"I'm calling the cops." Mrs. Newton turned to go into the house.

"Yeah, you go ahead and do that." Mrs. Gem held her purse tighter.

At the mention of the word "cops", Jake spoke up. "I didn't rape her, Mom. She wanted to have sex with me. I offered her a ride home and had to stop off to get something. She asked if could she come in, and one thing led to another."

Crystal's mouth dropped open. She looked at him in disbelief. "How can you stand there and lie like that? You raped me! I didn't want to have sex with you. You raped me!" she cried.

Hearing a car door slam, they all turned around to see Mr. Newton, all 6 feet 4 inches, 260 pounds of him, walking toward them. Seeing the look on their faces, he knew something was up. "What's going on here?"

"You want to know what's going on?" Mrs. Gem wasn't backing down from anyone. Her daughter was violated and she wanted justice her way. "You want to know what's going on? Your son raped my daughter."

Mr. Newton snapped his head in Jake's direction. Jake would not meet his eyes.

"Let's go in the house," Mr. Newton instructed.

"I don't want them in my house telling a bunch of lies," Mrs. Newton said.

Everyone ignored her while they followed Mr. Newton into the living room.

Putting out his hand, Mr. Newton introduced himself, "I'm Trevor."

Mrs. Gem ignored it.

Looking at Crystal, he asked, "Is this true?"

"Is it true? How could you ask her that? Of course it isn't true!" Mrs. Newton answered. "Jake would never do anything like that. You know how these young girls are always calling and throwing themselves on him. She's just trying to trap him."

"If you say another negative word about my daughter, it's going to be me and you," Mrs. Gem threatened. The tone of her voice told everyone that she meant it.

"Yes sir, it's true," Crystal said.

Jake looked at his father. He wanted to deny it, but he knew his father would not believe him. This was not the first time Jake had been accused of sexual assault. The first time was a little over year earlier, and his father took care of it then. He could only hope that his father would do the same now.

Mr. Newton turned toward Jake, eyes blazing. "Go to your room and don't come out. As a matter of fact, I don't want to hear you breathe. I will deal with you later."

Jake faced Crystal, started to say something, then thought better of it and walked away.

His mother started to follow behind him, but Mr. Newton placed his big hands on her shoulders and stopped her. "Go fix us some drinks. I think we all need one." He looked at Mrs. Gem and said, "I think the young lady needs one as well, to calm her nerves. Don't you think so?"

"No, I don't think so. If you have hot tea, bring that instead," she said, sitting on the couch.

Mrs. Newton left the room.

"Now, what are we going to do about this?" Mrs. Gem wanted to know.

"What do you recommend?" Mr. Newton asked.

Crystal wanted to say, "Call the cops. What do you think we're going to do?"

Mrs. Newton returned with the drinks and said, "I say we forget about it. After all, we don't know what really happened."

Crystal looked at her in disbelief. "I know what happened. Your son raped me. I thought he liked me. He offered me a ride and was flirting with me. He said he needed to come home and invited me in. I liked him, so I said yes, and maybe I shouldn't have. Maybe that was stupid of me, but how was I supposed to know he was lying to me?" Close to hysterics, Crystal went on to tell them what happened and how she got home.

They knew she was telling the truth. The pain in her voice spoke volumes.

Mr. Newton stood up and told Mrs. Gem they should go in the kitchen and talk amongst themselves. Mrs. Gem followed him, leaving Crystal sipping on her tea as Mrs.

Newton looked past her, avoiding all contact. Ten minutes later her mother and Mr. Newton returned.

"Let's go." Mrs. Gem took the cup out of Crystal's hand and placed it on the table.

"Why are we leaving? What did you and him talk about? Where are the cops?"

Grabbing her hand, Mrs. Gem pulled her up and practically dragged her toward the door. "Come on. Like I said, everything is taken care of."

"Everything can't be taken care of. The cops aren't here," Crystal said.

Her mother ignored her.

Crystal never knew what transpired between her mother and Mr. Newton. Jake never returned to school, and suddenly they had extra money. Her mother spoiled her for a good three months before things returned to normal. Well, normal as far as appearances. To Crystal, nothing would ever be the same. Her relationship with her mother had never been the same. She felt as though her silence had been bought.

Now, over a decade later, sitting in a bar, Crystal found herself reliving what happened that dreadful day. Not that she ever forgot, because rape is something a victim never forgets or gets over. She just stopped letting it consume her.

Now it appeared that if this was Jake's son—and Crystal knew in her gut that it was, he was stepping into his father's shoes. Crystal really hoped Tina would press charges, because this was a case she would do pro bono.

Could this have been what her dream was about? Was it a warning, telling her to be prepared?

"Excuse me, miss? Excuse me, miss?" Someone was tapping Crystal on the shoulder, bringing her out of her past. "Are you all right to drive?"

Looking down at the bar, Crystal had four empty glasses in front of her. She only remembered ordering one.

WILL THE TRUTH SET YOU FREE?

Susan pulled up into the driveway of her two-story, three bedroom, two bath house, and saw her friend Timothy sitting on the porch. When she bought the house six years ago, she thought she'd have a family by now. She was in what she thought was a committed relationship, then she found out she was pregnant and told her man. He left her. Maybe it was God's intervention that caused her to have a miscarriage. Whatever it was, she was thankful that her best friend Timothy was there to help her through it.

Susan and Timothy had been through a lot with each other and for each other. They denied they were in a relationship when confronted, stating they were just friends. She stood by him when he used women, dogged them out and when he fell in love and got hurt. One time he almost got married, but with her help realized it would have been a mistake.

She'd threatened many women behind him and helped him out with bills when he was getting his band together. He walked her through one abusive relationship, beat the guy's behind and went to court. He stood by her through an abortion and supported her when she was in school.

Susan turned off her car and looked at Timothy. She wasn't sure if she should be pissed or happy to see him. She hadn't heard from him in over a month and suddenly there he sat, like it was okay.

Getting out of her car, she slammed the door and walked right by him, not saying a word. She did, though, take note of how good he looked. He had on a pair of black jeans, Timberland boots and a mock turtleneck sweater. His hair was freshly cut and she noticed he wore her favorite cologne, Jean Paul Gautier.

"Susan," he called out, noticing the angry look on her face. "Don't just walk by me."

She ignored him.

"Don't do that. Don't ignore me."

She went into her house and closed the door in his face. *The nerve of him,* she thought.

Timothy knocked on the door. Susan wouldn't answer it.

"Susan, let me in!" he yelled.

"No, go away!"

"Please," he begged. "I'll stand out here and knock and yell all day if I have to."

"You think you can just not call me or come see me for a whole month and suddenly pop up like everything is supposed to be okay?" She stood near the door with her hand on her chest, feeling her heartbeat, angry because she cared more than she wanted to admit.

"I'm sorry," Timothy told her. "I was away on an emergency."

Susan snatched the door open. "Where the hell did you go for a whole month that you couldn't call me? We've been friends for a long time. I thought we were tighter than that. If I had an emergency, I would call you right away and I thought the same applied—"

Not letting her finish, Timothy admitted. "I was in rehab."

Susan blinked twice. At a loss for words, she let him in.

"I just got out today and came straight here." He followed her into the living room.

She sat on the couch. Timothy remained standing. Just in case she decided to throw him out, he didn't want to get too comfortable.

Susan faced him. "Why?"

"Why what?"

"Why were you in rehab?"

"Because I needed to go."

"Why?"

Timothy shifted in his seat. "What is this, twenty questions?"

"You don't have to get nasty. It's just that I thought we could confide in one another, and for you to just disappear like that, I didn't know what to think. I've been stressing and worrying about your black ass. I thought maybe something happened to you then you pop up like it's okay and announce, 'Oh, by the way, I was in rehab'."

Timothy sat next to her and placed her hand in his. "Susan, I'm sorry for stressing you out. I just had to do what was right for me. I know that sounds selfish and all, but I felt like I was losing control. I was in trouble and trying to hide it from you and my band, but most of all from myself. I couldn't take it anymore. I've been getting high now for over a decade and it was time for me to take a look in the mirror. I didn't like what I saw. It was time for me to stop."

"Why now? Not that I don't think it's a good thing, but I didn't have a clue anything was going on."

Ashamed, Timothy put his head down and revealed that he'd almost overdosed.

"What! When?"

"Well, the last time I was over here. When I left, I hung out with Jelly and his crew. We were getting high all night. I don't remember much. All I recall is waking up soaking wet with them sitting around me, looking scared shitless. They said I'd passed out."

"They didn't call anyone, or try to get you to the hospital?

"They were afraid."

Susan rolled her eyes.

"Anyway, it was a wake-up call. I could have died, and they probably would have left me there to do so."

Susan sat in silence.

"I think you should stop also, especially if we're going to be together." Timothy's words surprised her.

"What do you mean, if we're going to be together?"

Timothy got on one knee, looked up at Susan and popped the question. "Will you marry me?"

"Stop playing." They had always joked about getting married when they grew older, neither of them really meaning it. It was usually said in jest, while they were both in relationships with other people.

"Being away from you those thirty days and getting clean opened my eyes and my heart. It made me realize how much you mean to me, how special what we have is. All these years we've been fooling ourselves, denying what we both know."

Susan could feel the tears welling up. Clearing her throat, she asked, "And what is that?"

"That we love each other, or better yet, that we are in love with each other."

Susan stood up and started pacing. "I don't know, Timothy. Getting married might ruin what we have. You know how I am. You know I'm moody and a fly by night person. Even you can't stand to be around me for a long period of time. You've said so yourself."

"Are you telling me no?"

"I'm not saying yes or no. I need to think about it. Will you let me do that?"

"Yes, but don't take too long."

61

There was an awkward silence, neither knowing what to say. To break the silence, Susan asked Timothy if he was hungry. She needed some sort of distraction from the conversation they were having. "I'll cook you something to eat," she told him, "and while you're eating, I'm going to jump in the Jacuzzi."

"Can I jump in with you?" Timothy asked.

"I need some time to think about what you said."

"I understand," he told her.

As she cooked him a steak, potatoes and broccoli, Timothy dozed off on the couch. She woke him up with his plate made, and headed toward the bathroom.

She turned on the Jacuzzi and sat on the edge thinking about Timothy's proposal. Suddenly, she started to cry. She thought about everything that Timothy had said, especially the part about her no longer getting high. This might be just what she needed to stop. She had to admit she did love him, his company and his lovemaking skills. Yes, they'd made love quite a few times, and it was always phenomenal.

Twenty minutes later, Timothy knocked on the bathroom door and walked in before she had a chance to say anything. "The food was delicious. I need to run out. Are you going to be home?"

She nodded.

Timothy bent over the Jacuzzi and kissed her on the lips. "I'll call you later, okay?"

"Okay," she told him and watched as he walked out.

She couldn't help smiling. *Yeah, it would definitely be nice to get that on a regular basis.* Maybe now she would have that family she always wanted.

WHAT'S A GIRL TO DO?

Elsie was thinking about the family she wanted to have one day but didn't know if she would because of her sexuality. She was starting to get the Mommy itch, but after considering adoption, she wasn't too keen on the idea. She wanted to have a child come from her womb. She wanted the experience of carrying a child for nine months.

Summer was already a parent; her daughter was damn near a teenager. Elsie had yet to meet her, even though she and Summer were in their sixth month of dating. Maybe it was a good thing she hadn't, because Summer was pressuring Elsie to take their relationship to another level, meaning she wanted her to move in. Elsie wasn't feeling it, and didn't have the nerve to tell her.

When Elsie pulled into Summer's driveway, there was an unfamiliar car with out-of-state plates parked in front of the house. Summer's front door opened and out walked an older couple. Summer was behind them, holding a little girl's hand. The conversation between Summer and the couple looked intense, so Elsie stayed put.

Shit. She was not in the mood for any drama. After leaving the office, she attended her book club meeting and was in a relaxed state of mind. She thought they would just have a couple of drinks, maybe make love. It didn't look like that was going to happen. If she wasn't parked in the driveway, she would have driven away.

Sitting in the car trying to act preoccupied, Elsie looked up to see the couple walking past. She almost spoke until she realized they purposely didn't look her way.

Elsie looked at Summer, who was watching them with a frown. Once the couple got into their car and pulled off, Elsie climbed out of her vehicle and headed toward Summer,   who bent down and said something to the little girl. The child went inside.

"What's going on?" Elsie asked, following Summer into the house. "It looks like you've been crying. Is that your daughter?"

Instead of answering the question, Summer said, "I can't wait to start buying furniture."

Summer had just purchased the house and asked Elsie to move in. Elsie, caught in the after effects of an orgasm, told her she would move in as soon as the lease on her condo was up. Unbeknownst to Summer, it was up over a month ago. Elsie wasn't too sure about the cohabitation. She liked her space, and after having grown up in a foster home, the whole sharing a room bit didn't appeal to her.

For Elsie, living alone would be hard to give up. She was used to doing what she wanted, when she wanted, and not having to worry about the other person. She liked to think that living with someone she was dating would be different, because they were moving in together for the sake of love, but she still wasn't sure about it. She'd already had one bad roommate experience, an experience she was not ready to repeat.

The bad experience turned her off to rooming. If it wasn't for the fact that she was saving to start her own business, she would have never done it. Tish was her roommate's name, the roommate from hell. For the first couple of months, everything was fine. They got along great. Food was always in the fridge, rent was paid on time and the house was always clean. Elsie considered herself lucky. Things started to change overnight. Tish started having all kinds of company at all hours of the night. Elsie was always picking up after her and she grew tired of it. Still she didn't say anything. She needed the money. Elsie tried her best to make it work, until one day she came home from work and some man was walking around nude, like it was his house.

"Where's Tish?" Elsie asked, averting her eyes.

"She's not here," he told her, not even trying to cover up. That was the last straw. Elsie threw her out and vowed she would never again have a roommate.

She knew things would not be this extreme with Summer, but it still stressed her when she thought about the whole "moving in together" thing. Now on top of everything else, it looked like Summer' daughter would be staying a while. Elsie had not missed the stack of suitcases near the steps.

"What's going on?" Elsie asked again.

Summer looked toward the steps. "That's my daughter, Winter."

Elsie figured that part out already. She was the spitting image of Summer.

"Is she moving in?" Elsie wanted to know.

"Well, it looks that way. Her father, my ex-husband, was in a car accident, and those were my parents."

Elsie didn't know what to respond to first. "An accident? Your parents?"

For starters, Elsie knew that Summer was estranged from her family. They wrote her off when she came out of the closet. Summer cried when she told Elsie the story of when she realized she was gay and could deny it no longer. She had dated and married her high school sweetheart, became pregnant the first year of marriage, and she thought having a baby would complete her. It didn't. She just grew more depressed, and being married to James wasn't what she wanted anymore. She was tired of living to please her dad. She just couldn't continue with the charade anymore.

One night after dinner, Summer told James they needed to talk. Taking his hands in hers, she told him she wanted a divorce. She didn't love him anymore, and felt he deserved better. He refused to leave, telling her, "I won't break up my family."

She stayed in the marriage, unhappily, until she met someone, another woman, who she was willing to take a chance on. Broaching the subject of divorce once again, it fell on deaf ears. Unable to put off her desire, Summer started seeing the woman on the sly.

One day, the only day the woman had come to her house, James was supposed to be out of town. He arrived home two days early and busted them making love. Being a man of God, he granted her the divorce on the condition that he got custody of their daughter. It was the hardest thing Summer ever had to do, besides telling her parents why they were divorcing. Her father, a minister, told her she was going to hell and disowned her. James took Winter and moved to another state. Summer got to see her on holidays and in the summer. Now it looked like she'd be seeing her every day.

"Summer, what's going on?" Elsie asked again, growing agitated.

"James is dead," Summer told her, crying. "He was killed in a car accident, he and his new wife."

"Oh my God. When did this happen?" Elsie was shocked.

"A week ago."

"A week ago and you're just finding out now? I don't understand that."

Summer didn't understand it either. She was still processing the information and the fact that she would now be a full-time mother to an eleven-year-old.

"What about Winter?" Elsie asked.

"She's mine now."

Elsie wasn't sure if she was ready for this. Yes, she wanted children, but her own. How would she bond with a pre-teen?

The way Elsie figured it, Summer would need time to bond with her daughter. It gave Elsie the perfect excuse for not moving in as quickly as planned.

"You know what?" Elsie told Summer. "I think I'm going to leave and give you two some time alone."

Summer didn't want her to leave, but she knew it was for the best.

"I'm sorry about all this," Summer told her a couple of days later.

"There's nothing to be sorry about," Elsie told her. "It's as much a shock to you as it is to me."

"She thinks you're nice," Summer told Elsie. The day before, they all went out to dinner, Elsie being introduced as Mommy's best friend.

"Summer," Elsie caressed Summer's cheek. "You know we have to change our plans now."

"What plans?"

"Moving in together."

"Why?" Summer didn't think all that was necessary.

"Look at it from your daughter's perspective. She's an eleven-year-old child, thrown together with her mom, who she never really lived with, and her father's dead. She needs time alone with you, time to learn you, and you need time to learn her."

Moving Elsie's hand, Summer asked, "Are you breaking up with me?"

"No, of course not. I love you. I just think we need to put off moving in together."

Summer didn't have to say anything. The pain was written on her face. Wanting to make it better and not cause too much distress, Elsie asked, "How hard does Winter sleep?

"Hard. Why?"

Summer let Elsie lead her into the bedroom. They looked at one another, each wondering if it would be a while before they made love to one another again.

"You do know I love you, right?" Elsie asked, sitting on the bed.

Summer nodded.

Elsie leaned over, kissed her on the lips gently and pushed her back. She put her hands under Elsie's shirt, caressing her breasts. "That feels good." Summer moaned when Elsie pinched her nipples.

"I know something else that'll make you feel good," Elsie told her. She unbuttoned Summer's shirt and licked her down the center of her chest to the top of her pants, which she unbuttoned slowly and pulled down. She slid her hands up Summer's legs and palmed her pussy, grinding it against her panties.

Elsie knew she was wrong for trying to "make it better" with sex, but she didn't know what else to offer. For now, their worries would cease to exist.

GOING THROUGH THE MOTIONS

Another week lay ahead, and Jewell was tired and frustrated. Tired because she was up studying all night for an exam and frustrated because her car was out of commission. The night before on the way home from the movies with Tyson, not only did it start overheating, but there was a clinking noise. There was no way she would have been able to drive the car to work. Evan called her and she told him of her dilemma. He offered to drive her to work.

Climbing out of the car, she told him, "I'll talk to you later."

He wasn't letting her get away that easy. He got out of the car and started walking beside her.

"What are you doing?" Jewell stopped walking.

"I would like to walk you to the door."

That was something Jewell didn't want, but how could she tell him no? She was already hiding him, not sure if she was embarrassed or ashamed of dating a white man. Yes, she enjoyed his company. He made her laugh, took her out, and opened her eyes to things she wouldn't normally see on her own. They went to museums, the opera, and tried a number of restaurants. Jewell knew it was getting serious, but on the down low she wondered if she was giving up on the black man.

"Okay, come on," she told him, giving in.

When they got to the door, he kissed her on the lips. "I know that was hard for you," he told her.

"What are you talking about?"

"I don't think I have to get into it, but I will tell you this. You're going to have to let go of your fears and take a chance if you want to continue seeing me. I don't like being kept a secret. This is not an affair that we're having. I'm hoping it's the beginning of something special, and if it's not what you're looking for or hoping to do, let me know."

Looking at Evan, Jewell told him, "It's too early in the morning for this conversation."

Evan nodded and kissed her on the cheek. "Call me when you know what you want to do."

Watching him walk away, Jewell thought about how she and her girls were always complaining about how hard it is to find a good man, a man to take them places, show them things, and not press up too hard when it came time for sex. Now that she'd found one, here she was dissing him, and it was all because of his skin color.

"Scary, isn't it?"

Jewell jumped. "Where did you come from?"

"My car." Elsie was standing behind her.

"Oh. What's scary?"

"Taboo relationships."

Jewell looked at her. She wasn't sure if Elsie was talking about her own gay relationship or Jewell's interracial one.

"I know you know about me," Elsie said.

"It doesn't matter," Jewell reassured her.

"I'm glad to hear that."

Unable to hold it in, Jewell blurted out, "I just can't get past the fact that he's white. It's bothering the mess out of me. In my head, the perfect relationship would be with a fine, tall, black—and I stress a *black* man—who loves me for me. Someone I could talk to about anything, not feel like I have to put up a front. Now that I've found all that, it's in a white man. Ain't that some shit?"

"That ain't nothing," Elsie responded, opening up a little. "I've found it in a woman."

They looked at each other and started laughing. Together they walked into the building and waited for the elevator beside Lange.

Now, why can't I find a brother like that? Jewell wondered. *Fine, educated, built and polite.*

When they reached their floor and the elevator door opened, Lange spotted Crystal walking by. He stepped out behind Jewell and Elsie. "Crystal!"

She stopped in her tracks and turned around. "Yes?"

"Can we talk?" Lange asked.

"Sure."

They went into her office and closed the door. Crystal sat at her desk.

"Why have you been avoiding me?" Lange placed both hands on her desk and leaned over so that his face was in hers.

"What are you talking about? I haven't been avoiding you." Crystal was straight up lying. She knew it and he knew it. She was afraid of him, afraid of the temptation. Ever since the day they almost kissed, she could not get him out of her system.

"I think you have been," he insisted.

"Well, you're wrong," she told him, pretending to look in her desk for something, the lie evident in her voice.

"Look, let's be honest with one another."

She looked up at him.

71

"I can't stop thinking about you." Lange waited for a reply. When he got none he went on. "And honestly, I don't know what to do about it, if anything."

"There's nothing you can do. You're a married man," Crystal reminded him.

Rubbing the back of his neck, Lange confessed, "I've never been in a situation like this before. I mean, of course I've been attracted to other women. There's been a look here and a look there, but I've never wanted to act on it. Never, that is, until the other day in the elevator with you."

Crystal didn't know what to say other than, "We can't and we won't act on it, so standing here discussing it is a waste of energy."

Lange looked at Crystal with a longing in his eyes. "Are you sure about that?"

"Yes. Yes, I am."

"Can we be friends?" Lange asked.

"We are friends," Crystal answered

On that note, Lange leaned over the desk and kissed her briefly on the lips. He turned around and walked out of the office. Once the door closed behind him, Crystal put her head in her hands.

She was lonely and wanted companionship—true companionship. Not a date here or a date there, but someone she could call her own. She hadn't had sex in over six months, and it was of her own doing. She'd been asked out a time or two, but the way the men either looked at her or their aura turned her off. She was extra careful because the last relationship she had was a disaster.

She had met Lewis at the movie theatre. She was sitting home alone that night and decided she'd treat herself to dinner and a movie. She was at the counter buying popcorn when she felt someone tap her on the shoulder and say, "I'll pay for that."

Turning around, she found herself staring into the lightest eyes on the darkest man. "Won't your date mind?" she asked him, thinking a man that fine would not be at the movies alone.

"I'm by myself."

"Then sure, you can pay."

They discovered they were each going to see the same movie and sat together, talking all the way through. It didn't take long for them to start dating.

There was one drawback. She had yet to go to his house. He always came to hers. When she finally realized this, she asked him about it. "I'm having my house remodeled," he told her.

"Well, let me come by and see what you're having done," she said.

He made up excuse after excuse.

It was Susan who told her she was being played and needed to find out more about him. Crystal decided to have him followed. What she found out not only hurt her, but it made her give up on men for a while.

Lewis didn't have a home. He was basically a freeloader, staying the night at different women's houses. When he wasn't doing this, he stayed in a motel.

Crystal could not believe that she, an attorney, was taken for a sucker. So now here she sat, lonely and wanting to date a married man.

Shaking her head, trying to get back into her professional space, Crystal picked up the phone and dialed Tina's number. She had decided not to take the case after the conversation she had with Susan.

Crystal asked her, "Do you remember how we became friends?"

"Of course. I remember."

"It was the day my life changed."

"Why bring it up?" This was something they had not discussed in ages. "I thought you had put that all behind you."

"Well, I've found out that it's not something you really put behind you."

They both grew quiet while picking over their lunches. Breaking that silence, Crystal went on to tell her, "I may have a chance to represent a young girl that was raped."

Susan stopped eating, put her fork down and looked at Crystal. She knew Crystal volunteered at the Women's Crisis Center, that she counseled rape victims, but never before had she chosen to take on one of the cases.

"I know you're probably wondering why this one. Well, are you ready for this?"

Susan waited.

"The rapist is Jake's son."

Susan looked at her in disbelief. "What did you just say?"

"The rapist is Jake Newton, Jr."

Susan started shaking her head. "I don't know, Crystal. I don't know about this. I don't think it's a good idea to take on this case."

"Why not? It may be my only chance."

"Your only chance to what? To go through all that pain you went through before? What good would come out of that?" Susan placed her hand on Crystal's shoulder and looked her in the eyes. "You really need to think about this long and hard. Personally, I don't think it's healthy. I don't think you should have any part of it. But whatever you decide to do, I'll back you up. Okay?"

With teary eyes, Crystal told her, "Thanks. That's all I needed to hear."

"Please." Susan waved her hands. "That's what friends are for."

They continued to eat until Susan said, "Well, I have some news."

"Good or bad?"

Clearing her throat, Susan said, "I'm not sure yet."

Crystal waited.

"Timothy asked me to marry him."

Shrieking, Crystal was genuinely pleased. "Oh my God! Get out of here. That's better than good, it's great. Hell, it's about time. I know you said yes. When did this happen? Why are you just now telling me?"

"Hold up, hold up. I haven't given him an answer yet."

"Why not? You know you two belong together."

"I'm scared," Susan confessed.

"Scared of what? Girl, please. You and Timothy have been in love for over ten years but were too busy playing the friends role to realize it. He's finally able to admit it. Why can't you?"

"I don't know."

"Don't you love him?"

"Yes."

"Is the sex good?"

"How did you—Oh, never mind! It's the best I've ever had."

"Well, there you go. He loves you. You love him. The sex is good. He's been there for you and your moody ass all these years, and you've been there for him. What more could you ask for?"

Susan just shrugged. She had no answer for that.

That evening when Jewell arrived home, she decided to call Evan and invite him over for dinner. Tyson was with his dad for the week.

"Evan, it's Jewell," she said when he answered the phone.

"Hey there."

"Um, I was wondering if you'd like to come over for dinner tomorrow night."

There was no response.

Sensing his hesitation, she told him, "We need to talk."

"About?"

"Us."

"What time do you want me there?"

The night arrived quicker than Jewell wanted it to. First she couldn't decide what to cook, and then she couldn't decide what to wear. She decided on lasagna, salad, and garlic bread. To wear, she settled on a long, white spaghetti-strapped dress, something simple yet sexy.

On edge and unable to relax, Jewell popped in the Floetry CD and took a hot shower. After getting dressed, she went into the eating area, turned the lights down low and lit the candles in the center of the table. She was admiring the view and the mood when the doorbell rang. She took a deep breath, ran her hands down the front of her dress and opened the door.

Evan stood there in all his whiteness.

"Hey, sweetie," she greeted him, kissing him on the mouth.

"Oh, so it's like that today?" he said.

"Like what? What do you mean? It's always that way."

"Yeah, when we're alone. Never out in public."

Jewell looked at him and decided to get real. "Listen, Evan, this isn't easy for me. I've never dated a white guy and really had no intentions to before you came along. You've changed that, but you need to understand that I'm scared and I don't know what I'm doing or even if I'm doing the right thing."

"Why do you have to do anything?" Evan wanted to know. "Why can't you just let it be?"

"Because I don't know how to let it be. I've never been too comfortable with interracial relationships, and to find myself in one has thrown me for quite a loop."

They were in the living room and Evan sat down and patted his knee. She sat on his lap.

"Do you think this is easy for me?" Evan asked.

"What are you afraid of?" Jewell asked jokingly. "That some big black guy is going to see us together and jack you up?"

"As a matter of fact, yes. Not that I can't handle my own, but just like you, I see the stares, the looks and the snickers. I feel the discomfort. No, you're not the first black woman I've dated or spent time with. I've been through this before and couldn't handle it, but I'm ready to now. I enjoy being with you, and I'm willing to take a chance. None of that other bullshit matters to me. What matters to me is you. Are you willing to take a chance?"

After hesitating for a brief moment, Jewell said, "Yes, I am."

Evan touched her face and brought it closer to his, brushing his lips against hers.

Pulling away, Jewell said, "There is a condition, and that's that you can't stay here late or overnight when my son is around."

"I understand that, and I can live with it." Actually, he respected her even more because of it. "So, if I can't stay late or overnight when he's here, are you saying I can stay the night when he's not?"

Running her fingers through his hair, she said, "He's not here tonight."

Evan placed his hands around her waist. Jewell stood up, facing him. She knew tonight would be the night they made love. He put his hands on her ass and slowly massaged her cheeks.

"I want to make love to you." He ran his hand up her back to the straps on her shoulder. He pulled them down slowly while kissing her belly.

"I'd like that," Jewell told him, moving closer.

"What about dinner?" he asked.

"Dinner can wait."

Evan flicked his tongue over her belly button and licked his way farther down. Looking up at her, he asked, "What do you want me to do?"

"Whatever you want," she whispered.

He stood and scooped her up in his arms. "Where?"

She pointed to her room and he carried her in, gently placing her on the bed.

Evan ran his hands down her body and promised her, "I won't hurt you. I just want to make love to you. I want you to surrender to me." He placed his tongue between her breasts then traveled down and stopped at her thighs. He pushed them open. "You're beautiful."

Jewell couldn't say a word. She just lay in wait.

"This is for you," he told her as he spread open her pussy lips, burying his tongue deep inside her. All Jewell could do was moan in response.

Later that night, Jewell and Evan lay in the bed together. He was cuddling her from behind. "How are you getting to work tomorrow?"

"The bus."

"I'll take you."

Of course Jewell would rather that than ride the bus, but she told him he didn't have to.

"I want to. I also want to help you get another car."

Jewell turned to face him. "No, that's not necessary. I can handle it."

"I'm sure you can, but if you're going to be my girl, then it's my duty."

Jewell knew the right thing would be to turn down his offer, but damn it, she did need a new car, and he said help her, not get it for her. So, against her better judgment, she agreed.

SHOW AND TELL

The fourth annual office party was fast approaching. Crystal was running herself ragged trying to arrange everything. Their guests included clients, other attorneys and a judge or two. The first year Crystal suggested a party, Susan wasn't too keen on it, saying, "We shouldn't party with people we work with."

"You're acting like we're having a street party. This is a professional party with professional people. It's a time to relax and be ourselves. We're a new firm, and it's a good way to put us out there. Good PR, so to speak. Plus, when the suits come off, people are different," Crystal responded.

Elsie was indifferent, as usual. She told them, "When you decide, let me know."

Everyone had such a good time at the first party that it became a yearly event, something to look forward to. People were able to relax, if only for a night.

"Jewell, when you return from lunch, will you call the planners and see where everything stands with the party?"

"Yes," Jewell responded. She was glad Crystal told her to do it after lunch. She and Elsie were stepping out. They had developed a friendship outside of the office. It had a lot to do with the fact that even in this day and age, to some, their relationships were considered taboo.

Earlier that day, Jewell was staring out the window, looking stressed. Elsie took notice and asked her if everything was okay.

"Not really," Jewell told her.

"Want to talk about it?"

Jewell figured what the heck, might as well. "Let's talk at lunchtime. It's sort of private."

Elsie wondered if she was the one Jewell should be talking to. Then again, she did offer, and you never know, the tables might be turned one day and she may need someone to talk to.

Lunchtime didn't come soon enough. They decided to go to a little café around the corner

"So, what's up?" Elsie leaned back on the booth.

"Well, I think I'm falling in love with Evan. I'm just not sure if it's the right thing to do or if I'm even ready for it."

"Why not? Is it because you're afraid of what you feel or what other people might think?"

"I'm not sure. I always thought black should be with black, and white should be with white."

"Yeah, I always thought men should be with women."

Jewell decided to ask what she'd wanted to know all along. "Why do you like women? Are you attracted to men at all?"

Elsie didn't answer for a while. No one had ever just come right out and asked her personal questions like that before. She wasn't sure if she wanted to expose herself.

Sensing her discomfort, Jewell apologized. "I'm sorry. I didn't mean to blurt that out. I was just curious. If I'm prying, excuse me. You don't have to tell me shit."

80

"No, you're not prying," Elsie told her. "It's not that I'm not attracted to men. Occasionally I might find one appealing. It's just that my preference is women. They are what makes me happy. There was a time when I wished I could change it, but I realized I couldn't and I've decided to accept it."

Jewell slammed her hand down on the table. "You know what we should do?"

"What?"

"You should bring your lover and I should bring Evan to the office party. It'll be our coming out night."

"I already invited Summer," Elsie revealed.

"Get out!" Jewell was surprised.

"Now I'm wondering if I should renege on the invite."

"Why would you do that?"

"Fear," Elsie answered honestly.

Later that night, Elsie sat on the couch, looked at the phone and tried to figure out a way to uninvite Summer. What would she say? "The party has been canceled." That would be too obviously untrue.

Elsie was nervous about coming out to friends and coworkers. As it was, Crystal and Susan were wondering why she rarely went on dates. In the past, Susan even tried to set her up with a couple of Timothy's friends. Well, they were going to find out tonight if she didn't come up with a plan.

She picked up the phone, dialed the number, hung up, dialed the number and hung up again. After the third hang up, she decided to get off the couch and try to keep busy until it was time to get dressed. As she stood up, the phone rang.

Elsie hesitated before answering the phone. "Hello?"

"Why do you keep calling and hanging up?" Summer wanted to know.

Duh. Elsie forgot about caller ID. Before she could answer, Summer said, "You're nervous about the party, aren't you?"

That was one of the reasons Elsie loved Summer. She knew her so well. "I'm a little nervous."

"If you've changed your mind about me going as your date, I'll understand."

Elsie knew Summer meant what she was saying, and she appreciated it.

"Well?" Summer asked. She would do whatever Elsie decided, because she knew that Elsie's coming out at the workplace was a big deal, not something to be rushed into.

Summer was offering her a way out. If she was smart she would take it, but she didn't. "No, I haven't changed my mind. I want you to come. I'm tired of hiding you. I'm tired of hiding us. I'm ready for this."

"Are you sure?" Summer asked.

"Yes, I am." Elsie had to admit she was tired of not being able to be herself, of hiding what was a big part of her. She couldn't be in the shadows forever, this she knew. So, why keep putting it off? She was who she was and it was time for people to start dealing with it.

"Good. I was getting a little worried," Summer told her. "Now, I'm going to go find something to wear. Love you."

"Love you too," Elsie responded before hanging up.

In a boutique downtown, Crystal was looking for an outfit to wear to the party. As usual, she was pissed because she'd waited until the last minute.

While in the dressing room, she heard a deep, sexy laugh. When she stepped out of the dressing room, she glanced around, being nosy. Crystal noticed that the woman who laughed looked extremely familiar, although she couldn't place her. Normally something like that would not have bothered her, but this time it did. She wanted to ask her if they had met, but there was an intimacy between the woman and the man she was with, so Crystal thought it was best not to disturb them.

"I can't see you tonight," she heard the woman say. "I have other plans."

"You always have other plans," the man said.

"Well, you know my situation," she told him, kissing him on the lips.

"That I do. Just try to make time for me soon. I miss you." On that note, the lady walked away, glancing briefly at Crystal.

After choosing a white pantsuit and paying for her outfit, Crystal decided to go home and call Roger. When he had pulled her over, it was a shock seeing him. But once she'd had a chance to digest it, she had to admit it was nice, and the past was the past. Maybe it was time to let it go.

She and Roger had broken up a week after the rape when she told finally told him what happened. Instead of being there for her, he distanced himself. She was hurt by his response, which was to run the other way. Now she realized that it was because he was young and didn't know how to handle it.

Before going home, Crystal decided to drop by the bookstore. She hadn't read a good book in a long time. Reading used to be one of her passions, when she had time for it, and after hearing Elsie on the phone with one of her book club members, she'd decided to try to get back into it.

She pulled into the parking lot and wondered what was going on. It was packed. When she walked in, she read a sign announcing a book signing. *Essence* best-selling author Angel M. Hunter was signing her new book.

Might as well buy one of her books while I'm here, Crystal thought. Looking at the line and noticing how long it was, she decided to look around until the crowd thinned out.

She was glancing through magazines when she felt someone tap her on the shoulder. Lo and behold, it was Roger!

Crystal shook her head and laughed. "It's just funny seeing you here."

"What? A brother can't read?" he joked with her.

"No, no, nothing like that. I was thinking about giving you a call when I got home."

"Oh yeah?"

Boldly, Crystal told him, "I was going to ask you if you'd be interested in going out."

"Really?"

"Yes."

"When?"

"I know it's last minute and all, but my firm—"

"Your firm?"

"Yes, I'm an attorney. My firm is having an office party, and I was wondering if you would be my date."

"I'd be honored."

Crystal opened her purse, pulled out her business card and handed it to him. "Give me a call and I'll give you the details."

Roger gladly took the card and told her, "I will do that."

Suddenly Crystal felt uncomfortable and unsure of herself. "Um, well, I'll talk to you later." She left him standing there.

THE PARTY

They had rented out one of the ballrooms in the Sheraton for the party. Crystal arrived before anyone else. She wanted to make sure the planner had everything under control, and wanted to take a look around to feel the ambience. The decor looked spectacular. Crystal had to admit she was quite pleased with what she saw. The tables were set with purple satin tablecloths; the centerpieces held lilac and lavender flowers, there were aromatherapy candles throughout the room the DJ was playing Eighties music, and the seafood buffet looked delicious.

She glanced at her watch and saw that it was 6:30 p.m. Roger should be arriving any moment. She told him an earlier time than the other guests, so they would have a chance to talk and get reacquainted.

Crystal was talking to the party planner when she saw Roger walk in. "Excuse me." She went to greet him.

"Hey there." Crystal gave him a quick hug while she took in his attire—a cream-colored suit, cream shirt, burgundy tie and handkerchief. He was definitely a sight for sore eyes.

"You look handsome," she complimented.

"Thank you." He took a look around. He was impressed. "Where is everyone?"

"You're the first to arrive."

"Really?"

"I asked you to come a little early so we could catch up with one another."

Crystal noticed Roger taking her in.

"Why are you looking at me like that?"

He smiled. "Do you know that you still look the same, if not better?"

Crystal blushed. "Would you like a drink?"

"No, but what I would like is another chance." His answer caught her off guard. "Ever since that day I pulled you over, I've been thinking about you. Even before I pulled you over I wondered how you were, what were you doing, and what you'd be up to."

Crystal didn't know what to say.

"When I moved back here, I thought about looking you up, but chickened out." Roger was going for the gusto, and since he was putting it all out there, Crystal figured she might as well do the same.

"Well, you did break my heart."

"We were young, teenagers."

"Yeah, but I was in love with you, and when I told you what happened, you stopped dealing with me. You told me I shouldn't have gone with him. Do you know how much that hurt?"

"I couldn't handle it," Roger told her.

"It wasn't for you to handle. All you had to do was be there for me."

"I understand that now. I didn't then. Listen, Crystal, I don't know what to say, but you invited me here, and I hope it wasn't to beat me up over something that happened ages ago. I apologize. That's all I can do."

Crystal realized that she still held some resentment, and after hearing the sincerity in his voice, she felt embarrassed by it. She touched Roger's hand and said, "You know what? Let's start over."

"I think that's a good idea," Roger said.

"Roger, I'm glad you could make it." Crystal greeted him as if he just walked in the door.

"I'm pleased you invited me."

Together they laughed.

"How would you like a drink?" she offered.

"Sure."

They moved toward the bar.

Slowly but surely, people started to come in. First came Susan with Timothy. Crystal noticed that they were holding hands. She was delighted they decided to stop playing games and declare their love for one another.

"We know too much about each other," Susan would tell Crystal in the past when she'd ask why they didn't hook up. The pretense was finally over.

The second Susan spotted Roger, she recognized him. "Oh my God, what are you doing here? I haven't seen you in ages." She let go of Timothy's hand and gave Roger a hug, looking at Crystal with a question mark in her eyes.

"It's good to see you too." Roger smiled then turned to shake Timothy's hand. "What's up, man?"

After brief conversation, Crystal and Susan went to meet and greet their guests.

Timothy walked up behind Susan and whispered in her ear, "Will you look at that?"

Susan looked up to see Jewell and Evan walking in.

From across the room, Crystal spotted them at the same time. She noticed that Jewell looked a bit nervous. Approaching her, Crystal smiled. "Hey, girl."

"Crystal, this is Evan, my date." They shook hands, then in strolled Summer and Elsie. When Jewell saw them, she relaxed, because she knew that the focus would now be taken off her.

Timothy saw them as well. "There are all kinds of surprises tonight," he told Susan.

"What are you talking about?" Susan wanted to know.

"You'll find out soon enough." Timothy knew Summer from one of the clubs his band performed at. He'd asked her out quite some time ago and she politely refused him. She told him he wasn't her type. When he asked her what was her type, she told him flat out—women.

When Elsie reached them, she boldly introduced Summer as her date. Crystal almost choked on her drink. Susan's mouth was on the floor.

"Your date?" Susan repeated, checking to see if she heard right.

"Yes, my date."

"Well, aren't we full of surprises?" Susan said, looking at Timothy, who was smiling at Summer.

"Timothy! Long time no see," Summer said.

"You two know each other?" Elsie asked.

"Yeah, from Tigers. His band performs there occasionally." Looking at Timothy, she said, "I haven't seen you in a while. The band doesn't sound the same without you."

"I was on vacation."

"Hope you had a nice time."

"It was something I definitely needed," he told her.

When Susan and Timothy were alone, she asked him if he knew Elsie was gay.

"I didn't know Elsie was gay, but I knew Summer was, and it didn't take a genius to figure it out once I saw them walk in together."

Susan shook her head. "I can't believe it. How could I have missed something like that?" Looking in Summer's and Elsie's direction, Susan said, "I'll tell you this much, they don't look gay."

Across the room, Crystal was having a similar conversation with Roger. They were discussing how people aren't always who you think they are.

"I take it you're not close with the people you work with? Were you and Susan friends in school?"

"It's not that. We just don't share our business with one another, and yes, Susan and I were close, but sometimes you drift—" Crystal stopped mid-sentence. Her attention was directed to the door.

Roger followed her gaze. Lange had just arrived, and on his arm was the woman from the boutique. They were headed in her direction.

"Crystal," Lange said when he reached her. "You remember my wife, Lena, don't you?"

Crystal's glass slipped out of her hands. One of the waiters came running over. "Let me get that for you."

That's why she looked so familiar, Crystal thought.

"Hi, I'm Lange." He introduced himself to Roger. "This is my wife, Lena."

Lena looked at Crystal and remembered her from the boutique. "Nice outfit," she said in a tone that let Crystal know she recognized her.

"Thanks." Crystal needed to step away and get a breather. "Would you all mind excusing me for a moment?" Before anyone could respond, she was off.

Once in the bathroom, she closed the door behind her and leaned over the sink. Damn, here she was interested in a man whose wife was having an affair. Should she say something or not? If she decided to, would it be for selfish reasons only? If she didn't, would she be betraying a friend?

As she was splashing water on her face, Lena walked in. "We need to talk," she said as if they were friends.

Crystal placed her hands on her hips. "What could we possibly have to talk about?"

Clutching her Gucci bag, Lena said, "I know you saw me in the boutique."

Crystal remained silent.

"I also know you heard what was said."

Crystal crossed her arms. "Yeah, and?"

"I'm begging you not to say anything."

Crystal just looked at her.

"Please, this is between Lange and me."

Crystal interrupted her and said, "You know what? I really don't want to know all this. I think we should go back before they start looking for us." Crystal started walking toward the door.

Grabbing her arm, Lena told Crystal, "I know you're attracted to him."

Crystal looked at Lena's hand on her arm. "What you need to do is let go of my arm."

Lena let go and immediately apologized. "I didn't mean anything by that."

"I'm sure you didn't."

"I'm just asking you—"

Crystal threw her hand up. "I think the best thing right now would be for you to get out of my face."

Susan walked into the bathroom before Lena could reply. She felt the fireworks that were passing back and forth between Crystal and Lena. "What's going on?" she asked.

"Not a thing," Crystal told her.

Susan looked at Lena and back at Crystal. "Are you sure?"

"I just don't feel too well," Lena said and walked out.

Susan looked at Crystal. "What the hell was that all about? Isn't that Lange's wife?"

"Yeah."

"What were you two talking about? The tension in the air is thick as hell."

"Girl, you don't want to know."

Susan did want to know, but not just that second, so she didn't push it. She wanted to take a quick hit of the package she had in her purse.

"Maybe you'll tell me later."

"Yeah." Crystal turned and left the bathroom.

Susan went into one of the stalls, took her package out of her purse and breathed a sigh of relief. She'd been waiting on this hit for hours.

LADIES' NIGHT

In the two weeks since the party, two things had been bothering Crystal. One was the whole Lena/Lange situation. She had become obsessed with what she should do about it, if anything. On one hand, she wanted to tell him what she saw, and on the other, she wanted to mind her own business. Crystal knew she couldn't avoid Lange forever. She was glad that he was out of town at a law conference.

After going out a couple of times with Roger, she told him what she knew and asked for his opinion.

"Why are you so concerned?" Roger asked when she brought up the subject for the fourth time.

"Lange and I are friends."

"Is that all you are?"

"Why would you ask me that? Lange's a married man."

"That doesn't mean as much as it used to. Shit, as high as the divorce rate is, people don't care as much as they used to about marriage."

"Well, I care, and I resent your implying that I don't." On that note, Billie came running into the living room. He looked at Roger and growled.

"He doesn't like me much," Roger commented.

"Why would you care if he likes you?" Crystal thought he was talking about Lange. "He barely knows you."

Roger picked up on it and told her, "I'm talking about your dog."

"Oh."

The second thing that was bothering Crystal was that since the party, no one had commented on their dates, especially Elsie and Jewell. Not that she wanted to be all up in their business, nor were their relationships or sexual preferences an issue, but it seemed liked they were avoiding the subject altogether. They had talked about who was there and what went on, but they avoided the topic of themselves. Crystal couldn't help but wonder whether it was intentional. Were they purposely discussing only the surface stuff? She made the decision to connect, maybe have a girls' night out and get to know one another on a more personal level. Crystal had Jewell type up a memo requesting that they go out the upcoming Friday. They had never really hung out together. This would be a first. If they questioned her motives, she would be honest and tell them that it was because the office didn't feel like a team.

To her surprise, they all agreed.

Crystal picked out Blue Moods Comedy Club in Manhattan for their girls' night out. Depending on how they felt afterwards, they might go dancing. The girls couldn't wait for their night out. They decided to meet at Crystal's. They would ride to Manhattan in her truck. Since the ride was a little over an hour, Crystal knew it would make for an interesting conversation.

Crystal was pulling on her designer jeans and zipping up her stiletto boots when she heard the doorbell ring.

"Coming!" she yelled.

When she opened the door, she was surprised to see Susan, Jewell and Elsie standing there. "What is this? You all came together?"

Susan answered, "Nope. We pulled up within seconds of each other."

Crystal glanced at her watch. "Wow, I'm impressed. You're all on time."

"You threatened us, remember?" Susan joked.

Crystal smiled. She did tell them not to be late or else. What would go behind the or else, she didn't know.

"Well, come on in. Would anyone like a glass of wine?"

They all said no.

"All right then, let me run upstairs and get my purse."

Jewell wanted a tour first. "Can I see your house?"

"Sure. Follow me."

"Why don't we all get a tour?" Elsie asked, wanting to be nosy as well.

Susan had been to Crystal's on a number of occasions, so she went along just because.

After the tour, they stood in front of the mirror near the front door. Crystal wore Dolce and Gabanna jeans, a black leather tank vest with a black lacy bra underneath, and black stiletto boots. Susan had on black leather pants with a white v-neck bodysuit, and stiletto heels. Jewell sported a red miniskirt with a flowing black top, ultra-sheer black stockings, and boots, and Elsie had on black slacks, boots, and a black bodysuit, simple yet sexy.

"So, ladies," Crystal said, "do we look good or what?"

They all agreed.

Once in the truck, Crystal popped in the latest R. Kelly CD.

"That's one talented man," Jewell said. She loved herself some R. Kelly. It didn't matter to her what anyone said about him. She knew how to separate the music from the man.

"I agree. This is his best CD yet," Susan said.

"Crystal, having this ladies' night out was a good idea," Elsie said.

They all agreed.

"I wish I would have thought of it sooner. After all, we work together every day and sometimes we barely have conversation unless it's work related. I figured, what better way to bring us together than through laughter?"

"Laughter and honesty," Susan added.

"Why honesty?" Jewell wanted to know. If they wanted honesty, she was going to give it to them. She was dying to ask Susan why she gave her such a hard way to go.

"Well, for one," Susan started, looking at Elsie, who knew it was coming, "how come you didn't tell us you were gay? I thought we were girls. Maybe we're not the best of friends, but, well, something like that I'd think you would share."

"Well, to be honest," Elsie started, "I never really considered us girls. Like Crystal said, we barely talk unless it's work related, and I really didn't think my personal life was of any interest to y'all."

Susan didn't have a response.

"Well, maybe we need to change all that. Maybe we need to create another type of relationship between us," Crystal suggested, and they all agreed.

"Since we're doing the honesty thing, Susan, let me ask you something. Why do you give me a hard time?" Jewell asked.

Susan was all set to deny it.

"Please don't deny it. Lately we've been butting heads left and right. What is it about me that pisses you off?"

"You don't piss me off, Jewell. I'm just hard on you because I want you to succeed."

"Well, you get more bees with honey," Jewell told her.

"I know that, but I don't know. It's just that I see a young, single black mom trying to do her thing, and I feel some sort of obligation. I don't want you to get too comfortable."

"I thought you didn't like me, that you didn't want to hire me," Jewell said, recalling the conversation she overheard the day she was interviewed.

Everyone wondered how she knew that.

"I'll admit that when we first met you, I thought you were a little rough around the edges, and I wasn't too keen on hiring someone with no experience. Not only that, but you walked in chewing gum. Your first impression left a lot to be desired."

No one said a word. They were surprised Susan revealed that much.

Susan went on. "But I'm glad to say that you've proven me wrong. You're smart as hell, and I don't want to see you limit yourself. The way I figure it, if I'm hard on you, you'll reach higher."

Jewell kind of understood what she meant, but she still told her, "Wow, thanks. I've worked hard to prove myself. But you do need to lighten up, because I was beginning to take it personally."

"Don't. I just have my own issues." Susan felt put in her place.

"Heck, we all have our issues. I'm gay," Elsie said.

"Timothy asked me to marry him, and I'm scared it may mess up what we have now," Susan said.

"I'm falling in love with a white man," Jewell chipped in.

"Me, well . . . I'm interested in a married man whose wife, I know for a fact is having an affair," Crystal finally revealed.

They all looked at Crystal, surprise evident on their faces. "This is the stuff novels are made of," Jewell joked. They all agreed and laughed heartily.

The ride to the city went quicker than expected. Before they knew it they were pulling into the parking lot next to the club.

"Did you make reservations?" Susan asked Crystal.

"Of course," she replied.

"The couple you were talking about, it's Lange and his wife, isn't it?" Susan leaned over and asked in a hushed tone.

"How do you know?"

"Because of the look on your face at the office party and how you and Lange are around each other."

Crystal didn't even bother to ask what she meant by that. She just hoped her interest wasn't obvious to anyone else.

As they were heading toward the club, while Elsie and Jewell walked in front, Crystal told Susan what she knew about Lena. "What do you think I should do about it? Should I tell him?"

"If you told him, what purpose would you be serving?"

Crystal looked at Susan and wondered why she had to be so deep.

Blue Moon was packed. That was to be expected when Adele was performing. They waited patiently while the warm-up comedian did his thing. He was wack as hell. Crystal was relieved when she had to go to the bathroom.

"I'll be back. I'm going to the ladies room. Anyone else want to go?" No one did. Getting up and turning around, Crystal looked right into Lange's face. Sitting back down quickly, she tapped Susan on the shoulder.

"I thought you had to go to the bathroom," Susan said.

"I do," she whispered, while looking over Susan's shoulder. "Lange is here."

Susan turned around and her eyes met Lange'. He nodded and pointed to Crystal. "You might as well go now. He's spotted us and I think he wants you."

"I'll be back." Crystal stood up, ran her hands through her locks and headed in Lange's direction.

"Hey, lady," he greeted.

"Hey yourself. I thought you were away." Crystal eyed him up and down. She thought he was getting finer and finer. His attire was semi-casual, and it appeared to do him more justice than a suit. He was wearing a pair of off-white linen pants with a cream-colored linen shirt. His top four buttons were open and Crystal noticed his chest hairs peeking from beneath. She took it all in.

"You look good in those jeans," Lange complimented.

"You're looking mighty handsome yourself," Crystal told him. "So, did your wife go with you to the conference?" She knew that spouses could attend this one. It was in Vegas.

"No."

She couldn't help but ask, "Whose idea was that?"

"Both of ours."

I bet it was, Crystal thought.

"Hey, man," one of the men at the table said. "Aren't you going to introduce us to the pretty lady?"

"No," Lange told him.

Still in need of the bathroom, Crystal asked Lange to excuse her. Before stepping to the side, he asked her if she and her friends would like to join him and his boys after the show.

"I have to check with the girls first. Where are you going?"

"To a little spot in the Village. They have good food, strong drinks and a live band."

"Sounds like a plan. I'll let you know." Crystal turned and walked away with an extra pep in her step. Lange watched her with lust on his face.

From across the room, Susan watched him watch Crystal and thought, *Those two are definitely headed for trouble.*

"You did what?" Susan asked, knowing full well she had heard Crystal correctly.

"Well, I didn't tell him we would go with them. I said I had to ask you guys. I can always go and tell him no, that we have other plans."

"I thought this was supposed to be ladies' night," Elsie said.

"It is, and it still can be. I didn't tell him yes. We all have to agree or else the answer is no."

"I could care less," Jewell said. "We were talking about going out afterwards anyway. Does it really make a difference where?"

After the performance, the girls decided to go with Lange and his crew after all.

"I just hope they don't try to press up," Elsie said.

"Are you going to tell them you're gay?" Jewell asked.

"No, it's none of their business. I'll just let them know I'm not interested."

They asked Lange where they should meet. He gave them the address and introduced his boys as Lawrence, Dana and Smokey.

The second they stepped into the club, the men started pressing up. Elsie ignored it at first, even danced a couple of times, until Lawrence decided to let his hands roam.

"What are you doing?" she asked him and pushed his hands away.

"I thought we were enjoying each other," he said, obviously drunk.

"We were until you started touching and feeling." With that she walked away, leaving him in the middle of the dance floor.

Jewell had witnessed the interaction and was laughing. "I saw that," she told Elsie when she sat down.

"He was like an octopus."

Teasing her, Jewell said, "You know you miss a man's touch."

Elsie rolled her eyes.

"I was only kidding," Jewell told her.

"I know, I know. It's just that I feel guilty. I'm in New York, chilling, having a good time, and my girl is home waiting."

A few seconds later, Lawrence and Smokey sat down next to them. Smokey asked Jewell for her number.

"Sorry, can't give it to you. I'm seeing someone."

"Well, can't you have friends?"

Jewell looked at him and said, "Please. Don't you know that's the oldest line in the book?"

Smokey reached into his pocket and pulled out a business card. "Well, take this in case you need a doctor."

Jewell looked at the card and saw that he wasn't lying. He was a doctor. Had she not been involved with Evan, it might have moved him up a notch or two. But she also knew this was his way of letting her know what she turned down. Jewell handed him back the card and said, "I already have a doctor."

Meanwhile across the room, Crystal and Lange danced together a number of times.

Lange took a step back and asked her, "What are we doing?"

"I don't know," Crystal told him.

"I'm a married man," Lange said.

"But is your wife a married woman?" Crystal let that slip out.

"What do you mean by that?"

This was the moment she could tell him. She just couldn't bring herself to do it. "I mean letting you go away by yourself like that. If you were mine, I would have never allowed it."

"If I was yours, I wouldn't have agreed."

The band started to play "Secret Lovers" by Atlantic Star. Crystal took Lange's hands, put them around her waist and pressed up against him. She placed her head on his chest and they swayed to the beat of the music.

"This feels good," Lange groaned in her ear.

Crystal pressed up closer. She wished this moment could last forever.

When the song was over, Lange took her hand. "Let's sit down for a minute. I have to get my bearings."

They walked across the dance floor. "Excuse me," Crystal said to a couple that stood in the way. The man turned around and Crystal gasped. It was Jake Newton.

"Crystal? Crystal Gem?" he said as if everything was fine. "I haven't seen you in a long time. How's everything? You're looking good."

At that exact moment, Susan came out of the ladies' room, looked onto the dance floor and noticed Crystal with a shocked look on her face. Susan rushed to the floor when she saw Jake standing next to Crystal.

"Get away from her," Susan told Jake the second she reached them.

"I'm sorry," he ignored Susan, "about what happened all those years ago."

"Sorry this," Susan said and smacked the shit out of him.

He just stood there and took it.

Jake's dance partner looked like she didn't know what to do, and Lange looked just as confused.

Susan grabbed Crystal's arm and pulled her off the dance floor. She told Lange, "We have to go."

"Susan, who the fuck was that?" Lange asked, following her.

Rushing to the table, Susan told Elsie and Jewell, "We have to go." They looked from Susan to Crystal. "Come on."

"What's going on?" Elsie asked.

"We're leaving," Susan told them.

Once outside, Lange told Susan, "Give me and Crystal moment alone."

Susan looked at Crystal, who nodded.

"We'll go get the car. Give me your keys."

Lange looked angry. "What's going on? Talk to me. Tell me what happened in there." He felt concerned for Crystal and angry because it was obvious that guy had done something to her. He wanted to know what, so he could handle it.

Crystal didn't have the energy to lie. She decided to be truthful. "Lange, I was raped a long time ago, and that was the guy."

Lange didn't know what to say. This was the last thing he expected to hear. He had a million questions, but he knew that this was neither the time nor the place to get into them. He pulled out his card and wrote down his cell number. He told Crystal to call him the minute she got home.

"I will," Crystal told him. She sensed his anger and was touched by his concern. "Lange, please just leave him alone. It happened a long time ago." Lange kissed her on the cheek without making any promises then went back inside.

When Crystal climbed into the car, Susan was in the driver's seat. Jewell and Elsie asked, "What the hell happened? What's going on?"

Crystal told them who Jake was.

"And he had the audacity to speak to you?" Jewell said.

Elsie didn't know what to say.

"Let's just leave," Susan said.

"I'm sorry, y'all. I didn't mean to ruin the night out with my drama," Crystal apologized.

"Girl, please," Elsie reassured her. "It's late anyway. Don't worry about that."

The ride home was quiet. Everyone fell asleep and that left Susan driving alone and high. She'd spent most of the night in the bathroom taking hits of cocaine.

"I think I'll tell Timothy yes," she said out loud. When no one answered, she glanced at all the girls and laughed.

When they pulled up to Crystal's, she woke them. "We're here."

"Does anyone want to come in for coffee or anything?" Crystal asked, hoping they would say no. She was just trying to be polite.

"No, I'm going home to call Evan, plus I have to pick up my son from his father's in four hours," Jewell said, glancing at her watch.

"I'm going to Summer's," Elsie said.

"I'm going home," Susan said.

Hugging each other goodbye, they told Crystal to call one or all of them if she needed to talk.

"I'm okay," she reassured them, letting herself in the house. Once inside she went upstairs, took a shower, put on her flannel gown, the one that comforted her, and tried to put Jake out of her mind. She looked at the phone and wondered whether she should call Lange. She was worried about what may have taken place after they left the club. The look on his face when she told him who Jake was scared her.

Crystal retrieved her purse and pulled out his cell number. She dialed the digits. The phone rang three times and she was about to hang up when she heard, "Hello."

"Lange?"

"Crystal?"

"Yes, it's me. I just wanted you to know I made it home and I'm okay."

"Are you sure?"

"Yes." She didn't hear any loud music in the background, so she asked him, "Where are you?"

"On the turnpike. Do you want me to come sit with you for a while?"

Before she could think about it, she responded, "Yes."

"What's your address?"

She told him. After they hung up, she asked herself, "What are you doing? He's a married man. You should not be letting a married man in your house at four in the morning."

She decided to keep on her gown. She didn't want it to appear as if she'd "gotten ready" for him. "He's just coming by to check on me. He saw how upset I was and he's being a good friend," she said out loud trying to calm her nerves.

Crystal sat on the couch and wrapped a blanket around her body. She was just about to doze off when she heard a car pull into the driveway. She jumped off the couch and ran to the door. Just as Lange was about to knock, she pulled it open, causing him to jump back.

"Whoa," he said.

"I heard you pull up. Come on in," she told him. "You got here fast."

"I was near the exit."

He followed her into the living room while Billie sniffed behind him.

"You want something to drink?" she offered.

"No thank you."

They sat down, neither saying a word.

Lange took Crystal's hand in his and caressed it. "Are you okay?"

"I'm fine. I was a little shook up. It was a surprise to see him. It happened so long ago, and for some unreal reason, I thought I'd never see him again."

"Is there anything I can do for you—to him?" She could tell Lange meant it. "When did this happen?"

"In high school."

"Did you report him?" Lange asked.

"No, but I did tell my mother. Back then people were quick to cover things up. Namely, our families."

Lange didn't know what to say.

"The funny things is," Crystal continued, "when I used to think about confronting him, I had this big 'Why' speech prepared. To finally get that chance tonight and freeze up pisses me off."

"So, this was first time you'd seen him since it happened?"

"Since that day." She proceeded to tell him how she and her mother went to their house with a gun and Jake's father bought their silence.

"Damn, Crystal. I'm so sorry this happened to you. Have you ever discussed it with your mother?"

"No, it's like it never happened."

"Have you ever gotten counseling?"

"No."

"You know it's never too late."

Crystal nodded.

Lange sat back on the couch. "Crystal, can I be straightforward with you?"

"Of course."

"I know I shouldn't be here, especially this late, but I wanted to check on you, make sure you were okay. I'm here to hold you if you need to be held, talk if you need to talk. Even if you just want to do nothing but sit quietly, I can do that."

She glanced at the clock on the wall and asked him, "Aren't you going to get in trouble for being out like this?"

Just because she didn't acknowledge what he said didn't mean that his words escaped her. He could have meant anything, but they both know what he was saying. She knew they shared something special, and it scared the mess out of her.

"I'm a grown man, Crystal."

"Yes, but you're also a married man."

"Lena is with her sister in Connecticut."

"Oh. You two are apart a lot lately." Crystal was fishing.

Lange shifted uncomfortably. "That we are."

"You don't seem too happy about it."

"Honestly, I don't know what I am."

"Do you want to talk about it?"

He looked her straight in the eyes and said, "What I want to do is make love to you."

"We can't." She moved away.

"I know," he replied while putting his lips on hers.

Crystal felt the moistness between her legs. She threw common sense to the wind, took his hand and placed it between her legs. "Touch me," she demanded.

"How about I taste you instead?"

Now that was what she wanted to hear. It had been so long since she'd made love with a man, much less had oral sex performed on her. *Please let this man do this right.* Crystal always loved this part of foreplay and hated when she got disappointed by a man going down there and eating like it was a snack instead of an entrée.

Lange put his hands on her hips and stood her up. He pulled up her gown and placed his face on her love spot.

"Your scent is divine," he told her.

Thank God I showered, she thought as she pushed her hips forward, hoping he got the message.

He pushed her legs apart.

"I need to sit," she told him as she anticipated the rush.

"No, I want you to stand. It's more intense that way." Lange ran his tongue on the insides of her walls. He played with her lips before finding her clitoris.

Crystal went weak in the knees and started to grind against his mouth. Unable to stand it anymore, she felt her knees buckle and called out, "I'm about to come."

After he felt her shudder, he looked up at her, put a finger inside her and said, "Are you sure about this?"

She laughed a low, deep laugh. "It's a little late for that now, don't you think?" She started moving against his hand. "Lange, I want to put you inside me." She took a step back and bent over to unzip his pants.

"Do you have any condoms?" Lange asked.

Crystal looked at him, ashamed because it slipped her mind. "I believe I do."

Crystal went upstairs and searched her drawers. Growing discouraged, she went into the bathroom and under the sink in the back was a box of unopened condoms. "Thank you," she said and took one out.

When she returned, Lange was sitting on the couch with his pants undone. She was pleased at the sight. "Where were we?"

"I believe you wanted me inside you."

They started to kiss and Crystal pulled Lange's pants down and off. She faced him and straddled him slowly. She took in every single inch.

"You feel as good as I thought you would." He placed his hands on her hips and tried to control her movements. She pushed them away.

"Let me be in control." She proceeded to ride him slowly.

Lange put his head back on the couch. "What are you doing to me?" he kept repeating over and over. "What are you doing?" Suddenly his body tightened up, he grabbed Crystal's hips, and said, "I'm about to come."

When he was done, she relaxed on his chest and said, "I'll go get a towel."

"Can I stay with you tonight?" he asked.

"Yes," she told him. "Come with me upstairs."

She climbed off him and he took the condom off. Embarrassed, he wanted to apologize for coming so quick, but didn't want to bring attention to it.

"Flush it down the toilet. The bathroom is down the hall to the right. I'll meet you upstairs."

When he entered the bedroom, he took off his shirt and entered the bathroom where Crystal was washing off. He stood behind her. "You're so beautiful." Crystal turned to face him. She ran her fingers through his soft and curly chest hair. She moved her hands over his shoulders and across his back. "Let's take it to the bed."

The lovemaking they shared that night was the most intense experience each had ever had. They brought each other to new heights. It was as if their bodies were made for one another.

After they showered together, they lay in the bed and Lange held Crystal to him. They both knew that this was a mistake, but both wanted it to happen.

Lange knew that getting involved with Crystal would only make matters worse. How could he have been so stupid? He had let his feelings get the best of him—his feelings and his libido. He didn't want anyone to get hurt, himself included.

"Stop," Crystal said out of nowhere, feeling his vibe.

"Stop what?"

"Thinking so much."

"How did you know?"

"I could feel it. Lange, let's not regret tonight. It happened, and it's obviously something we both needed. Let's just enjoy the moment."

On that note, he pulled her even closer. "Let's not fall in love," he whispered in her ear.

It was too late for that.

BUSTED

Susan was driving home from a party she attended alone. Ever since he got clean, Timothy didn't want to do much of anything other than attend Narcotics Anonymous meetings. Sometimes Susan felt as though he had become obsessed. It was like the meetings had become another addiction. It was all he talked about, and she was tired of hearing it. She was tired of him questioning her on whether she was still getting high, tired of him staring at her the second she walked through the door. He would look into her eyes like he could read her. She was even tired of him being at her house when she came home from work everyday. Don't get it twisted, Susan enjoyed his company, but she felt like he was there to check up on her, and she didn't appreciate being treated like a child.

She didn't tell Timothy about the party. She lied and told him she was doing something with the girls. "This is bullshit. I'm too old to be lying," she said out loud. She wanted to go to this party. The people throwing it had the best supply of cocaine in the area, and she wasn't concerned with the word getting around because this crowd was one of professionals. They had just as much to lose as she did.

109

Susan had finally told Timothy that she would marry him. She just hoped this whole marriage thing would work out for her. Susan thought about suggesting they get pre-marriage counseling. She knew that in order to do that, she'd have to stop sniffing first. She knew he expected her to stop getting high, and she planned on it, after tonight.

Marriage and the prospect of doing it was frightening to Susan. Over fifty percent of couples that married got divorced. She knew for a fact that it wasn't just a statistic, because almost everyone she knew was separated, divorced or unhappily married. After representing several divorce cases, she'd come to the conclusion that relationships changed and people changed once they said those two magic words, "I do." The obsession, expectations and disappointments became magnified.

She really liked things the way they were between her and Timothy. He wanted more than what they had now. He wanted her to be his wife. Either that or he would be out of her life. She thought his attitude about it was messed up, but she loved him, and she was going to try harder to get clean after tonight. There was no way in the world she would allow Timothy to marry someone else.

After the party, Susan was driving nervously. "Just let me make it home, just let me make it home," she prayed out loud. "A few blocks to go." Susan was high as hell. Her eyes bulged out of her head, her pulse was racing, and her was nose running.

She tried to drive extra carefully. Trying and doing were two different things, though, because she went right through a red light and realized it a little too late. A cop car was right on the corner, and the officer quickly flashed on his lights. For a second, she thought about trying to outrun him. This caused her to snicker. She always thought that shit was funny as hell, when people tried to outrun the police. Like they weren't going to get caught. She looked in her rearview mirror and pulled over. "Please, God, don't let them search my purse."

Susan had a small package of cocaine on her. She considered trying to dump it out, but knew there wouldn't be enough time. "Maybe he'll just give me a ticket and send me on my way," she said hopefully.

Two cops got out of the car. She noticed that one of them was Roger, but didn't know whether to breathe a sigh of relief or to panic even more.

When they reached the car, Roger was surprised to see Susan behind the wheel. "Susan, what the—? Do you know you ran a red light?"

"No."

Roger's partner peered into the car. "Are you okay? You were also weaving a little."

"I . . ." She didn't know what to say.

"I take it you and Officer Soloman know each other?"

"Yes, we do," she said, trying not to look in the officer's face.

The other officer noticed and looked at Roger, eyebrows raised.

"So, where are you coming from at two in the morning?" Roger asked.

None of your damn business, was what she wanted to say, but instead she told a lie. "From my boyfriend's house."

Roger's partner opened the door and told her to get out of the car. "Officer, what's your name?" Susan asked.

"Officer Patrick Brown."

"Well, Officer Brown, do you really think this is necessary?"

"Yes, I do. Now, miss, please get out of the car."

"What are you doing?" Roger asked, thrown off by this sudden aggression.

"Stay right here," Officer Brown told Susan then gestured for Roger to follow him.

Roger met him behind the car. "What's up?"

"Something's not right. I think she's high."

"What? You don't know what you're talking about. I know her. She's an attorney. Drinking maybe, but high? I doubt that very seriously."

"Take away what she does for a living and the fact that you know her. Look at her eyes."

Roger noticed her eyes the second he saw her, but he didn't want to tell his partner.

While in the car, Susan prayed they would let her go. If they searched her purse and found her stash, the repercussions would be serious. Timothy had always told her, what's done in the dark will come out in the light. She should have listened.

"You check her bag and car while I run a check on her," Officer Brown told Roger.

Roger didn't have much of a choice but to go along. He had to admit, her whole aura was off, and he could recall Crystal expressing concern for Susan.

Officer Brown walked back to the car and told her to give her purse to Roger. She did so, reluctantly. Roger noticed.

"Let's have her take the sobriety test," Brown suggested.

"You think all that is necessary?" Roger asked.

"Yes, I do."

Asshole, Roger thought.

While Patrick administered the test, Roger checked her purse and came across a lipstick holder. He shook it. It sounded like something other than lipstick was inside. He took the top off to find a piece of wrapped aluminum foil. He knew what people carried in folded up foil—cocaine. The last thing he wanted to do was bust her. If he did, not only would he be hurting her, but Crystal as well. If he let her go, he would be putting his job on the line.

Office Brown came back with Susan by his side. "She failed. We're taking her in. Did you find anything in her purse?"

Roger looked at Susan, who was tearing up. "No."

Susan looked at Roger, relieved and confused. She wondered why he was covering up for her. Surely he had found something. They made her get into the back of their car and placed a call to the station. "The car will be towed. You'll get all the information at the station," Roger told her.

They rode to the station in silence. When she and Roger got a second alone, he told her she could make one phone call. Her dilemma was who to call. Because Roger knew her, they didn't place her in a cell. They allowed her to sit in one of the waiting rooms under supervision. Susan wondered why he still hadn't said anything about the package. Officer Brown left the room and Roger turned to Susan. "You know we need to talk."

Susan just looked at him.

"What were you thinking, Susan? What the hell is going on with you?"

She didn't answer him. She didn't know what to say.

"Listen," he whispered. "You have two choices. Either cooperate and let me know what's going on with you, or be prepared to suffer the consequences. I'm trying to help you and save your ass."

Susan broke down. She said, "Roger, I'm falling apart. I feel like I'm losing control. I know you know what I had and—"

"Shhh." He interrupted her. He didn't want her to say too much. "I'm going to call Crystal to come pick you up." He stood up. When he reached the door, he turned around and asked her, "Or would you like me to call Timothy?"

That was the last thing she wanted. "No, Crystal's fine."

Crystal was lying in her bed. For some reason she couldn't fall asleep, so she started watching *A Thin Line Between Love and Hate*. She had her popcorn and was chilling. The last thing she expected was a call from Roger telling her Susan was in jail.

"What!" she yelled and turned the volume down on the television. She must have heard him wrong. As a matter of fact, she was sure she heard him wrong.

"Susan's in jail. You need to come get her," he repeated.

"For what? What happened? Why is she there?" Crystal asked.

"I'll fill you in when you get here. Just come as soon as possible."

Crystal threw on a pair of jeans, a T-shirt and some sneakers. She washed her face and brushed her teeth while she wondered what the hell was going on.

While on the road, she glanced down at her gas gauge and noticed it was on empty. "Damn." She pulled into the gas station and told the attendant to fill it up. As soon he started pumping the gas, she realized she left her purse home.

"I can't believe this shit!" She placed her head on the steering wheel.

"That'll be $28.00," the gas attendant said.

Crystal looked up and started explain her dilemma when she saw Lange getting out of his car. On the passenger side sat his wife.

"Excuse me for a second. I need to go inside first." Crystal climbed out of the car and followed Lange inside. He hadn't noticed her yet. Crystal tapped him on the shoulder.

He turned around, "Crystal." He was surprised to see her out this late. Lange almost bent over to kiss her, but caught himself and glanced out the door.

"What are you doing out so late?" he asked her, concerned.

"An emergency," she told him, hoping he just assumed it was one of the girls from the rape crisis center.

He did. "That's unfortunate," he told her.

The gas attendant was still waiting to be paid, so in an embarrassed tone, Crystal cleared her throat and said, "Lange,

God works in mysterious ways. You couldn't have come at a better time."

"Why do you say that?"

"I'm embarrassed to ask you this, but I left my wallet home and can't pay for my gas."

"I'll take care of it for you."

"You'll take care of what?" Neither of them noticed Lena had walked up behind them.

"Hi, Lena," Crystal said.

"You go ahead and do what you have to do, I'll tell her," Lange said.

"Thank you," Crystal said and walked away with an ache in her heart.

"The gentleman inside will take care of it," she told the attendant.

Crystal went home, got her wallet and pulled up at the police station forty-five minutes after Roger's call. "What took you so long?" Roger asked the second she walked in.

"I left my purse home," Crystal said in an exasperated tone.

"Come into the conference room so we can talk before you see Susan."

Crystal followed him.

"Susan got pulled over for driving under the influence," he told her.

"What?"

"She got pulled over for—"

"Did you say for driving under the influence?"

"Yes."

"Driving under the influence of what?"

"Alcohol."

Crystal shook her head.

"Well, that's not the worst part." Roger pulled the lipstick holder from his sleeve and gave it to her. "This was in her purse."

"Lipstick? Why are you giving me her lipstick?"

"Open it."

She did and knew instantly what was in the aluminum foil. Crystal was at a loss for words.

"Did you know about this?"

Crystal looked at Roger like he was crazy. "What kind of question is that? Of course I didn't know." She started to pace the floor. "This is it! This is what's been making Susan act so erratic." Crystal stopped pacing and looked at Roger. "What are you still doing with the packet? You didn't turn it in?"

"No, and what you need to understand is that I risked my career holding onto it," he whispered.

"Why?" Susan asked. She didn't want to think he did it for her, because then she would feel like she owed him something.

"I don't want to see a sister go out like that."

Crystal didn't know what to say. "Thank you," she told him.

"I took a chance," he told her. "Let her know that, because if it ever happens again, I won't."

"Take me to her," Crystal said, pissed.

Roger looked at her. "Are you all right? Can you handle this? Do you have the money for bail?"

"I have it. You know what? Before I see her, maybe I should take care of that first. That way we can just leave this place."

"I think that would be a good idea," Roger responded.

After paying bail, Crystal entered the room where Susan was being held. When Susan saw her walk in, all she could do was hold her head down in shame. Crystal started to say something, but decided now was not the time. "Come on, let's go."

As they walked toward the car, neither said a word.

Once in the car, there was so much Crystal wanted to do and say. She wanted to call Susan a freaking maniac, a fool, to tell her she was disgusted with her and to go upside her head. Emotions were running on high.

"I'll pay you back," Susan said, not knowing what else to say.

Crystal didn't respond. She just started up the car.

"Do you think this is going to affect the practice?" Susan asked.

Crystal was afraid to open her mouth because she didn't know what would come out if she did.

"I apologize for all this," Susan sniffled.

Crystal wanted to tear into her, but remained calm as she said, "Don't apologize to me. You should be apologizing to yourself for the chance you took. What would you have done if Roger had turned in your little package?"

"I don't know."

"Yeah, I bet you don't," Crystal said. "I'm not taking you home. It's late, I'm tired, and I think you should stay with me tonight."

Susan didn't have the strength to disagree.

By the time they pulled up to Crystal's house, they were both exhausted for different reasons.

"We'll talk in the morning," Crystal told Susan. "Take the extra room. The towels are in the hallway closet."

Susan was relieved and surprised that Crystal left her alone. She needed the time to get her thoughts together and relax. A shower would do the deed. She also had to call Timothy so he could pick up his car.

Picking up the phone in the living room, she dialed Timothy's number. There was no use in putting it off. "Susan?" he asked.

"How did you know it was me?"

"Who else would be calling me this early in the morning? Is everything all right?"

Susan hesitated.

"Is everything all right?" He asked again.

"No."

"What happened?"

"I was on my way home tonight and had a bit too much to drink. I got pulled over in your car and arrested for driving under the influence. You have to call the police station and they will let you know what towing center it was sent to."

"I'll do it first thing this morning. Where are you?"

"At Crystal's. She came and got me from the police station."

"How come you didn't call me?"

Susan could hear the hurt in his voice. Once again she chose to tell a half-truth. "Her boyfriend Roger is a cop and he called her."

"Oh." Timothy paused. Something in her voice didn't sound right. "Is that all?" He wanted to tell her she had that "just coming down from a high" tone, but thought better of it. They would discuss it tomorrow.

"Yes, that's all. I'm tired. I need to get some rest. How about I call you when I wake up?"

He didn't want a damn phone call. He wanted to see her face, but she'd been through enough. "Make sure you do that."

"Okay, bye."

"I love you." Timothy wanted her to know this didn't affect them.

"I love you too."

AFTERSHOCK

Susan barely slept. Her eyes were swollen from crying. Her face was puffy and her hair was all over the place. She glanced at the clock. Eight o'clock a.m. She'd only gotten four hours of sleep, definitely not enough.

Crystal was in her room on the phone with Roger.

"Did you talk to her?" He wanted to know.

Before she could answer, there was a knock on the door.

"Come in," Crystal said.

Susan walked in. "When you get off the phone, can we talk?"

"Roger—"

"I heard. I'll call you later."

They hung up.

Susan sat on the bed. "I messed up, didn't I?"

"That you did. What were you thinking?" Crystal asked.

"That's just it. I wasn't."

"You know what gets me?" Crystal said, "I knew something was going on. I just didn't know that you were destroying yourself. What's so bad that you had to turn to drugs?"

119

"I don't know."

"You don't know?"

"All I know is I'm unhappy and I feel like I'm drowning. It's not any one thing, either. It's everything."

"Why didn't you say anything?" Crystal wanted to know.

"I didn't want anyone feeling sorry for me. I feel sorry enough for myself as it is."

"I'm your friend, Susan. I'm supposed to look out for you."

"Roger did just that, didn't he?"

"Yeah. Does Timothy know you've been getting high?"

"Timothy just got out of rehab," Susan blurted out.

Crystal was shocked.

"When he asked me to marry him, one of his requirements was for me to stop getting high."

"So, he's known."

"To an extent. You know, it's funny, because last night was supposed to be my last hurrah. I guess I should have stopped while I was ahead."

They shared a pathetic laugh.

"Have you thought about counseling?" Crystal asked. Heck, she'd just looked into it for herself and found someone she might go to.

"Actually, I have." Getting up off the bed, she said. "I'm going to call Timothy and see if he would like to go to breakfast. Then we should call Elsie and tell her what happened."

"Tell her everything?" Crystal asked, expecting a "No."

Susan surprised her by saying, "Yes, everything. After all she is a partner."

When Susan left the room, Crystal got down on her knees and thanked God for her life and the fact that she was healthy and sane. She knew she often took things for granted, things like her business, her home and her health. After praying, she decided she would go for a quick run. As a matter of fact, she'd ask Susan to join her.

When she knocked on the guestroom door, Susan was just hanging up the phone. "Timothy wasn't home. He probably went to get his car."

"You spoke to him last night, right?"

"Yeah."

"You told him everything?"

"No."

"Don't you think you should?"

"I will, but not over the phone."

"Don't start off your engagement with lies."

She already had.

"I came to see if you would like to come running with me," Crystal told Susan.

"Running as in jogging?"

"Yeah. The air will do you some good."

Susan wanted to say "hell no," but she felt somewhat obligated. "I don't know about running with you, but I might walk behind you."

Crystal laughed. "Good. That's better than nothing. I'll bring you down a pair of sweats and a T-shirt."

Once at the track, the air did them some good. Susan surprised herself, running at a slow but steady pace. It allowed her to think about her life and how she was messing it up.

"How often do you run?" Susan asked when they were done and heading back to the house.

"Not often enough, but I think I'm going to pick it up again."

"It actually felt kind of good."

Looking at Susan, Crystal said, "I heard that about people who used to get high. Once they start working out, it helps with sobriety. The endorphins become their high."

"I just might try it." Susan was willing to try anything at this point.

"Why don't we all have dinner tonight?" Crystal suggested.

Susan knew she meant the girls in the office. "That's fine. Listen, just drop me off at my house. I'm sure Timothy is there waiting."

"What about your clothes?"

"I'll get them later."

When they pulled up Timothy's car was in the driveway. Susan's stomach started to do flip-flops. She was nervous and tried to brace herself for his blow-up.

When she walked in the door, Timothy greeted her with a hug. He held her tight and long.

"Hey, sweetie." Susan kissed him on the cheek.

"Hi." He let her go and looked her up and down. "What's up with the sweats?"

"I went running with Crystal."

Timothy looked confused.

"I need to take a shower."

He following her into the bedroom, where she immediately started to undress. "You know, when we got off the phone, I was thinking. The only time you drink is when you're high," he told her.

Busted and too tired to play it off, she decided to tell him the truth. Standing in her panties and bra, she told him, "It was supposed to be my last night."

"Did you get busted with anything?"

"No." She went on to tell him what Roger had done for her.

"I have to thank him," Timothy said.

Still waiting on a blow-up, Susan was surprised when Timothy reached over and kissed her instead. "We'll get through this." he told her.

This loving gesture made Susan cry. "I honestly thought I had everything under control."

"People who are addicted tend to do that. We convince ourselves that we know what we're doing, that we can stop when we want to, that we have it and our lives under control, when in reality it's controlling us."

"Timothy, I'm sorry," she told him. "I know I let you down."

"Don't worry about letting me down. Worry about letting yourself down. And you don't have anything to be sorry for. I'm the one who started you getting high."

Susan placed her hands on his chest. "Stop. Stop right there. You're making excuses for me. I've been lying to you and to myself. I need help. It's just that simple. I've been jeopardizing everything. My job, us, my life—and for what?"

"Why don't you come to a meeting with me?" Timothy asked.

Susan took a step toward the bathroom. "I don't know. What if one of my clients are there?"

"The meetings are confidential. What's said in the room stays in the room. As a matter of fact, I'm going to a meeting tonight."

"I can't go tonight. Everyone from the office is having dinner tonight at Crystal's to discuss what happened."

"Can you handle that?" Timothy asked.

"I'm going to have to."

Susan had just finished telling the girls what happened and Elsie was looking at her with a look she couldn't describe. She couldn't tell if it was anger, disgust or disappointment.

"Why are you looking at me like that?" she asked Elsie.

That was the opening Elsie had been waiting on. "You really want to know?"

"Yes, I do," Susan replied, already knowing but wanting Elsie to get it off her chest.

"How could you have been so stupid? You of all people should know better than to drink and drive. We represent people like that! What would you have done if you'd gotten into an accident or something? You put your life on the line."

Jewell surprised herself by siding with Susan. "Damn, Elsie, she made a mistake. We all do. Give her a break."

Looking at Jewell, Elsie said, "Yeah, but it could have been a deadly mistake."

"You think I don't know that?" Susan asked. "You think I don't know that I could have hurt not only myself but someone else as well? Well, I do. I realize that what I did was dumb, and that I should have known better, but we don't always think about things until it's too late. I'm sorry if I hurt you in any way."

"It's not that you hurt me," Elsie said. "It's just that I don't feel I should have to pay for your mistakes."

"How will this affect you? Will you lose any clients because of it?" Susan asked.

"No. Thanks to Roger."

"Then why stress yourself over something that didn't happen? It's my problem to handle. Not yours, not Crystal's, not Jewell's, but mine."

Elsie knew Susan was right. She also knew she was displacing her anger. It wasn't about Susan, so after a brief silence, she revealed, "I apologize, Susan. I'm just going through some stuff myself and I didn't mean to take it out on you."

"I saw Summer in the mall with a little girl yesterday," Jewell said, feeling Elsie's unease. She thought she was changing the subject, but instead was digging the hole deeper.

"That was her daughter."

Everyone looked at Elsie.

"Her daughter?" Jewell asked.

"Yeah, she was married a long time ago. She got divorced, and the father got custody of her."

"She was married?" Jewell asked.

"Why are you repeating everything I say?" Elsie asked with annoyance.

"I don't know. I'm just surprised."

"Anyway, her ex was killed in a car crash and her daughter now lives with her," Elsie continued.

"Is that what's been bothering you? Is that what's going on?" Susan asked.

"Yeah. Before all this happened, me and Summer were going to move in together, but I told her it should be put on hold. She barely knows her daughter and they need time alone."

"Kids adjust, you know," Jewell said, thinking of her relationship with Evan and hoping.

"Yeah, but this isn't a simple thing. Summer and I are lovers. Can you imagine how that little girl is going to feel when she realizes this? She may even think her mother left her for me."

"But that's not the case. You can explain that to her," Jewell told her.

"Yeah, we could, but I'm also not so sure I'm ready to be a step-mom."

"Oh, so now you don't want to date a woman with kids?" Jewell couldn't believe what she was hearing. "Just like a man."

Crystal and Susan decided to stay out of this conversation.

"What do you mean, just like a man?" Elsie was insulted.

"You just said you've not ready to be a step-mom. That sounds like you don't want to date women with children."

"I didn't say a damn thing about not dating a woman with kids. I just know that having a child is a big responsibility and I'm not sure if it's one that I'm ready for. That may sound selfish, but if it does, so be it."

"You love Summer, don't you?" Jewell asked.

"Yes. I think so."

"Well, if you truly do love her, her having a child shouldn't even play a part in it. When you love someone, it should be unconditionally. You have to love her and her child. It's a package deal. You can't love one and not accept the other."

"I know that."

"Do you?" Jewell knew that if Evan didn't express an interest in Tyson from day one, they wouldn't have gotten this far.

She recalled a relationship she was in when Tyson was about three. She was in love with this guy. Actually she was in love with the sex. No, to be more precise, she was in love with the size of his manhood. Somewhere along the line, she got it confused with real love. She would go see him whenever he called. This went on for over a year. He'd call, she'd show up, or if she got the itch, she'd call and he would show up. One day, she was at his house, looking at a picture of his daughter and it hit her. Even though he knew about her son, he never asked about him. So one day, she showed him Tyson's picture, hoping he would express some interest, maybe even that she and Tyson, along with him and his daughter would do something together. He didn't. That was the end of their relationship.

"I'm sure that Summer needs you more than anything right now," Jewell told her. "Shit, being a single mom is not easy. To have the support of someone you love is everything."

Elsie didn't know what to say. She knew Jewell was right.

Crystal decided to just keep her mouth shut. She had said enough to Susan earlier, and she was all talked out. The only person she wanted to talk to now was Lange.

COINCIDENCES

A couple of weeks had passed since Crystal and Lange's rendezvous. Neither had told a soul and they had barely talked about it with each other. It wasn't that they were trying to pretend it didn't happen. They just wanted to prevent it from happening again.

Crystal's thoughts were consumed with Lange—the way he made love to her, the way her body felt as if she were floating and like every nerve in her was being touched. She yearned to feel that way again, but she knew that was not likely to happen.

Since they'd made love, they'd spoken on the phone quite a few times. He wanted Crystal to know he was thinking about her and didn't want her to feel that he'd taken advantage of her.

Take advantage of me. I'm a willing participant. That's what she wanted to tell him, but kept the thought to herself.

She glanced at the clock and sighed. This was going to be a long day and a long weekend. Tina and her mother were coming into the office to discuss the case and what they should do. After going back and forth with it, she decided to tell them there was no way she could represent them. Lange agreed to take the case, and she would be there for support.

A big week lay ahead for Crystal. Later that night, she was going out with Roger. They still hadn't slept together. She'd thought about it more than once, hoping it would get her mind off Lange. It wasn't a good reason to sleep with someone, but for her, it might be good enough.

Her mother was also coming to visit. She hadn't seen her in six months since she moved to Charlotte, North Carolina. She told Crystal there was something very important she needed to discuss with her.

Crystal's intercom came on. "Your appointment is here," Jewell informed her.

"Okay, Jewel. Please seat them in the conference room."

"Will do," Jewell replied.

Crystal stood up and took several deep breaths before she headed toward the door. Just as she was about to open it, the knob turned.

Jewell stuck her head in. "They're waiting on you."

"Just give me a couple more seconds."

Jewell closed the door and informed Tina and her mother that Crystal would be with them shortly.

When Crystal entered the conference room, Tina gave her a hug.

"Hi, Ms. Crystal."

Crystal hugged her back and felt a pang of regret that she couldn't be her attorney.

"This is my mom, Brenda Lord."

Crystal offered her hand. "How are you?"

Tina's mom just looked at her. Crystal looked at Tina, who shrugged. She and Tina had spoken on the phone at least once a week since the incident. Just like Crystal did when she was younger, Tina blamed herself. Crystal had to tell her a number of times not to do that, but that it was normal to feel this way.

Crystal pulled out a chair and sat down to face Tina. Since her mother wanted to be an ass, she figured this was best. "Tina, I'm proud of the fact that you've decided to stand up for yourself and not let your rapist get away with what he did. You're an extremely brave person for coming forward."

"Thanks," Tina replied. "I just hope it's the right thing to do."

"It is," Crystal reassured her.

"How do you know?" Ms. Lord asked.

"How do I know what?"

"That it's the right thing to do."

"Well, why shouldn't it be?" Crystal looked at Ms. Lord like she was crazy. "Your daughter was attacked, forced to have sex, and you don't think she should press charges?"

"I think she should just let it go. It's not like she was a virgin."

Crystal wanted to smack her clear across the face. "Excuse me?"

"Think about it. What will she gain from it? Money? No. Popularity? No. Embarrassment and shame? Yes. What good will that do?"

Crystal could not believe what she was hearing. She wanted so bad to curse this woman out.

Tina faced her mother and said, "Ma, this is something I have to do. So what if I wasn't a virgin? Does that make you not believe me? What if he does this to someone else?"

"Then let that someone else report his ass."

On that note, Crystal stood up. "You know what? I need some air. I'll be right back." Before they could say a word, she was in the hallway. Susan was passing by and saw the look on Crystal's face.

"What's up?" Susan asked. "Why are you looking like that?"

"Tina's mother is more concerned about her reputation than about her daughter. She doesn't think Tina should report the rape. I needed to get out of there because I was two seconds away from smacking the bitch."

"Did you explain to them that no matter what, since she went to the hospital, the state has it on file and can start a case and force her to testify?"

"No."

"Why not?"

"I didn't have a chance. Her mother pissed me off so bad."

Meanwhile, in the room, Ms. Lord looked at Tina, who was staring her down with tears in her eyes. "What's your problem? You asked me to come, knowing how I felt."

Tina didn't respond.

When Crystal returned, she pulled her chair up close to Ms. Lord and said, "Listen, I'm going to be real with you. Young girls get raped every day. Some are strong and can deal with it, but there are others who have breakdowns, turn to drugs, become promiscuous, you name it. Luckily, Tina is one of the strong ones who can stand up for herself."

"Ma, I don't want him to hurt anyone else," Tina interrupted.

"With Tina's stepping forward and trying to put this boy behind bars, it may save someone else's life. How do you know he's going to let the next one get away?" Crystal was trying her best to reach this woman.

"Listen," Ms. Lord said with an attitude, "I understand what you're saying, and I appreciate what you're trying to do. My concern is that everyone will know, that it's going to be in the paper and she'll be ridiculed."

"Mom, are you sitting there saying your reputation is more important than my well-being? Well, you know what? Forget you! I don't need you or your support."

Ms. Lord wouldn't give anyone eye contact.

"She needs your support," Crystal said.

Ms. Lord looked at Crystal with tears in her eyes and suddenly it hit Crystal like a ton of bricks. Ms. Lord herself was once a victim and she was the one not believed.

"Tina, will you excuse me and your mother?"

Tina stood up and walked out.

Crystal waited until the conference room door was closed. "All right, what's really going on?"

"What do you mean?"

"I find it hard to believe you would let someone get away with hurting your daughter. Did something happen to you? Were you raped and not believed?"

From Ms. Lord's silence, Crystal knew she was right.

"I was raped repeatedly when I was younger by a cousin." She waited for Crystal's response. When she received none, she went on. "It started when I was eleven and continued up until I was fourteen. By that time, I wasn't scared of him anymore. The last time he tried to come into my room, he was eighteen and I fought him tooth and nail. Scratched him up good, too. My mother came home and saw the scratches on his face and asked him what had happened. He said I had a boy over and we were having sex. He told her he tried to stop it and I attacked him. Of course I denied it and tried to tell her what he had been doing to me, but she didn't believe me. She loved him and favored him. My mother had a twin that died and this was her son. Me, I was a bastard child. My father left her and she took it out on me. She went around and told the family I was spreading lies. I was shunned. The day I turned sixteen I dropped out of school and moved out." Ms. Lord looked at Crystal and asked, "So, you see why I don't want Tina to speak up?"

Crystal sympathized with her and told her this, but also told her, "You can't let your past affect Tina's future. This is a different day and age. She went to the hospital. They have evidence." She took Ms. Lord's hand. "I feel for you, I really do, and because of what happened to you, you should support your daughter. Maybe you and her can get counseling together, because obviously you're still holding on to the past. Let her get justice for herself and for you."

"Justice for the both of us?"

"Yes."

Ms. Lord stood up and went toward the door. Crystal thought she was going to leave, but Ms. Lord called Tina back into the room.

Tina came in and sat down. She looked at her mother and waited to hear what she had to say.

"Tina, I'm going to support you."

She was surprised. "You are?"

"Yes."

Tina looked from her mother to Crystal and back toward her mother. "What made you change your mind?"

Not ready to reveal what happened to her, she said, "I just did, all right."

Tina knew not to say anything else.

"Okay, ladies, there's something you need to know. I am going to refer your case to an excellent attorney, a friend of mine. His name is Lange Houston."

"What are you talking about? I thought you were going to be Tina's attorney."

"I would love to be, but there's a conflict of interest."

"What?"

"I too am a rape survivor, and the boy who raped your daughter is the son of the man who raped me when I was a teenager."

Ms. Lord shook her head in disbelief. "Are you serious?"

"Very, and because of the nature of the case, we want this to go as smooth as possible."

I understand," Tina said. "But you will be there every step of the way, right?"

Crystal took Tina's hand and said, "Of course I will." She handed them Lange's card. "I will be there for you every step of the way."

"Crystal, you have a phone call." Jewell stuck her head in the conference room.

"I'm in a meeting," Crystal said.

"Whoever it is said it's an emergency."

Ms. Lord, Tina and Crystal stood up at once. "We're leaving anyway."

KEEPING IT REAL

"Hold on a second." Jewell was on the phone with Kim. She waited until Tina and Ms. Lord walked out before she finished her conversation. "Anyway, as I was saying, girl, I might be biting off more than I can chew. I mean, I let him give me money for the down payment on my new car, and I told you King found out about it."

"No, you ain't tell me that shit. What happened?" Kim asked.

"Listen, meet me for lunch and I'll give you the run down."

"Bet."

Jewell and Kim met at TGI Friday's and Kim was anxious to find out what happened.

"Girl, King popped up one day. Now, you know I don't like that as it is. I don't just pop up at his house. The least he could do is pick up the phone and let a sister know he's coming," Jewell said.

"Yeah, yeah. Go on."

"Anyway, I almost cursed his ass out, but I noticed he looked upset. I asked him what was wrong and he told me he'd just found out that his father died."

"His father? I thought he didn't know his father."

"He didn't until recently. One of his family members told him where he was and he went looking for him."

"Damn, that's deep. A grown-ass man still wanting his daddy."

Jewell looked at Kim, and not for the first time realized how ignorant she was. "Anyway, they were just getting to know one another, and for him to just up and die, King was devastated."

"So he came to you?" Kim asked, thinking that was a little weird.

"Yeah, he came to me. Why you got to say it like that? He and I have been through a lot. You know that, and I'm the only one who understood how he felt about growing up without a dad. He needed to talk to someone he could trust."

"Uh-huh," Kim said. "He wanted you to feel sorry for him and give him some ass."

Jewell rolled her eyes, glad she didn't tell Kim everything about how they sat on the couch all night watching movies and ended up kissing. The kiss surprised King as much as it did Jewell. Every now and then he would try to press up and reconcile with her, convince her they should be a family, but she always shut him down. It wasn't because she didn't care for him. Hell, King was her first love and her son's father. He would always have a special place in her heart. She just didn't want to go backwards.

"Anyway," Jewell went on with the story, "Evan had sent me some flowers and a card, and I forgot they were in the kitchen on the table. King went to get something to drink and when he came back, he was holding the card in his hand."

"And?" Kim wanted her to hurry up and get to the good part.

"The card said 'Enjoy the car, and if I can do anything else for you, just ask'."

Kim started laughing. "You're straight lying."

"What the hell is so funny?"

"That's what his ass gets for snooping," Kim said.

On one hand, Jewell agreed, but then again, she had been enjoying their time together. There was something intimate about it, and for a second she pretended that they were still a family. When King came back into the living room, Jewell was in the middle of wondering what it would be like.

"What the hell is this?" King threw the card at Jewell.

She looked at it. "A card."

"I see that," King said. "Who the hell is Evan?"

"Someone I'm seeing."

"What?"

"Come on, King. I know you don't think I'm an old maid and don't date."

"Dating and letting a man buy you a car are two different things."

"He didn't buy me the car."

"Did he help you get the car?"

Jewell wanted to lie and say no, but King wasn't stupid. He could read between the lines and he could read her face.

"You let another man give you money for a car?"

"He loaned me money for my down payment," Jewell said, though the truth was he gave her money.

"How come you didn't come to me? I'm your son's father. I'm the one who should be taking care of these type of things."

Jewell didn't know what to say. She didn't agree with him—he wasn't her man—but standing there in the middle of the chaos, she couldn't blame him for being upset.

While they argued back and forth, Tyson came out of his room, rubbing his eyes. "What's going on?"

King went over to him, gave him a hug and said, "Nothing, son. Daddy's just leaving."

King walked out without saying another word to Jewell.

Kim listened to this story and said to Jewell, "Girl, I wouldn't even stress over that mess. King ain't going nowhere. He might be angry right now, but he loves his son. He'll get over it."

Jewell wanted so badly to believe her. She glanced at her watch and told Kim, "I've got to get back to work."

"You want to go out for drinks tonight?"

"Nah, I'm going out with Evan," Jewell answered, thankful for her babysitter.

Later that evening when the doorbell rang, she knew it was Evan. The time had finally come for her, Evan and Tyson to do something together.

"Mom, your friend is here," Tyson yelled as he ran to the door.

"Wait. Let me answer it."

Tyson trailed behind her. She opened the door and was shocked to see King.

Oh, shit, she thought. This was the last thing she needed.

"Listen," she told King, "I'm getting to ready to go out."

Looking her up and down, he said, "I can see that."

"Why don't you call me later?"

From the look on her face, King could sense something was up. "What? You're not going to let a brother in to see his son?"

She opened the door. "Only for a minute or two."

"Dad!" Tyson was glad to see him. "What's up?"

King bent down and gave Tyson a hug. "I just needed to see you and speak to your mother real quick." When King had spoken to his son earlier, Tyson told him that he and his mother were going out with her boyfriend. There was no way King could let this opportunity pass him by.

"Well, can't it wait?" Jewell asked. She wasn't ready for King to find out Evan was white.

"Maybe."

King still cared for Jewell. When they first got together, he was young and wild. He still needed to sow his oats, as the old-timers like to say. The only problem was he kept getting caught. Finally, Jewell couldn't take it anymore and told him it was over. That was something she had threatened him with many times, and once again he thought she was playing. She wasn't. After spending two nights out, he came home. She was gone, along with all her belongings. She left a note telling him she was pregnant and that it was his loss. King wanted to be a father so badly. He knew he would make a great one.

Jewell had no family, at least none that she kept in contact with, so when he went to look for her, he had no idea where to start. He tried calling her friends, but they were ghetto whores and hung up on him. He went as far as to file a missing persons report, but when he told them she left a note, they told him there was nothing they could do.

One day while walking through the mall, he heard a laugh just like Jewell's. Turning around, he saw that it was her.

"Jewell," he said.

Recognizing his voice, she kept walking, quickening her pace.

"Please don't walk away. If you do, I will make a scene."

She knew that he would. She placed her hand on her belly, which was protruding now that she was six months along. "What do you want?"

Going for it, he told her, "I want to be with you and raise our child together."

Looking at her friend, Kim, with a "can you believe him" expression, she put her hands on her hips and said, "I don't want that, King. Why do you think I left? I can't trust you. I can't be with a man I don't trust. I can't even believe you have the audacity to stand here and talk about raising a child together. You were barely around when it was just you and I. What would make me think you're going to be around now that a baby is in the picture?"

"Please just give me a chance. You can't raise a baby by yourself." He was prepared to beg.

Kim decided to put her two cents in. "Didn't you hear her? She said no."

King looked at her. "You need to mind your business." The tone in his voice implied that he was serious. "Jewell, please, I'm begging you. Let's give us another chance. It's not just you. There's a child involved. Had I known you were pregnant, I wouldn't have done all the things I did."

"That's just it. Listen to yourself. It shouldn't take a child to make you do right. You should do right because you love me."

"A child needs two parents. Stop being selfish."

He was right about that, and she knew it, but he had hurt her one too many times. Crying, she told him, "I can't do it. I don't trust you."

"But you still love me, don't you? I see it in your eyes." He still loved her, and he was sincere about trying to do the right thing. He knew he was out of control and that he'd done his thinking with the wrong head.

"Love has nothing to do with it. I loved you before, and look what happened." She started to walk away.

"I'll take you to court to see the baby." He was adamant on this topic. He grew up without a father, and he refused to see the same thing happen to a child of his.

Stopping in her tracks, Jewell asked, "What did you say?"

"I'll take you court, and I mean it," he said harshly.

"You would really do that to me?"

Softening up, he told her, "Jewell, you know my father was never in the picture and that caused my mother a lot of pain and resentment. I'm not going to allow that to happen to my child. I will do any and everything to assure that it won't."

139

Going into her purse, she pulled out a pen and asked Kim for a piece of paper.

"Are you sure?" Kim asked, pulling out the paper.

"Yes, I'm sure." She wrote her phone number. She didn't give him her address because she didn't want him to know where she lived. "Call me and we'll talk more."

As it turned out, they didn't get back together, but he'd been in Tyson's life ever since.

"I'm going somewhere," she told King again, hoping he would get the message.

"Are you leaving this second? There's something I really need to talk to you about."

"We're not leaving yet. We're waiting on Ma's friend. We're going out for pizza," Tyson chipped in.

King raised his eyebrows. "Well, how about I wait with you?" He took a step toward the couch.

"I don't think so," Jewell said and stood in front of him. "How about you call me later and we can talk then or I'll call you the second I get home?"

Before King could respond, there was a knock at the door. Jewell panicked. *Please let it be someone else,* she said to herself. But she knew it wasn't. Unable to move, she watched Tyson run to the door, swinging it open. There stood Evan, looking whiter than ever.

"Hi," Tyson said, not letting him in.

"Hey, young man. Is your mother home?" Evan asked.

"Let him in, Tyson." Jewell was busted. There was no hiding now.

Evan walked in and looked right in King's face.

"Who is this?" King looked him up and down while pulling Tyson to him.

"I'm Evan. You must be King, Tyson's father." He put his hand out, but it went ignored. Evan got the hint. He looked at Jewell and asked her, "Are you two ready?"

King just stood and stared at Evan in shock. He looked at Jewell and shook his head. "I don't believe this shit."

"Please, King, don't start," Jewell begged.

"So," King asked, "this is your new friend?"

"Yes, he is."

He looked at Evan and asked, "How long have you been seeing each other?"

Before Evan could get a word out, Jewell said, "I don't think that's any of your business."

"I think it is," he told her, still holding onto Tyson.

"Daddy, you're hugging me too tight," Tyson whined.

"Tyson, go to your room and get your jacket," Jewell said. She turned to Evan.

"Will you excuse us for a minute? I think King and I need to go talk in the kitchen."

"We can talk right here," King told her.

Jewell pulled him along and said, "In the kitchen."

Once in the kitchen, she asked him, "What are you trying to pull?"

"I'm not trying to pull a damn thing. You're the one dating a cracker."

"King, please leave."

"I don't want my son around-"

"Around what? White people?" she finished for him. "Do you know how that sounds? He has white classmates, white friends, white neighbors—there's no way."

"You know what I'm talking about. Don't play dumb," King said.

"You can't pick and choose who I date."

"I don't want to, but I can pick and choose who my son is going to be around."

"What do you mean by that?"

"What I came over here to discuss with you is Tyson moving in with me."

This caught her off guard. "I'm going to ask you once again to leave. I don't want to turn ghetto on your ass in front of our son." She knew that would get him.

"You know this talk is not over, and you know you should have discussed this with me."

"You don't discuss with me who you're dating."

"I wouldn't date outside my race either. I don't want my son to see it and duplicate it."

"You sound like a racist, King."

"I'm not a racist. I'm just proud of who I am and my heritage."

"This is a new day and age."

King just looked at her. "Make sure you call me," he told her and left her standing in the kitchen.

This is where she stayed until she heard the front door slam shut

"Is everything okay?" Evan asked.

"Yes, everything is fine," she lied.

Later that night, Jewell and Tyson were lying across his bed watching a movie when out of nowhere he asked, "Ma, if I liked a white girl, would you be happy?"

"I'll like whoever you like, as long as she's good to you," Jewell told him. In reality, she wasn't sure about that. She wanted her baby to date and marry a black woman. Double standard? It certainly was. Did she give a damn? No. King had touched a nerve.

LET'S GET IT ON

While Crystal was getting dressed for her date with Roger, Marvin Gaye's song "Let's Get It On" was playing on the radio. She knew that was what Roger wanted to do tonight, get it on. She was nervous about it, not too sure if she would go through with it. Crystal knew she needed to move past Lange, get him out of her system, but was another man the way to go about it?

Crystal decided to wear a black mini dress with slit sleeves and a plunging neckline. Her locks were pinned up. She wore gold stiletto heels that matched her necklace, a thin gold chain with a diamond in the middle, which fell between her breasts in just the right way.

"You look beautiful," Roger told her when he arrived to pick her up. They were going to the policemen's ball.

"Thank you. You don't look so bad yourself."

He turned around and struck a pose. "GQ style, baby."

Crystal smiled as she took him in with her eyes. He did look extremely handsome in his black tux. The jacket was one of those long ones she liked, the shirt was a cream-colored, as was the handkerchief in his pocket.

"Before we go, I need to ask you something," Roger said, sounding serious.

"What is it?" Crystal asked.

"I just want to know if I can kiss those beautiful lips of yours."

Crystal leaned forward in response.

He brushed his lips across hers lightly and wrapped his hands around her waist. He pulled away and asked, "How do you want it? Passionately or playfully?"

"However you want to give it to me," she said.

He kissed her passionately.

When he pulled away, Crystal still had her eyes closed. "That was nice," she told him.

Taking her hand, they walked out the door.

It was after midnight when they returned. They were sitting in the car and Crystal could feel the beat of her heart. She'd decided to invite Roger in, and she knew he wouldn't be leaving until the next morning.

"I had a good time," she told him and meant it.

"I did too." This was the moment he had been waiting on for a long time. He wanted to make love to her when they were younger, and again the moment he saw her when he pulled her over. From the way she let him hold her, the looks that passed between them at the dance and the way she touched him when they talked, he had every reason to believe tonight was the night.

Roger didn't want to beat around the bush. He asked Crystal, "Am I coming in?"

"Yes," she told him, knowing what he really wanted to ask.

They got out of the car, walked up to her porch and into the house. Crystal flicked on the lights. Billie was waiting on the steps. When he saw Roger, he started to whimper.

Crystal laughed and headed in the direction of the bedroom with Roger behind her. "I think he knows. Do you want something to drink?"

"No," he told her. "All I want is you."

Once in the room, she said "Make yourself comfortable. I want to freshen up."

When she entered the bathroom, Crystal decided to take a shower. She stuck her head out the door and told Roger, "I'm going to jump in the shower. You can take one after me." She didn't wait to see if he'd ask her if they could take one together.

When Crystal was done, she dried off and threw on her plush pink robe. She walked into the bedroom and saw that Roger had undressed down to his underwear. "Your turn," she told him.

As Roger stood up, Crystal looked him up and down. She was a little disappointed to notice a slight budge around his mid-section. Thank God it wasn't too much.

"I left a washcloth and towel out for you," she told him.

After he closed the bathroom door, Crystal pulled out a thong and slipped it on under her robe. She lay across the bed and waited.

Less than ten minutes later, Roger returned. The towel was wrapped around his waist. He sat on the bed next to her and said, "I've waited for this a long time."

"Do you have any massage oil?" Roger asked.

Crystal started to get up, but he told her, "Don't move. Just tell me where it is."

"In my bathroom, under the sink."

He went to retrieve it. When he returned, he told her, "How would you like a massage?"

"I'd like that."

"Take off your robe."

Crystal did as requested and turned over on her stomach. Roger poured just a drop of oil on her back and thighs, then massaged some in his hands. The house was quiet. There was no sound other than their breathing.

He started at her shoulders, moved down her arms, then up and down her back in slow circular motions. When he arrived at the arch of her back, he slowly pulled her panties off, bent over to kiss her buttocks, opened her thighs slightly and touched her gently.

"Mmmmm."

He continued to tease her as he ran his hands down her thighs to her feet, gently massaging each toe and then back up again. He concentrated on her buttocks. "You have such a nice ass," he told her as he bit down gently. "Turn over."

She did and looked him in the eyes.

He kissed her on the mouth as she glided his hands between her legs and let his fingers enter her. She started to move against his hands, the feeling becoming more intense. Roger put his mouth on her breasts, his hands still inside her, and started to bite down on her nipples. Crystal was on the verge of an orgasm. His fingers were working wonders. As soon as she felt like she was getting to her peak, he pulled his fingers out. "What, what are you doing?" she asked.

"Shhh." He replaced his fingers with his tongue.

"Oh," she said and lay back to enjoy the pleasure. Next thing she knew, her body started to quiver. She began to move her hips and placed her hands on either side of his head. "Right there, right there," she said as she arched her back. "Yes, Yes, Yes!" Crystal yelled. When she was done, she looked up at him and said, "Let me get on top."

At this point, Roger was willing to let her do anything she wanted.

The next morning, Crystal kept catching Roger staring at her while she made breakfast.

"Why are you staring at me like that?" She was ready for him to go. Her mother was coming soon and she had to get the house prepared.

"I'm just wondering what this means," he answered.

"What does what mean?"

"Your allowing me to make love to you," Roger said.

She hoped he wasn't making more out of this than she was. To her, it was a night of lovemaking. A relationship it did not make.

Before she could reply, the doorbell rang. "Excuse me," she told Roger and went to take a peek out the living room window. She was surprised to see Lange standing at the door. "Fuck," she said in a low tone. Crystal looked down at herself and frowned. All she had on was a sweatshirt.

She went to the door, opened it and stepped outside. "Lange, what are you doing here?"

He noticed that she was almost naked and apologized for popping up unannounced. "I just needed someone to talk to."

"This isn't the time," she said and glanced behind her. Damn it, why didn't she throw Roger out when they first woke up?

"I'm sorry, it's just that—" Lange saw a shadow move behind the curtain. "You have company?" he stated, looking at her car and another car in the driveway.

"Yes." What more was there to say?

"I'll call you later." Lange turned and walked away.

"Lange, wait." She didn't want him to leave like that.

He stopped at the bottom of the steps. "I'll call you later."

Crystal stood on the porch and watched him walk away. When she walked back into the house, Roger was no longer in the kitchen. She headed upstairs and heard the shower running.

"Was that your friend Lange?" Roger asked as he stepped out of the shower.

147

"Yeah, we're working on a case together. He wanted to discuss it."

"You don't owe me an explanation." Roger said, not meaning a word of it. As he pulled on his pants he asked "Can we have lunch later?"

"No. I have a lot of things to do, but I'll call you later."

As Crystal walked him down the stairs to the door, he turned to her, kissed her on the mouth and said, "I could fall in love with you."

Before she could reply, he was out the door. "Please don't do that," Crystal said out loud. "That's the last thing I need."

Crystal went back into the house, picked up the phone and dialed Lange's cell number. The answering service came on. She didn't bother to leave a message. He'd see her number on the caller ID.

THE CONFRONTATION

Jewell was waiting for King to arrive. She glanced at her watch and noticed that he was fifteen minutes late. She decided to give him five more minutes. If he didn't show up by then, she would be out. Just as she made that decision, King walked in. He looked around the restaurant, spotted her and frowned.

From the look on his face, Jewell knew this wasn't going to be good. She had been avoiding King for over a week now. She would drop Tyson off at his house and leave the second he stepped foot in the door. She'd even rush him off the phone. She knew that wasn't going to last too much longer, especially after she received the message from King saying he would come to her job if she didn't stop avoiding him.

King pulled his chair out and sat down. He got right to the point. "Why have you been avoiding me?"

"I haven't been avoiding you," Jewell denied. They both knew she was lying.

"You have and you know it."

"Listen, let's eat first, then we can discuss whatever it is you would like to discuss," Jewell suggested then picked up a glass of water and took a sip.

"I feel he needs his father," King continued.

"He sees you every weekend and sometimes during the week."

"Yeah, but it's not enough."

"To you," Jewell said.

"Yes, to me. He's getting to be that age where he's going to have a lot of questions, start liking girls, and well, I want to be there for him on an everyday basis. Shit, it won't be hard. I'm self-employed. I work from home, and business is doing great. I go to clients occasionally. He can come with me or I can get a babysitter. Damn it, you've had him long enough. It's my turn to have him."

His being able to take care of Tyson wasn't an issue. Aside from designing websites, King was a master electrician who owned his own general contracting business, and he had several men working for him. Jewell informed him that a child isn't a thing, something you take turns with.

"You know what I mean. Remember in *Boyz In The Hood*, how Lawrence Fishburne—"

"King, this is not a movie. This is real life with a real child. I don't give a damn about a movie." Did he really think she would just agree to this, to giving up her son? Yes, he was Tyson's father, but the arrangement they had was working. Why disrupt it?

"I've spoken to Tyson about it." King surprised her by saying. "He's excited about the idea."

"You did what?"

"We've talked about the possibility of him coming to live with me."

Jewell didn't know what to say. She wanted to reach across the table and punch King in the face, she was so pissed. "I can't believe you did that." She shook her head. "If he's so excited about it, how come he hasn't discussed it with me?" Jewell's voice was getting louder.

"Shhh. Lower your voice." King looked around and noticed that people were looking in their direction.

"Maybe I don't want to lower my voice. How could you discuss this with him without talking to me about it first? I can't believe you did that."

"He's my son too, and he probably didn't mention it because he knows how sensitive you are. He didn't want to hurt your feelings."

Jewell was tripping. She couldn't believe what she was hearing. "He knows how sensitive I am? Where the hell did that come from?"

The waiter came over to take their orders. Jewell shot him the evil eye. "We're not ready yet."

"Think about it, Jewell." King reached for her hand and she snatched it away.

"Don't touch me!" She was clearly upset.

The waiter pointedly asked Jewell if everything was okay.

"Everything is fine," King told him.

"I'm talking to the lady."

"And I'm talking to you. If you don't leave us alone, everything won't be fine."

Jewell looked at King. "Is all that really necessary?" She then told the waiter everything was fine.

"If you say so." The waiter walked away.

"Why'd you threaten him?"

King ignored her question. "What is this, white men just flock to you now?"

"What are you talking about now?"

"You know damn well what I'm talking about—your white man, the white waiter."

"Oh, so that's what this is all about? Is that why you're trying to take Tyson away from me, because I'm dating a white man?"

151

"No, Jewell, it's not. That night I came over to talk to you about this, I had no idea your new man was white as rice."

She knew he was telling the truth.

"Answer this for me," he said. "If I was dating a white girl, how would you feel?"

She knew it would irritate the hell out of her, but she chose to lie. "It wouldn't bother me at all."

"Yeah, okay," King said, wondering who she thought she was fooling. "You forget how well I know you. Remember, I was your first love."

"Well, people change." She crossed her arms.

Neither of them said a word. They just sat across from one another. Finally King said, "Let's get back together. Let's see if we can make it work."

"Don't do this to me, King. Not now."

"I've never stopped loving you Jewell. I'm ready to settle down, have more kids, and the thought of having a whole bunch of baby mamas is not appealing."

"Stop it, King."

"Think about how good we could be together, and how happy it would make Tyson to have both of us."

"He has both of us now."

"Not in one household, not together."

"That's not fair," Jewell protested.

"Just consider it, think about it. If not, consider him coming to stay with me."

The waiter came over again and asked if he could take their order. Jewell stood up and said, "I'm not hungry."

King watched her walk away.

"Can you believe him?" Jewell asked Evan. She was having dinner at his place.

"That's his father, Jewell, so I do believe it," Evan told her. "It's only natural that he would want more time with him. Me, I think you should consider it. You women are always complaining that black men don't spend enough time with their children and—"

Jewell looked at Evan and told him, "Watch yourself. You're crossing boundaries." She hated when he did that, tried to explain something about black people as though he had a clue. Then on top of everything else, he said "you women."

"Well, you asked me for my opinion," he told her, confused.

"No, actually I didn't. I was just telling you what happened today."

Actually she wasn't telling him everything. Jewell excluded the fact that King asked her to consider them being a couple again. She knew if she told him that, he wouldn't be so, "oh, you should consider it." What concerned her was why she was withholding information, why she chose to keep that part of the conversation from him. What was the big deal? Was it that she was considering it? Was it because even with all King had put her through, she still loved him?

"Listen, I'm sorry if I upset you," Evan reached for her hand and kissed it.

"I know you are. You just need to be more aware of your words."

"I will, I promise. Did you think about what we discussed?"

He had asked her to move in with him. "I did, and I can't do that, Evan. We've only been dating for a short period of time and well, I'm not the type of woman that just moves in with someone."

"But I'm falling in love with you," he declared.

"How about this?" Jewell tried to pretend he didn't say what she thought he'd said. "I'll stay the night occasionally and we'll see."

"That's not the answer I was hoping for," he told her.

"Well, we can't always get what we hope for," she told him. Jewell didn't want to commit to anything right now, especially after this afternoon. King had messed everything up by saying he still had feelings for her after all these years.

"I'll accept what you feel you can give me then. Are we still on for this weekend?" he asked.

Evan's parents were coming to visit him, and he wanted them to meet her. She wasn't crazy about the idea and she let him know it. "I'm just not sure about this meeting your parents thing."

"Why not? We are a couple. I want them to meet the person I'm involved with."

"Do they know I'm black?"

"I'm real close to my parents," he went on to say.

"That's not what I asked you. I asked you if they know I'm black."

"Does it make a difference?"

"To me it does."

"No, they don't know, but it wouldn't make a difference anyway. If you make me happy, which you do, that's all they're going to care about."

Jewell didn't reply, because she knew better.

THE MEETING

Why she agreed to do this, she didn't know. Susan decided to attend a Narcotics Anonymous meeting with Timothy. It was being held at a church, the last place she wanted to be. When they walked through the doors, she regretted it immediately. She felt as though all eyes were on her.

"You're just being paranoid," Timothy told her when she expressed this. "When I came to my first meeting, I felt the same way."

"Are you sure these meetings are confidential?"

"Yes, Susan."

She knew she'd asked him that question before leaving the house, but he didn't have to give her attitude. "How do you know?"

"Because I know, Susan. We've had this conversation numerous times."

"Why are you talking to me in that tone?"

With love in his eyes he told her, "Listen, sweetie, you're making me nervous, and I've been here before. I'm going to the bathroom, and when I return, we're going to take a seat."

Susan wasn't stupid. She knew he needed to take a breather, so she let him go. She looked around the room to see if there was anyone she knew, any faces she recognized. Thank God, there weren't. Then again, there probably wouldn't be, considering the fact she made Timothy take her to meeting over an hour out of town.

"How are you doing?" someone asked her out of the blue, causing her to jump. "Is this your first meeting?"

"Is it that obvious?" Susan asked.

"Well, I haven't seen you here before, plus you have that nervous first-timer's look on your face. Did you come alone?"

"No, I came with a friend," Susan told her.

"My name is Dasha."

"I'm Susan."

Before they could converse any longer, Timothy walked up. "Hey, sweetie, let's go have a seat."

"Timothy, this is Dasha."

"How you doing?" Timothy greeted.

They went to find seats. Susan really didn't know what to expect, but for people to stand up, give their names and identify themselves as addicts was a bit much. As they went around the room, it was getting closer and closer to her turn and she was obviously nervous.

"Don't worry," Timothy told her. "You don't have to say anything."

I wasn't planning on it, Susan said to herself as she looked around the room, surprised at the diversity amongst her. It was mind-blowing. Of course, she knew drugs could beat anyone down, regardless of class or color. Heck, it got to her, but to be sitting here staring it in the face was a whole different matter.

A young girl who looked to be all of sixteen years old stood up and told her story. She said that she had tricked for drugs, and never considered her body as something sacred. She had been a victim of incest, and would give her dealers her body instead of money. Now she had HIV. She wasn't diagnosed until she'd been clean for three months.

Hearing the stories, feeling the emotions, was a bit much for Susan. She found herself getting antsy, squirming in her seat.

"Are you okay?" Timothy asked.

"I need to go to the ladies' room," she lied.

Timothy knew she didn't have to go to the bathroom. He knew she was feeling overwhelmed. "It's always hard in the beginning," he said to reassure her.

The ride home was a quiet one.

"You want me to come in and stay the night?" Timothy asked as he parked the car.

"Yes." She didn't want to be alone.

Together they went into the house, climbed up the stairs, got undressed, turned the television on and cuddled.

"Let's start praying together," Timothy blurted out.

Susan looked at Timothy, surprised by his suggestion. "When did you start praying?"

"I've always prayed off and on. What do you think, I'm some kind of heathen?"

"No, of course not. I've just never known you to be religious. How come you never shared this with me before?"

"Prayer is normally a private thing."

"I'm just surprised."

"Well, do you want to pray or not?" Timothy figured that since they were both trying to stay clean, if they could connect spiritually, it would increase the chances of sobriety and their becoming one.

"I don't know how to pray," Susan admitted. "What am I supposed to say?"

"Say whatever comes to mind. Say what's in your heart. It doesn't have to be poetic or fancy. God knows what you feel. If you don't want to say anything out loud, you don't have to.

You can pray to yourself and I'll do the same. We'll still be praying together." On that note, Timothy took her hand.

Susan watched him close his eyes, closed her own and said to herself, *Damn, I love this man.*

A NEW DAY, A DIFFERENT WAY

Susan climbed out of the bed, but not before kissing Timothy on the cheek. "Good morning," she told him.

"Good morning," he replied.

"You want some breakfast?"

"No."

Susan smiled because she knew when he was short with her, it only meant one thing. He wanted more sleep. Recalling how she and Timothy prayed together the night before, she told him, "I'm going to church today."

"Repeat that?" Timothy looked up at her in surprise. He wanted to be sure he heard her right.

"I said I'm going to church today."

"I thought that's what you said. Do you want me to go with you?"

"Nah, I need to do this by myself."

Timothy understood.

She kissed him again and said, "I'm going to make a quick breakfast and some coffee." She left the room.

Susan was in the kitchen, pouring herself a cup of orange juice when Timothy came in and hugged her from behind. "So, do you think you'll be attending another meeting?"

She didn't want to tell him no because he swore by them. They might have been the answer for him, but Susan knew they weren't for her.

"I don't know," she told him.

"Why not?"

"I don't like the group thing. I'd rather do one on one."

Timothy pulled away. He was disappointed to hear her say this, because he'd already put it in his mind that they would attend the meetings together. To hear her reject his idea threw him for a loop. "Well, you need some kind of help," he told her. "You're not going to be able to get clean on your own."

Felling insulted, Susan snapped, "Well, maybe your kind of help isn't the kind I need."

"Listen, I'm just concerned. I didn't mean to upset you."

"I know, I know. It's just that I have to do this my way, not your way. It's not a rejection of you or your solution, but I need to find something on my own. I know you love me and that you want to rescue me, and I appreciate it, but you have to let me do this my way. Okay?"

"Okay," he told her.

Susan placed her cup on the counter. "I have to get dressed."

While in the shower, Susan thought about Timothy and wondered if his insistence on her attending the meetings would become a problem between the two of them. She hoped he would stop pressing the issue because it was bound to push her away. She told him she needed to do this her way, and although she didn't know what her way was, she needed to explore some options. Right now there were only two: God and counseling.

While Susan was getting dressed, Timothy asked her, "What church are you going to?"

Susan told Timothy that she'd heard Crystal mention a church she went to quite a while ago. It had a "come as you are" policy. You didn't have to dress up, there was no trying to outdo one another and the congregation was mixed. Non-denominational, she believed it was called.

The church parking lot was full. *Good*, she thought. *This way I won't stand out.* Little did she know she didn't have to stand out in this church to be noticed. People approached newcomers whether they knew them or not. Everyone that walked through the door was welcome this way.

"Welcome. Praise the Lord. God Bless you." People approached her left and right. All this attention brought tears to Susan's eyes.

Damn, she thought. *Here I am getting all emotional.* She glanced around and found a seat in the back of the church. She sat down and closed her eyes while she listened to the choir. Susan started to cry because she found herself moved by the emotion and the depth of the lead singer's voice.

"Are you okay?" the man next to her asked. "Do you need a fan or some water?"

"No, no thank you. I'm fine. I'm just, I'm just . . ." She couldn't finish.

He took her hand in his and told her, "The Lord knows and understands all. You heard what the preacher said. Cast all your cares upon him."

Susan removed her hand from his and thanked him. She looked up at the preacher as he said, "Be not anxious for anything, but by prayer and persistence . . ." Prayer and persistence, Susan repeated to herself. She was going to put prayer in her life and be persistent about becoming whole again.

When church was over, she was headed toward her car when someone called out her name. She turned around and saw that it was Crystal.

"What are you doing here?" they both asked at the same time.

"I don't know," Susan told her. "Heck, with all that's been going on in my life, who better to turn to than God?"

"I know that's right. Do you want to go get something to eat?" Crystal asked.

"Your mother is in town, right?"

Crystal rolled her eyes.

"It's like that?" Susan asked.

"It's worse. Let's talk about it over lunch."

Susan could feel Crystal's despair. "Let me call my house and let Timothy know I won't be right home."

She pulled out her cell phone and dialed the number. "Hey baby, me and Crystal are going to grab a bite to eat. Yeah . . . yeah . . . love you too." Susan hung up. "Where to?"

"Perkins?" Crystal suggested.

"Perkins it is."

When they arrived at the restaurant, Crystal proceeded to tell Susan about her mother's visit.

She should have known something was up when her mom told her she would catch a cab from the airport.

"Are you sure?" Crystal asked, silently thanking her because it gave her time to clean up and run to the gym.

"Yeah, baby, Mommy's sure."

That should have been the second clue. Her mother was never one to be overly sweet, calling her baby and all. That definitely wasn't her style.

When her mother arrived, she didn't have any bags.

"Where are your bags?" Crystal wanted to know.

"At the hotel."

"At the hotel? What are you talking about? You're staying here with me. Why would you want to stay at a hotel?"

Mrs. Gem didn't answer her.

Standing back, Crystal said, "Okay, Mom. What's up?"

"What do you mean what's up?"

"Something's not right," Crystal told her.

"Let's go inside," Mrs. Gem said. "We need to talk."

They walked through the door and Mrs. Gem glanced around. "I see you made some changes with your décor. How about you give me a tour?"

"Mom, what do you want to talk about? What's going on?" Crystal had a bad feeling in the pit of her stomach.

Her mother moved toward the couch. "Let's have a seat," she said.

They did.

"I'm staying at a hotel because I brought someone with me," Mrs. Gem revealed.

"A man?"

"Yes, a man, and not just any man. He's someone I care for very deeply."

This wasn't as bad as Crystal thought.

"Mom, that's wonderful. Why didn't you bring him with you?" Her mother had been alone for as long as she could remember. "When can I meet him?"

Clearing her throat, Mrs. Gem said, "You already know him."

"I already know him? What do you mean I already know him? Who—" Crystal stopped speaking when she saw the look on her mother's face.

Mrs. Gem folded her hands in her lap. "I'm tired of hiding this from you. I wanted to tell you for quite some time."

"Spill it, Mother. You're scaring me."

"Trevor Newton."

"Trevor Newton." Crystal repeated the name. "Trevor Newton." Then suddenly it hit her. It hit her so hard that she started to hyperventilate.

"Bags, bags, where are they?" Mrs. Gem asked in a panic.

Crystal pointed to the kitchen.

Mrs. Gem came back and assisted Crystal in putting a paper bag over her mouth. When she was finally able to speak, she looked at her mother in disbelief. "How could you do this to me?" she gave a pathetic laugh and shook her head. "I can't believe this. How long has this been going on?" The words couldn't come out quick enough.

"Hear me out, Crystal."

Crystal stood up in a rage. "Hear you out? Hear you out? You're dating the father of the boy who raped me! I can't believe this shit. How long has this been going on? Oh my God! Is this why we didn't sign a complaint?" She looked at her mother with disgust. "You are seeing the father of the boy who raped me. I can't believe this. No, I don't want to believe this."

"Crystal, please sit down and let me talk to you about this."

Crystal felt like her whole world was falling apart. She collapsed onto the couch.

"What could you possibly say to me that's going to make this any better?" Crystal asked.

"This wasn't going on back then."

"Then when, mother? Tell me when. And why did we let Jake get away with what he did to me, if it wasn't to screw his father?"

Mrs. Gem pointed her finger in Crystal's face and told her, "You will not talk to me that way. I am still your mother."

"A mother is someone who truly loves her daughter, and someone who truly loves her daughter wouldn't betray her this way. Do you have any idea how this makes me feel? Did you think about that?"

"Crystal, you know that all my life I've put you first. I wasn't seeing Trevor back then. It didn't start until three years ago. We didn't press charges because Trevor offered me money, a large sum, to keep quiet. I know how that may sound, but being a single parent and all, it helped us to live just a little bit better, and you never had to set eyes on Jake again. They sent him away."

"I never had to set eyes on him again until recently," Crystal informed her.

"What do mean, until recently? What are you talking about?"

"Never mind."

"It's been fourteen years, Crystal."

"I know that, mother, but it still doesn't excuse the fact that you're seeing his father."

"That's another thing. He's not Jake's father. About seven years ago, Jake got into an accident and lost a lot of blood. When Trevor went to donate his, he found out Jake wasn't his son. He divorced Jake's mother and moved to North Carolina."

"And that's supposed to make it better?" Crystal couldn't believe her mother was telling her this. "Is that why you moved to North Carolina?"

"No, no, that was a coincidence."

Thinking of Tina, Crystal said, "A lot of coincidences have been happening lately."

"Why do you say that?"

"It doesn't matter. Go on."

"Anyway, one day I went out to dinner with some friends and Trevor walked into the restaurant. We spotted each other at the same time and he came over to the table."

Crystal interrupted. "That's when you should have left."

Mrs. Gem ignored her. "We spoke briefly and he gave me his card."

"You should have thrown it out."

"I did."

"Well, how did you end up together?" Crystal wanted to know.

"He knew one of the people at my table and tracked me down that way."

"Mother, how could you not tell me this? How could you keep it a secret for so long?"

"I was afraid of your reaction, of how you would feel."

"And rightfully so," Crystal told her.

Mrs. Gem sat down. Neither of them said a word. They were both exhausted from the news, telling it and receiving it.

"And that's when I stood up and told her I needed to lay down," Crystal told Susan. "I just couldn't deal with her at that moment. I needed some time to process what she'd told me."

"Wow! That's messed up," Susan said.

"I know," Crystal told her. "She thinks that just because he's not Jake's real father it makes it okay, but it doesn't. I still feel betrayed because he was the one who paid us off."

Susan didn't know what to say because the points Crystal was making were valid and legit. Crystal continued, "So the end result was, my mother left and went back to the hotel, but not before trying to make me feel guilty. She actually had the nerve to say that instead of me being selfish and thinking of myself, I needed to realize how lonely she's been and for how long, and that I could at least give him a chance, hear him out. You know what? I ain't giving him shit."

Crystal waited for Susan's response. When there was none, she asked her, "Do you think I'm being selfish?"

"No."

"Good, because I don't want to see her or him right now, much less talk to them."

Susan didn't reply because she knew that she wouldn't handle news like this well either. Heck, it would probably cause her to get high.

"We don't see each other for months at a time and she pops up with this, and on top of that, I've got Lange to worry about."

This caught Susan's attention. "Lange?"

Crystal leaned across the table and spoke in a whisper. "I'm a ho."

Susan laughed. "What are you talking about?"

"Remember that night at the club when we ran into Jake?"

"Yeah?"

"Well, Lange came over and well . . ."

Susan looked at Crystal in disbelief. "Y'all did it?"

Crystal nodded.

"Girl, do you know what you're getting into? He's married. Shit, you know that. I don't know what to say other than be careful. In the end, you may be the one hurt."

"I know. I can't believe I did something so stupid. Then I keep trying to justify it by saying his wife is cheating on him. I don't know." Crystal shook her head. "Let's talk about something else. What's going on with you?"

"Well, I went to a NA meeting yesterday."

Crystal was surprised to hear this. "Really? Wow, that's big."

Susan said, "I know, I know. I can't believe I did it either."

"Well, how did it go?"

"All I can say is I don't know if I'll be returning. Standing up, introducing myself as an addict, that's not my cup of tea. But I am going to try to start counseling next week. I think I'll do better one on one."

"I'm happy for you. Proud of you too."

They finished eating their meals and stood up to leave. Susan reached over to hug Crystal and told her, "Listen, I know you're going through a lot mentally. We both are. Let's just be there for one another."

Crystal teared up and responded, "I like how that sounds."

SURPRISE, SURPRISE

Elsie and Summer were cuddled up on the couch, watching a movie when in walked Winter, returning from church. She'd gone with one of her classmates. Since she moved in, she'd had no problems making friends, and this made things a little easier on Summer.

"I'm home," Winter said as she stood behind the couch.

Summer and Elsie jumped apart.

"Hi, Ms. Elsie," Winter said.

Elsie felt like she was busted. "Hey, sweetie. How was church?"

"It was okay."

Winter turned to leave the room, but Summer patted the seat next to her. Winter took the hint, sat down and crossed her legs like a little lady. She looked from Summer to Elsie and asked, "Are you two best friends?"

"Yes, honey, we are," Summer told her. "Why do you ask?"

"Because she's always here."

Elsie shifted in her seat.

"Ms. Elsie might be moving in with us. What do you think about that?"

Elsie looked at Summer with a question in her eyes. They hadn't discussed talking to Winter about it.

"Well, I'll have to think about it," Winter told them.

Caught off guard, Summer said, "Okay, you do that."

Standing up, Winter asked, "Can I have a snack?"

"Of course."

Winter went toward the kitchen. The second she was out of sight, Elsie tore into Summer. "Why would you do that?"

"Do what?"

Elsie rolled her eyes. "Tell Winter that I was moving in."

"You are, aren't you?"

"Once again, I think we need to wait until things are smoother with Winter."

"I'm the mother, she's the child."

"I understand all that, but just the other day you were complaining that this is harder than you thought it would be."

"I'm not going to front. It is. Sometimes I feel like she's not responding to me at all. She will stay in her room, and barely says a word."

"I know you didn't think this would be easy," Elsie said.

"No, I didn't think it would be easy, but I thought we'd at least bond with one another."

"You have to give it time," Elsie told her.

Summer looked into Elsie's eyes and asked, "Like I'm giving us time?"

Elsie didn't reply.

"I want more than what we have. I feel like we're falling apart. If something is wrong, you need to tell me. If I didn't do something or if there's something I can do, you need to tell me. I want us to be more like the couple we were up until a month ago."

Elsie knew what Summer wanted, knew what she needed. She just couldn't give it to her.

"Please, Elsie, be honest with me. Are you doing this because you no longer love me? Do you not want to be with me anymore?"

"Of course I want to be with you. What are you talking about? I'm just thinking about your child. She just moved in, and you two barely know one another."

"I know all that, but this is my life also. And if you're going to be in it, I think we should go ahead and make this move."

Elsie felt caught between a rock and a hard place.

"Please, Elsie," Summer begged. "She's going to find out about us sooner or later. It might as well be sooner. That way this little drama thing that's going on right now can happen all at once and be done with. I need you and your support."

Summer was winning her over. She always did. Summer did have a point. If she moved in now, everything could be handled at once. "But what if it got to be overwhelming? What if it didn't work out? What if—?" Elsie had to stop right there, because she could "what if" all night and it would get her nowhere but frustrated.

"Okay," she found herself saying against her better judgment. "I'll move in. I just need a couple of weeks. I have to talk to my landlord and get a few things situated."

Summer gave Elsie a tight hug and told her, "I love you, and you won't regret this. I know you're worried and all, but it'll work out. I know it will."

Summer initiated a kiss, but Elsie wasn't into it. Her mind was wandering and wondering.

On the way home, Elsie decided to stop off for a drink at a nearby gay bar. She was at the point where hiding her sexuality was no longer an option. She pulled into the parking lot and saw that it was full. She parked down the street, and as she walked up to the bar, a car with a bunch of teenagers rode by. They slowed down and yelled "Dyke!" out the window. She knew she should ignore them, but chose not to. Elsie turned around and stuck her middle finger up at them.

"Use it on yourself," they yelled back.

Kitty Kats was the name of the place. There was a small dance floor and two bars, loveseats positioned strategically around the room. There was also a pool table. She glanced around to see if there was anyone that she knew.

She walked up to the bar. The bartender's back was turned. "Excuse me," Elsie called out.

When the bartender turned around, they were both surprised. It was Janay, Elsie's first female love. They hadn't seen each other since their breakup over two years ago.

"What are you doing here?" Elsie asked, shocked.

"Is that all I get?" Janay came from behind the counter and gave Elsie a hug, which went unreturned.

"What are you doing here?" Elsie asked again. The last she heard, Janay had moved to California to pursue acting.

"This is my bar," she told Elsie. "I just bought it a month ago."

Elsie took in Janay's appearance. She was still beautiful— a little thin, but the curves were noticeable in the jeans, white "Fetish By Eve" T-shirt that was cut in all the right places, and stiletto boots.

Janay called someone over from the dance floor to handle the bar and asked Elsie, "You want something to drink?"

Elsie needed something strong. "Yes. A martini on the rocks."

After getting her drink, Elsie allowed Janay to take her hand and pull her toward a table, where they sat across from one another. Elsie asked for the third time, "So, what are you doing here?"

"Is that all you can say? How about I'm happy to see you?"

"I am happy to see. I'm just surprised. Very surprised." Elsie was also nervous. Seeing Janay stirred up emotions that she thought were gone. "What happened to California? Last I heard you moved there to pursue an acting career. As a matter of fact, isn't that why you left me? We wanted different things. We were going in different directions is what you said, if I remember correctly."

"Now, why do you have to go there?" Janay asked.

"Go where?"

"To the past. Let's leave it behind and concentrate on the here and now. Yes, I did go to California to pursue the arts. I did a couple of commercials and got a part in a movie that's coming out next year."

"Well, if you were having so much success, what brought you back out this way?"

"My niece has cancer and my sister needed my support," Janay answered bluntly.

"Oh, and you're here bartending?"

"No, this is my bar."

Elsie was impressed.

"You still look good," Janay told her.

"Thanks. So do you."

"Are you seeing anyone?" Janay wanted to know.

Elsie hesitated. "Yes. Yes, I am."

"Are you happy?"

Again Elsie hesitated. "Yeah, considering." As soon as she said that she regretted it.

Not one to beat around the bush, Janay said, "So, that's a no."

"I didn't say that."

"You didn't have to."

Elsie picked up her drink and started sipping.

"Well, would your friend mind if we hung out?"

"Probably." Elsie knew the answer was more like "Hell yes." Summer would freak.

"How about I give you my number? If you can sneak away or just want to go to lunch or something, you give me a call."

"I'd like that," Elsie said, knowing she was dead wrong.

Later that night when Elsie arrived home, there was a message on her answering machine from Jewell. "Call me. I don't care what time it is. I need to talk."

"What's up?" Elsie asked Jewell the second she heard her voice. "Is everything okay?"

"Dinner with Evan's parents did not go well at all. I don't know what he was thinking, talking about we should meet," she told Elsie.

"Why? What happened?" Elsie asked.

"It's not that anything happened. It was more about the look on their faces when they met me. I told Evan that he should have told them about us, but no, he didn't want to listen. 'My parents are open-minded', he insisted. Open-minded my ass." Jewell was pissed at Evan. She felt like he put her on the spot. The whole night was one of discomfort.

After they left, Evan had the audacity to say, "I told you they would like you." *Even he couldn't be that blind,* Jewell thought.

"So, are you going to continue going out with him?" Elsie asked.

"Yeah, I think so. He's just scaring me a little. It's like he's moving too fast, wanting me to meet his parents. Who knows what's next? And on top of that, King asked me if Tyson could come live with him."

"Wow, that's a big one. Are you thinking about it?"

"I don't know. What do you think?"

"I'm the wrong person to ask. I mean, I don't have any children, and well, off the top of my head, I'd say you should."

"Why?"

"Well, he is his father, and you are in school. You work full time, and it'll allow you time for you. You'll be able to concentrate on school more and get yourself together without

173

the disruptions of a child. Plus, it's not like you're giving him away. I'm sure you'll have all the access you want to Tyson."

"I have to be honest and say I'm actually considering it, I can't help but feel like I'm abandoning him, though."

"Girl, please."

"I know it sounds silly, but I can't help it."

"It doesn't sound silly at all. It's understandable."

"So, what's been up with you?" Jewell asked.

"Well," Elsie said, "I ran into my old girlfriend tonight. Actually, she was the love of my life."

"Get out of here."

"Yeah. She's moved back into the area."

"Did you tell her about you and Summer?" Jewell wanted to know.

"I did." Elsie wanted to talk more about Janay and how she realized she still had feelings for her, but she wanted to be in denial about it too.

Jewell could read in Elsie's voice that something was up. "And?"

"Girl, I think I still have feelings for her."

"How long ago did you two break up?"

"A little over two years ago. We were together in college, broke up then reconnected years later. She left me to pursue the arts, and because she felt like we were headed in two different directions."

"Damn, so y'all never had closure?"

"Nope."

"What are you going to do about it?"

"I have no idea."

IT'S OVER

When Crystal arrived home, the first thing she did was check the messages on her answering service. There was one from Lange. They had not had a chance to talk since the day he came over and Roger was there. She wanted to call him, but had gotten caught up at work. She didn't want him to be angry with her for having Roger over, especially when it was obvious that he stayed the night. She knew she shouldn't feel this way, because it wasn't like they were a couple. After all, he was married, she was not. She had to keep telling herself this.

"I'm sorry for the way I ran off that day. I should know better than to just pop up like that. It was selfish of me to think you would be available at the drop of a dime. I need to see you. Some events have taken place, and well, I need to talk to you. Call me at home." He left his number and then there was a click.

He needed to speak with her, not *wanted* to but *needed* to, and on top of everything else, he'd left his home number. She didn't know if she felt comfortable calling him at his house, but since he'd left the number, it must be okay. Crystal picked up the phone and dialed his number.

175

"Hello." It was Lange.

"Lange. Hi, it's Crystal. I got your message. Is everything okay? It sounded important."

"Are you busy?" Lange asked.

"No, I just walked in the door."

"Are you alone?"

"Yes."

"Do you mind if I stop by?"

"Come on. I'll be here."

They hung up.

Crystal wondered what was going on. Lange didn't sound like himself. She wondered if he'd found out about Lena's affair or if Lena had found out about them.

"Stop trying to guess and be patient," she told herself.

Crystal didn't know what to do with herself until he arrived. She tried to sit down and relax, but it didn't work. She found herself glancing toward the door every few minutes.

"Stop it," she told herself. "You're getting yourself all worked up and it could be something petty." But she knew it wasn't.

"Billie!" she called out. She decided to take him for a short walk. That way she'd get some of the nervous energy out of her system.

Thirty minutes later, she and Billie were approaching the house as Lange pulled into the driveway. She tried to appear calm, cool and collected as she approached the Jeep.

"Hey there," she greeted.

"Thanks for letting me come by at the last minute." He kissed her on the cheek.

"Anytime," she told him then led the way inside her house.

He followed her through the door into the living room.

"Have a seat. Do you want something to drink?" she asked.

"Rum and Coke."

Crystal went into the kitchen and returned with a rum and Coke for him, water for her.

She passed him the glass and sat next to him. "What's causing a brother to drink?"

"Lena and I are separating," he announced.

Crystal wasn't surprised. "Why?"

"She had an affair." Lange put his drink down and dropped his head. "She's been having one for quite some time, actually."

"How did you find out?"

"She told me."

"She told you?" That was the last thing Crystal expected to hear.

"Yeah, and you know what?"

"What?"

"I kind of suspected it all along."

"You did?"

"Yeah, women aren't the only ones with intuition, you know."

Crystal stood up and told him she'd be back. Heck, she needed a drink as well. When she returned with her drink in hand, he continued, "Our marriage has actually been falling apart for quite some time. I think we were both in denial."

"I don't know what to say, Lange."

"There isn't anything to say."

Crystal could see that Lange was hurt, and she knew that all she could do was be there for him. "What exactly did Lena say to you? If you're willing to share."

"She said we have to talk. Now, when a woman says we have to talk, you know it's something serious. Immediately, I thought she knew about us or maybe suspected something. So, we decided to talk over dinner. She picked our favorite spot."

"When did all this happen?" Crystal asked. She wondered if it happened before the day he popped up.

"The night before I came over here and you had company."

Crystal ignored his snide remark.

"Anyway, she asked me if we could have an honest conversation. Of course I told her yes. She asked me if I was happy. I told her I was comfortable and content, that happiness comes and goes. She went on to tell me she's not happy anymore, and that she's not even comfortable. She said she doesn't like her life, where she's at or where she's going. That this was not the life she had planned. Then she blurted out she wanted a separation."

"Damn, just like that?"

"Not exactly. I mean, we exchanged dialogue but that was the gist of it."

"How did that make you feel?" Crystal wanted so bad to wrap her arms around him.

"Surprised, maybe a little hurt, even a sense of relief. I mean, if I were all that happy, you and I wouldn't have made love. So of course, me being a man asked her if there was someone else."

Crystal almost feel off the couch. "And?"

"She told me there was, but that her wanting a separation had nothing to do with this person. She just needed to come clean with me."

"Wow! That was bold."

"As much as I wanted to be angry and cause a scene, I couldn't. I had no right to, but I'll tell you what. I feel like I've failed. When I first knew the marriage was in danger, I should have stepped up to the plate, suggested counseling or something."

"It's not too late for that." Crystal was trying her damnest to be a good friend, but that shit was easier said than done, especially when her attraction for him was involved. She wanted to say, "Forget about her. You can have me." But could he really have her? Would she trust him not to cheat on her?

Damn it, friendships become complicated when you put sex in the picture.

Finishing off his drink, Lange told her it was too late. "When I got married, I thought it would last forever."

"Most people think that."

"Yeah, well, I believed it."

"So, what are you going to do now?"

"I don't know. What am I supposed to do other than move out of the house I paid for?"

"Is that what Lena wants?"

"Actually, no. She said she'd move out into an apartment or condo until we could figure out what we're going to do as far as dividing up our assets."

Crystal didn't understand. "Then what's the problem?"

"I can't allow that. It's just as much her home as it is mine." Lange grew quiet and Crystal could tell he was deep in thought. "You know what? When Lena and I first got together we were teenagers, still in high school, actually. I was her first love, her first lover, and I have to admit I wasn't the most well-behaved back then. She came from a single parent family, her mother was an alcoholic, and I rescued her. She used to say I was her hero, and that's just what I wanted to be. She told me she lost herself in our marriage, that she never got a chance to grow up."

"That sounds like a bunch of crap. I believe it's the woman that allows her individuality to be taken away. We allow ourselves to get so consumed with our partner that we forget about our wants, our needs, and ourselves. The second she realized this, she should have said something," Crystal said.

"I never held a gun to her head and said do this, do that, don't do this, don't do that."

"Look," Crystal said, "let's get to the heart of the matter. Do you still love her? Do you still want to be married to her?" That's what Crystal wanted to know. That's what she needed to know.

Lange was honest and said, "I really don't know. I'm not in love with her anymore, but she's familiar. You're single. You know how hard it is to put yourself out there. I don't think I can go through that process again."

Trying to ease the mood, Crystal shoved him and said, "Believe me. You won't have problems with the ladies."

Lange passed Crystal his glass. "Can I have a refill?"

She took his glass and said, "Listen, I rented a couple of movies. Do you want to watch them with me?"

"Yeah, I'd like that."

DECISIONS, DECISIONS

Susan was sitting in the waiting room of the therapist's office. She'd canceled two of her appointments so far. It wasn't because she was busy. She was just afraid. What the hell was she going to talk about for an hour? Other than, "I've been getting high for over ten years and have decided it's time for me to stop," she couldn't think of a damn thing. She already knew that she was angry about her childhood, angry with her mother for not being there for her during her teenage years when she needed her most. She already knew that she was an overachiever and that she obsessed over everything being perfect and in place. If she knew these things already, why the hell was she going to the therapist?

When she posed this question to her friend, Crystal told her, "Although you know these things, you don't know how to deal with them. Maybe getting high is your way of numbing yourself, of pretending that things are better than they actually are. Counseling will help you figure that out." Crystal's theory sounded good, but who knew what this would do for her?

Earlier that day, when she'd spoken to Crystal on the phone, she told her, "Girl, I don't know what to do. I feel so much pressure with this wedding thing, and on top of that, I'm trying to stop getting high. I don't know if I can do it." Ever since Susan got busted, they'd talked openly about her addiction.

"If you feel that way, maybe you shouldn't get married," Crystal advised.

"That's what my mind says, but my heart is saying something else. I can't imagine myself growing old with anyone other than Timothy. I don't want him to be with anyone else, and I'm not looking to be with anyone else."

"Then what's the real problem?"

"I just have so many other things going on. All this mess is taxing. It's draining me."

"Have you spoken to Timothy about it?"

"I've tried to."

"And?"

"And it goes nowhere. I might as well be talking to myself. I mean, I end up feeling how I felt in the beginning of the conversation, and he ends up being upset."

"Maybe the therapist can help you out."

So, here she sat in the waiting room. The door to the office opened and out walked Dr. Elliot. Susan felt a sense of reassurance the second she saw her. Dr. Elliot possessed a motherly, caretaker's air. Susan had searched high and low to find an African-American therapist. She hoped for someone older because she felt that with age came wisdom. She sensed a whole lot of it from the woman who told her to "come on in."

Susan stood up and entered the room. She took a quick glance around, taking in the homey feeling of the room. It was definitely decorated for comfort. The color scheme was various shades of blue. Susan knew what Dr. Elliot was trying to accomplish—serenity. It worked with her. On top of the navy blue plush carpet sat the most inviting looking sofa. It was a couple of shades lighter than the carpet. There were also two chairs, pictures of the sunset, oceans, and people at play. There were plants in every corner, and a coffee table in the center of the room. In front of the window was Dr. Elliot's desk. It was the neatest desk Susan had ever seen.

"Where are your file cabinets?" Susan couldn't help asking.

Dr. Elliot pointed toward two closed doors and said, "Behind there. Have a seat." She went toward her desk, opened the drawer and pulled out a micro-cassette recorder.

Susan sank into one of the chairs. "This is nice."

Dr. Elliot sat on the sofa, close to Susan. "So, Susan, what brings you here today?"

Damn, I didn't think she'd get straight to the point. "Um, I'm here because I need help."

"In?"

"In my life. It's falling apart," Susan told her.

"Falling apart how?"

Susan looked at the doctor and wanted to say, "You know, forget it. I'm out of here." Dr. Elliot must have seen this, because she told Susan, "Listen. You only have to tell me what you want to. Nothing more, nothing less. We can talk about your day, the people in your life, or we can just jump right into what you feel you need help with."

Susan thought jumping right into it would be best. "I'm here because I've been doing cocaine for over ten years and want to stop, because I'm engaged and terrified of the whole marriage thing, because I'm an attorney and after years of education and starting my own business, I'm not sure if I want to continue doing it." Now, that revelation shocked Susan. She didn't even know she was thinking that. "Because I'm tired and feel like I'm going crazy."

Susan held her breath and waited for Dr. Elliot's response. She waited to be told that she had too many issues, that maybe she needed to go to NA. Dr. Elliot said none of this.

"What we'll work on first," Dr. Elliot said, "is getting you clean. As that happens, solutions to all the other issues you seem to having will become clearer."

Susan breathed a sigh of relief. "So, there's hope?"

Dr. Elliot smiled. "There's always hope."

The hour Susan spent in therapy left her feeling exhausted. Once she started talking, she couldn't stop. It was weird to Susan how she exposed herself to a stranger, but between Dr. Elliot's kind eyes and reassuring smile, she felt for the first time in a long time that her life just might be okay. It wasn't anything the doctor said. It was more of what Susan felt from releasing all that had been pent-up in her for so long.

Now all she wanted to do was go home, close her eyes and soak in a hot tub. No such luck. Timothy was on the couch, notebook and pen in hand, when she walked in.

"Hey, sweetie," he greeted as he stood up to kiss her on the cheek. "How was your first session?"

"Tiring. All I feel like doing is relaxing."

"I thought we'd talk about the wedding. You know, pick a date, make up a guest list."

"Timothy, that's the last thing I feel like doing." Susan couldn't decide what kind of wedding she wanted, and he kept pressuring her about it. Almost every damn day it was one thing or another.

When she really thought about it, she figured eloping would be the best idea. She just didn't feel the need to put on a show for others. That's what big weddings were to her, performances. But when Susan would suggest this, Timothy would give her a look that said, *Are you crazy?*

Sitting on the couch, Susan looked up at Timothy and said, "Timothy, we need to talk."

He sat next to her and faced her expectantly.

"We need to come up with a plan that's feasible for the both of us. We keep going back and forth and nothing is being accomplished. I can't have this stress over me. You know I'm trying to stop getting high. You're rushing me to plan an elaborate wedding. It's too much and frankly, I can't handle the shit."

"Whatever you want to do is fine with me," Timothy told her.

This surprised Susan because the way he'd been talking is like he wanted to go all out. "Let's show our love to everyone," he'd told her.

"Why the sudden change of heart?" she asked.

"Because I love you and I don't want to lose you by pressuring you."

"What if I wanted to elope?"

"Anything but that."

"Why not? You said whatever I want is fine."

"I know, but you also said something that's feasible for the both of us, and I want to exchange vows in front of family and friends."

"What friends? What family? We're both loners."

"My family from the meetings, your co-workers. Damn, girl, this is supposed to be your big day, our big day, and I feel like you're trying to minimize it."

"I'm not minimizing it, I just, I just—"

"How about inviting just fifty people?"

"All right," she gave in.

"I'll plan everything. All you have to do is pick out what you're wearing and a maid of honor."

Susan knew that would be Crystal.

Timothy took her hand. "So, how many kids are we going to have?"

Susan looked at him like he'd lost his mind. How did he go from the wedding to kids? This was not the time. When she walked in the door, she was tired. Now she was exhausted. She barely had the energy to tell him, "Timothy, you know that I've always said I didn't want any kids, and that's what I meant."

She saw the sadness in his eyes and added, "But now . . ." She hesitated.

Timothy's eyes lit up. "But now, what?"

"Well, it's something I've been thinking about on the down low. I may have changed my mind."

"Really?" He was getting excited.

"I said *may* have. I need to think about it a little more. Having a child is serious business. It's life altering. Once you have a child, your life is kind of put on hold, and I don't know if I'm ready to put my life on hold. I may be one day, but not right now."

"I'm not asking you to make a decision right now," Timothy told her. "I'm just glad to hear you're considering having a little me and you."

Susan smiled, stood up and asked, "Can I go take my bath now?"

Timothy stood up and pulled her to him, "Of course."

Heading toward the stairs, Susan looked over her shoulder at Timothy and surprised herself when she asked, "How often do you stay at my house?"

"About four times a week."

"Why don't you just move in?"

"Are you sure?"

"I said it, didn't I?"

Timothy nodded. "That you did."

FOR OLD TIMES' SAKE

Jewell was dropping Tyson off at his classmate's house, then she was headed to his new home with his dad. She'd decided to let him move in with his father. They'd agreed to have dinner together to discuss King sending Tyson to a private school. The first few days without Tyson were hard. She'd labeled herself everything from a bad mother to a neglectful one, and finally she sat still and listened. Silence,—it shocked her. There was no Tyson running around saying "Mommy, Mommy, Mommy. I want, I want, I want. Can you do this? Can you take me here? I need, I need, I need." Jewell had to admit that the silence was nice. The first couple of days she moped around, but after day four, she felt a sense of freedom, something she hadn't felt in a long time. She even walked around the house butt-ass naked.

They pulled up in front of Tyson's friend's house and he jumped out of the car. "Bye, Mom!"

Before he could run off, she told him, "Come here."

Jewell watched as Tyson huffed and puffed his way to her. "Yes?"

"Are you in hurry or something?"

"Yeah, Ma."

"Who do you think you're talking to like that?" Jewell asked.

Tyson looked down at the ground and replied, "No one."

"That's better. Now give me a kiss."

He looked around to see if anyone was watching. This tickled Jewell because it seemed like yesterday he couldn't bear to be away from her. She teased him and grabbed his face and kissed him all over. "Now," she noticed a half smile from him, "be good!"

When Jewell arrived at King's, she couldn't bring herself to get out of the car. The night before, she'd had an erotic dream about him and felt uncomfortable with it.

"Are you coming in or what?" King yelled from the porch.

She stepped out of the car and headed toward the house, looking everywhere but at him.

She noticed King was looking at her in a weird way, "What's wrong with you?" he asked.

"Nothing. Why you ask me that?"

"Well, you looking around like you've never been here before."

Instead of denying it, Jewell chose to ignore his observation.

"Something smells good. What's cooking?" Jewell could smell the aroma of dinner before she hit the door. It was even stronger once she walked in the house.

"Follow me," he told her.

They went into the kitchen, where the table was set with placemats, napkins, candles, real plates, and what looked like the good silverware. In the center of the table was baked salmon, a salad, and sweet potatoes. There was even a bottle of wine.

"All this for me?" Jewell put her hand on her chest and pretended to swoon.

"I hope you're hungry," he told her.

"That I am."

He pulled out her chair. "Have a seat."

Sitting across the table from him reminded Jewell of their better days. They each made their plates and ate mostly in silence. Jewell tired of the silence. Picking up her glass and taking a sip, she said, "King, I appreciate all you've done."

"You appreciate it?"

"Yes."

"You make it sound like I'm some kind of stranger doing you a favor. I'm Tyson's father. I do what I do because I'm supposed to and I want to. I told you from day one when you tried to run from me that I would be there."

"Now, why do you have to go and bring up the past?"

"And I've kept my word," King told her.

"King, the reason I appreciate it is because there are a lot of absent fathers out there, and I just want you to know that what you do does not go unnoticed. And as for the whole private school idea, if you think it's best, I do too."

"Are you done?" King asked.

Jewell nodded.

King stood up, walked around the table and put out his hand. "Come on."

She grabbed her purse off the counter, where she placed it when she came in, and King led her into living room.

They sat on the couch. King still had her hand in his, "Listen to me now. I love Tyson just as much as you do. I've done what I've done because it's my job, my responsibility. You've taken good care of him. In a way, you've put your life on hold—your dreams, your wants, your needs and your desires to raise our son. Let me stress *ours*. What I'm trying to do is give you an opportunity to do you. Go back to school, or whatever it is you want to do. You don't have to worry about childcare, you can date—although I would prefer you didn't—but if you do, try to have it be with a man of color."

Jewell looked at him.

"Just being real," he told her.

"Anyway," Jewell said, "just know that I'm going to be over a whole lot more. You're going to think I've moved in or something."

"You're more than welcome to. You know what I asked you before."

Jewell ignored him.

"Want to look at Tyson's room?" King asked. "I changed it around and bought him a few things."

"Of course," Jewell answered.

Jewell followed King to Tyson's room. When she looked around, all she could do was shake her head. No wonder he liked coming to his father's house, she thought as she looked around. He was spoiled rotten—a big TV, his own DVD player and PlayStation II, all the latest technologies for little boys. Jewell found herself feeling slightly jealous because she could never afford all this for her son. She told King, "You know you can't spoil him like this."

"I don't spoil him," King lied.

Jewell gave him the "yeah, right" look.

King laughed and said, "He's not spoiled. He's just loved."

"Yeah, a lot," Jewell joked.

Together they laughed then went back into the living room.

"So," King said.

"So," Jewell repeated. "What do we do now? We've talked, we've laughed."

"How about making love?" King blurted out.

"Why do you have to go there?" Jewell asked.

"I was just playing."

190

Jewell didn't believe him. She knew if she said yes, he'd be all on it.

"How come you won't give me another chance?" he asked.

"We're the past. I'm living in the future."

"Is it because of your white boy?"

"No. That has nothing to do with it." Jewell knew she should leave, especially with the way the conversation was going.

"Then what is it?"

"I can't, that's all."

"You can't or you don't want to?" King wasn't stupid. He knew she still had feelings for him. He could see it in her eyes. He could feel it.

Jewell thought about the question. She couldn't answer him. Why? Because the answer wasn't that she didn't want to. She did, she just couldn't. King did have, and always would have, a special place in her heart. She had finally admitted that to herself and to her friend.

"Girl, I still have feelings for that boy," she told Elsie.

"Well, what are you going to do about it?"

"Not a damn thing. Shit, he's my past." Jewell had finally acknowledged her feelings out loud and it messed up her mind because there wasn't anything she could really do. She had convinced herself that it was a bad idea, and told Elsie this.

"Why do you think that? He's your son's father. Families should be together."

"That's an old fashioned way of thinking," Jewell told her, even though she agreed. She didn't want to have more than one baby daddy, be a statistic, but it looked like that might happen.

"It sounds to me that you've made your decision," Elsie said.

Jewell grew quiet because she really hadn't decided. Evan was a good man and he could offer her the world. He was kind, gentle, everything she thought she wanted. The sex was good, too, but her heart just wasn't there, and in relationships that's what matters the most. She didn't want to use him or walk all over him and she could see that happening. Evan didn't "move her." She had to admit that King still did. She was still attracted to him, and it seemed to be getting stronger by the day. It bugged her out.

Jewell stood up. "I think it's time for me to leave."

Before he could reply, her cell phone started to ring. She picked up her purse and pulled it out. "Hello."

"Tyson is at the hospital," a kid on the other end said.

"What!" She screamed into the phone. "What do you mean Tyson is at the hospital?"

King snatched the phone from Jewell. "What happened?"

"A car hit him. My aunt took him to Jersey Medical."

"Call your aunt and tell her we're on our way." King hung up the phone and told Jewell what happened.

Immediately, she started crying. "Oh my God. Oh my God."

He grabbed her hands and told her, "Calm down, sweetie. Get it together. We'll go to the hospital together. I'll drive."

She nodded and followed him to the car.

"It'll be okay. Trust me," he told her.

"Okay." She was in a daze.

They drove to the hospital in silence, both too nervous to say a word, but each of them prayed silently. They pulled up to the emergency entrance. King told Jewell to go inside while he parked the car.

"Please, God, let my baby be okay," Jewell repeated over and over. As she was headed to client information, she spotted the mother of the boy whose party Tyson had attended. She walked up to her, all set to go off until she saw that the lady looked almost as worried as she did.

"Jewell, I'm so sorry."

Jewell didn't want to hear any apologies. All she wanted was to know where Tyson was.

As the women led her to Tyson, Jewell asked, "What happened?"

"They were playing ball and it went into the street. Tyson ran after it and a car came from nowhere and hit him."

King walked up on that note and said, "Just take us to him and to the doctor. We can get the details later. Right now we just want to see our child."

When they entered Tyson's room, he was in the bed, bandaged up but conscious.

"Mom, Dad," he mumbled.

They both went to his bedside.

"I'm sorry," he said.

"Shhh," King told him. "You don't have anything to be sorry for."

Jewell kissed him on the forehead, looked at the little boy's mother and thanked her for getting him to the hospital. What she really wanted to do was ask her, "Weren't you watching them? How could you let my baby get hit by a car?" But she knew this wasn't the time or place.

"We love you," King told Tyson. "I'll be back. I'm going to go talk to the doctor."

While King was gone, Tyson closed his eyes. Jewell sat and watched him. When King returned, he told Jewell that the doctors wanted to keep Tyson for a couple of nights.

"For what?" she wanted to know.

"For observation. They believe he has a concussion."

"Well then, I'm going to stay here with him."

King pulled up a chair, looked at Tyson and smiled. "He looks just like you."

"No." Jewell took his hand. "He looks like us."

They held hands and watched Tyson sleep.

Before they knew it, the sun was rising and the doctor walked in. "Why don't you two go home and get some rest? There's nothing you can do here."

Jewell didn't want to leave, but King suggested they at least go shower, get a change of clothes and some things for Tyson.

"Well, can I shower at your house?" she asked.

"Yes, of course you can."

They walked out of the hospital unconsciously holding hands. Little did Jewell know a friend of Evan's was outside the hospital and spotted them.

When they arrived at King's, Jewell told him that maybe a bath would be better. It would relax her.

"The towels and wash cloths are in the closet in the hallway."

"I'll also need something to put on," she told him.

"I've got a pair of sweats you can wear."

"Thanks." Jewell grabbed her washcloth and towel, went into the bathroom, ran the water and sank into the tub. "Ahhh . . ." She closed her eyes and found her thoughts drifting to Tyson. She started to cry because she realized she could have lost her son.

"King!" she yelled out.

He was outside the door in no time at all. "Yes."

"Will you come in here with me?"

Silence.

"King?"

"Yes?"

"Did you hear me? I asked you to come in."

Hesitating, he opened the door and walked in trying to avert his eyes. "What's wrong?"

"Everything," she told him. "I don't want to be alone. Can you just sit in here with me?"

King looked at her and said, "I don't know, Jewell." He eyed her body and said, "It's going to be hard, but I'll do it." He sat on the toilet, crossed his legs and closed his eyes.

"King?" Jewell said. "Can you wash my back?"

"You're reaching with that one," he told her with lust in his eyes.

"Please," she begged.

"I'm giving you fair warning," he told her.

He reached for the washcloth and soap. She turned her back toward him. The second his hands touched her bare skin, she knew she wanted more. She took his hands and moved them toward her breasts.

"What—" King started to ask.

"This is what you wanted," she told him as she stood up and climbed out of the tub.

"Do you know what you're doing?" he asked, knowing he should put a stop to this.

"Yes, I know what I'm doing, and I know what I want you to do to me."

Jewell watched as he struggled with a response. There was none. He just picked her up and carried her into the bedroom. He placed her on the bed gently.

"What does this mean?" he asked.

"Let's not analyze it, King. Let's just enjoy this moment," Jewell responded.

WHAT WAS I THINKING?

Elsie wondered what she was going to do about Janay. She'd been on her mind constantly since they ran into each other at the bar. She wanted to call her, but talked herself out of it.

That morning when Elsie arrived at work, there was a message on her desk. Janay had called. That didn't surprise her because back in the day when she and Janay were involved, Janay was very aggressive.

She decided to call her back. What harm could it do? Elsie picked up the phone and dialed the number on the message pad.

"Hello," a male answered.

"Um, hi, may I speak to Janay?"

"Who's speaking?"

"Elsie."

"Hold on, please."

"Hey, you. How come you haven't called me?" Janay asked immediately.

"I've been busy working on a new case," she told her, half truth, half lie. The real reason was that she didn't think it would be right. She believed she still had unresolved feelings. After all, there was never any real closure between them. On top of that, she didn't trust herself with Janay.

"Would you like to go out to lunch?" Janay asked.

"Lunch?"

"Yes."

"When?"

"Today."

"Yeah," Elsie told her while she wondered if she was out of her mind. She knew she was wrong for accepting a lunch date with Janay. She tried to justify it by saying better lunch than dinner. It was safer in the daytime because she was less likely to do something she might later regret.

"How about I come to your office?"

"No, how about we meet somewhere?" Elsie suggested in return. There was a buzz on her phone. "Can you hold on a second?"

"Yeah," Janay replied.

Elsie pressed the intercom and asked the temp secretary, "Who's calling?"

"Someone named Summer," she answered.

Was this a coincidence or what? Summer and Janay were calling her at the same time. "Tell her I'll be right with her."

She clicked back to Janay and told her she'd meet her at one. They agreed on the place and hung up.

Elsie picked up the line Summer was on. "What's up?"

"I just wanted to know what you were doing for lunch."

Something I shouldn't be doing, Elsie thought. "I'm meeting with a client," she said.

"I was going to stop by. What time will you be returning?"

"I'm not sure," Elsie told her.

"Are you bringing any of your things over tonight?" Summer asked. Elsie still hadn't moved her things in. Although she stayed the night occasionally, they slept in separate rooms for the sake of Winter. When they wanted to be next to each other, they would sneak. Of course, this caused an even bigger strain on the relationship.

"Elsie, is everything okay between us?" Summer asked.

"Of course. Why would you ask me something like that?"

"I don't know. I just feel like things are changing between us, and not for the better. We don't do things together like we used to."

"Well, we can't. There's a child in the picture now," Elsie said, feeling like shit for blaming it on Winter.

"Are you sure that's all it is?"

"Isn't that enough?"

"I guess so. Are you staying the night tonight?"

"No. I need to go to my apartment and pack up some things," Elsie lied. She just wanted to sleep in her own bed.

"So, I won't get to see you at all today."

Elsie thought for a moment. "I'll stop by briefly."

"Okay."

"Bye." Before Elsie could hang up, she heard Summer say her name. She placed the phone near her ear. "Yes?"

"I love you."

"Same here," Elsie said and placed the phone on its cradle. She sat down at her desk and stared out the window. Why was she making her life more complicated than it needed to be? If it blew up in her face, it would be her own fault.

Elsie pulled out a case file she was working on and became engrossed in her work. Before she knew it, lunchtime had arrived. She had to admit that she was nervous about going out to lunch with Janay. She knew she was playing with fire.

Elsie and Janay arrived at the restaurant at the same time. While looking over the menu, Janay asked her about Summer. "So, tell me about the woman you're seeing."

"What is it you want to know?"

"How about her name?"

198

"Summer."

"What does she do for a living? So I can know what I'm up against."

"What makes you think you're up against someone?"

"Do you love her?"

Elsie shifted in her seat. "Why don't you answer some questions for me?"

"Shoot." Janay leaned back in her chair, ready.

"Are you seeing anyone?"

"No."

"Why not?"

"I've been concentrating on the club, haven't had the time."

"Were you seeing anyone out west?"

"Yes."

"Well, what happened?"

"I knew I would be coming out here, and I didn't want a long—distance relationship. I also knew I would be looking you up when I got in town."

"Oh, you did, did you?" Elsie didn't believe a word of it, although she wanted to.

"Is that all you have to say?"

"What more is there for me to say?"

"I don't know. How about you're glad I'm back?"

Elsie didn't comply. Instead she looked at her watch. "Let's order." She waved the waitress over and they placed their orders.

The second the waitress walked away, Janay leaned over the table and placed her chin in her hands. "Still avoiding the obvious, huh?"

"What are you talking about?"

"You never could be up front," Janay told her.

"Up front about what?" Elsie had no idea what she was talking about.

"Nothing. Just let it go."

Elsie wrinkled up her brow, but decided to do just that—let it go. The waitress returned with their food and they made small talk while eating. It really just seemed like they were getting to know one another again.

When they were done eating, Elsie told Janay, "I have to get back to the office."

"Why don't you stop by the bar later and join me for a drink?" Janay asked.

Elsie knew she should say no, but she heard herself saying yes. *Looking for trouble,* her inner voice chastised.

Back at the office, Elsie was surprised when she walked through her door to find an arrangement of flowers. They could only be from Summer, she thought, picking up the card and turning it over. It read: *Thanks for lunch. Janay.*

Elsie always had been a sucker for flowers. She smiled and wondered when Janay could have done this. It must have been as soon as they hung up the phone that morning.

Elsie looked at the phone and debated whether to call Jewell. She knew Jewell was taking care of her son. She decided to dial Jewell's number. The answering machine came on. "Hey, Jewell, it's Elsie. Just calling to say hello, see how everything is going and if you need anything. Give me a call when you get a chance." She hung up and threw herself into work.

Before she knew it, it was time to leave. What Elsie really wanted to do was go home and relax before going to the bar, but she'd promised Summer that she would stop by. She grabbed her briefcase and headed out the door

When she arrived at Summer's house, the door was wide open, so she let herself in. Winter ran up to her and held out a piece of paper. "Look what I did." She showed Elsie a picture she had drawn. In it were three people holding hands. "That's you, me and Mommy."

Elsie took the picture from her. "That's sweet." She kissed her on the cheek then looked around and asked Winter, "Where's your mom?"

Summer appeared out of nowhere. "I'm right here."

"Winter, sweetheart, can you leave us alone for a minute?" Summer said, her eyes never leaving Elsie's face.

"Awww, Mom, do I have to?

"I would like for you to."

Winter stomped off. As soon as she was out of earshot, Summer asked Elsie, "How come you didn't tell me Janay was in town?"

Talk about catching someone off guard. At first Elsie was going to deny it, but thought better of it. She decided to play it down. "I didn't think it was important," Elsie told her.

Summer looked at Elsie in disbelief. "I can't believe you would stand here and say that you didn't think it was important. I think having your ex move back in town is of extreme importance."

"Not to me," Elsie lied. "Anyway, that relationship ended years ago. What difference does it make?"

"Maybe it wouldn't matter under different circumstances."

"What do you mean under different circumstances?"

"I mean when we were doing better as a couple. When I felt like I was loved, wanted, desired. When I felt like you wanted to be around me."

Elsie told Summer, "Look, I don't know what you're talking about. I don't have time for a jealous fit. I had a long ass day and I'm tired. I could have gone home and laid down, but I decided to stop by here first, and this is what you greet me with. I'm going home." She turned to walk toward the door.

Summer grabbed her arm. "Elsie, don't leave."

Elsie looked at her, "What, Summer? What do you want me to say?"

"I don't know, but I do know that I'm not crazy. I do know that something is off between us. I feel it in here." She touched her heart.

"Relationships can't be perfect all the time."

"I know that. I don't expect it to be, but I do expect you to be up front with me," Summer said. "I'm ready to tell Winter about us."

"I don't think that's a good idea . . . at least not right now. We need to figure out what's going on with us before you bring Winter into it."

"So, something is going on?" Summer asked.

"I'm going home. I'll call you later." Elsie did something she had never done before. She walked out on Summer.

"You made it," Janay said. She was almost certain Elsie would flake out on her.

"Yes, I made it," Elsie replied, stepping into the bar.

"You look sexy," Janay told her.

"So do you."

They stood in front of one another, neither saying a word, just taking each other in.

Taking her hand, Janay said, "Come on. I want you to meet some people."

"No, no, I don't want to meet anyone." Elsie was afraid that whoever she was about to meet would know Summer. She couldn't for the life of her figure out how Summer knew Janay was back in town.

"Listen, stop being paranoid and enjoy yourself. Damn. The people I want to introduce you to aren't even from here. Come on. Loosen up." Janay pulled her along.

After she hesitated for just a second, Elsie made up her mind to enjoy her night. Tomorrow was another day. When she saw Summer, they would talk and try to figure out what was going on. After a few drinks and a couple of dances, Janay asked Elsie, "Stay with me until closing time."

Elsie told her she would. After everyone had left, they were sitting at the bar having one last drink. Elsie finished hers off and said, "Well, I guess I'll be leaving now."

"Are you okay to drive?"

"Honestly, no," Elsie said. "I mean, I'm not drunk, but I think it would be just a wee bit safer with me off the road."

"How about I drive you home?"

"What, and leave my car here?" Elsie didn't think that was a good idea.

"No, I'll drive your car. You can bring me to mine in the morning."

"In the morning? Do you plan on staying the night at my house?"

"If it's a problem, I'll sleep on the couch."

"Okay then, let's go."

When they arrived at Elsie's house, Elsie turned on the television and sat on the couch next to Janay.

"Why are you turning on the TV?" Janay asked. "It's late, I'm tired, and so are you."

Elsie stood. "You don't have to sleep on the couch, I have an extra bedroom."

"Where is it?"

"Down the hall to the right." Elsie led the way. When they reached the door, Elsie told Janay, "If you need anything, my room is down the hall."

Janay stared into Elsie's eyes. "Okay."

Once in her room, Elsie closed the door and undressed. She wondered what Janay was doing. She threw on her robe and opened the bedroom door. Janay was at the door about to knock.

Elsie looked in her eyes and immediately wanted her. She held Janay's face between her hands and kissed her on the lips.

Janay pulled away. "What are you doing?"

"Kissing you." She went to kiss her again, but Janay pulled back again.

"Are you sure? I thought you didn't want this."

"A girl's entitled to change her mind," Elsie said.

"Maybe we should wait until you're sober."

"I don't want to wait."

Janay stepped into the room. "I've missed you."

"I've missed you too," Elsie said and removed her robe. She let it fall to the floor and walked over to the bed. "Come join me."

Janay stood in front of Elsie and slowly undressed. Elsie could feel her body shivering. She reached out and caressed Janay's breasts.

Janay removed Elsie hands and put them over her head. She pushed Elsie back on the bed and said, "Let me be in charge."

Elsie closed her eyes and waited for the wave to arrive.

The next morning when Elsie woke up, Janay was gone. She left a note on the pillow. It read. *Didn't want to wake you. Took a taxi to my car. I enjoyed every bit of you last night. Please call me. Don't run. We need to talk. Love, Janay.*

Looking at the letter, Elsie wanted to smack herself. How could she have been so stupid?

WHAT NOW?

Ever since Lange told Crystal about his impending divorce, they had been seeing a lot of each other, but they had yet to be physical again. He had moved into a hotel until he could find an apartment and had asked her to visit him there. She turned him down. Crystal felt that it was better to play it safe.

Crystal and Lange were in his office going over Tina's case when her cell phone rang. Normally she would look at the caller ID, but without thinking, she just picked it up and answered. "Hello."

"Hello, gorgeous." It was Roger. "I was just calling to confirm our date for tonight."

"I'll be ready." Crystal tried to be short.

"Are you busy?"

"I'm in a meeting right now."

"I'll let you go. See you tonight."

When Crystal hung up the phone, Lange was staring in her mouth. He had heard Roger's voice through the phone. "That was your cop boyfriend?"

Crystal caught the jealous tone and decided not to feed into it. "Roger's not my boyfriend. He's just someone I'm dating."

"Isn't he the one who was over your house that day you wouldn't let me in?"

Crystal raised her eyebrow and answered, "Yes."

"So, then you're sleeping with him?"

Before she responded, Crystal cleared her throat. "Lange, we have feelings for each other, yes, but who I choose to date isn't really any of your concern."

Taken off guard, Lange said, "It's not any of my concern?"

Crystal stood her ground. "No, it's not."

They fell into an uncomfortable silence and just sat looking at one another. Crystal finally said, "I think we're done." She stood up, gathered her papers and placed them in her briefcase.

"I'll call you later," Lange told her as she headed toward the door.

When Crystal returned to her office, she sat at her desk and thought about her feelings for Lange, which included a fierce attraction. When she saw him, she felt as if she were in high school and sneaking to see her first love behind the school. Her feelings for Roger were calm and peaceful. She enjoyed his company. He made her laugh, and he always made sure she was having a good time. She just didn't feel as much of a physical attraction toward him, and she felt like he hounded her, wanted to be around her too much. It scared her just because it felt like she was being pressured.

There was a knock on her office door. "Come in," she called out.

In walked Susan. "What's up, girl?"

"Nothing. About to close up shop."

"Wanna do something tonight?"

"Nah, I've got a date with Roger," Crystal said.

Susan took a seat across from Crystal and said, "You're seeing a lot of Roger. Is it serious?"

Crystal relaxed in her seat and said, "I don't know about all that, but I am feeling him, even if he is a little overwhelming at times."

"And what about Lange?"

Crystal rolled her eyes. "That's another story altogether. I don't feel like getting into it right now."

Susan stood up. "Call me over the weekend."

That night while Crystal waited for Roger, she tried to find a way to let him know that he was being too aggressive. She wanted to be polite with it, not hurt his feelings but every idea she came up with sounded harsh. Crystal was in the bathroom putting on her makeup when the doorbell rang.

"Coming," she called out. As she walked down the hall to get the door, the telephone rang. She snatched it off the hook and didn't bother to find out who it was. "Hold on," she said into the phone. She placed the phone on the table and ran to open the door.

"Hi, sexy." It was Roger. He kissed her on the cheek.

"Come on in. I have a phone call."

He followed her into the living room.

Crystal picked up the phone and said, "Hello?"

"Hi, Crystal."

The voice wasn't familiar. "Who is this?"

"It's Lena."

Crystal almost dropped the phone. Lena was the last person she expected to call her. What could she possibly want? Did she find out about Crystal and Lange's affair? Did Lange know Lena was calling her? Trying to sound in control, Crystal told Lena, "I'm about to run out. Is everything okay?"

"Yes, everything is fine. Do you mind if I call you later? I need to talk to you."

Crystal wanted to know what she had to talk to her about, but with Roger standing there, she didn't want to take a chance. "I won't be in 'til late. Call me tomorrow."

"Okay. Talk to you then."

They hung up.

"Is everything okay?" Roger asked.

"Yeah. Why?"

"You're all frowned up."

Crystal brought her hands up to her face. "Am I?"

"Yeah."

"Oh, it's nothing. Listen, give me one more minute. I have to go upstairs and get my purse." She left him standing there with a puzzled look on his face.

In the car, Crystal kept trying to make small talk. She was trying to keep her mind off Lena's phone call, but Roger wasn't cooperating.

"Roger, why aren't you talking to me? I feel like I'm having a one-way conversation."

"I'm sorry. It's just that I know something is bothering you and I want you to be able to talk to me. Who knows? I might be able to help."

"I told you it was nothing," Crystal snapped at him.

When he didn't reply, she apologized. "I'm sorry. It's just that I don't open up often, and when I'm having a problem, I feel like it's just that my problem. I don't want to be a burden."

Roger didn't respond.

"Do you accept my apology?" Crystal didn't want to ruin the night. She leaned over and kissed him on the cheek. When she noticed his smile, she took his free hand in hers.

"You're lucky I can drive with one hand and that you're irresistible," he told her. "But I can't help but wonder who could get you all worked up like that."

"My mother," she told him. He was aware that they weren't speaking at the moment.

"You know you need to resolve your differences. She's the only mother you have."

"I know, but it's hard to let go. She's with the man who raised—"

Roger removed his hand to turn the corner. "I know. You told me all that, but you have to let it go sooner or later. You only get one mom."

Crystal turned her head and looked out her window. "How about we change the subject?"

"I can do that. How about this? There's something I need to have clarified between us," he said.

"What?"

"I need to know what we are."

"Huh?" Crystal looked at him with raised eyebrows.

"Are we a couple or are we just friends?"

"Why do we have to put a title on it?" Crystal asked. "Why can't we just be?"

"Because I'm ready to settle down. I'm ready for a relationship. We both know I've wanted to be with you for a long time. Now that the opportunity is here, well, I don't want to mess it up. So, I guess what I'm doing is asking you if you'll be my lady."

Crystal just smiled. She didn't want to say yes but she couldn't come right out and say no either. What she chose to say instead was, "I have to think about it, Roger. I've been single for a while now, and to just jump into something this soon . . . I don't know. Will you give me some time?"

Roger looked over at her and said, "I'll give you some time. Just know that I don't plan on waiting forever."

"And I'm not expecting you to."

That night after Roger dropped her off, she lay in bed and wondered why this was happening now. Why did Roger, who was a good man, have to come into her life when there was a slight chance with the man she lusted after? Crystal picked up her phone and dialed Lange's number at the hotel. He wasn't

209

in. Crystal wondered if he was with Lena. She left a message.
"I need to talk to you about something. Call me first thing
tomorrow morning."

The next day when Crystal woke up, she thought about
calling Lena back, but first decided to call Lange. She tried the
hotel first.

"Good morning," Lange answered.

"Good morning. Where were you last night?" Although
she had no right to ask, she couldn't help it.

"I went out for drinks with some friends."

"Oh. Your wife called my house last night. Do you know
what she could want?"

"She what?" Lange sounded as surprised as Crystal felt
when she first heard Lena's voice.

"She said she needed to talk to me about something. Are
you positive she doesn't know about us? Maybe she's been
having you followed or something."

Lange started laughing.

"Why are you laughing?" Crystal asked him. "This is
serious. It's not a joke."

"I know that, but you're getting all worked up and
paranoid. So what if she had me followed? We're attorneys and
you're assisting me on Tina's case."

"I'm glad you can be all calm about this," Crystal said.
"How did she get my number anyway?"

"She must have looked in my directory. I don't know."

"You think I should call her back?" Crystal wanted him to
say no.

"Yeah, and then call me back."

When they hung up, Crystal decided to take a shower
before she returned Lena's phone call. After drying off, she
wrapped a towel around herself and dialed the number.

"Hello." It was Lena sounding sleepy.

"Good morning, Lena. It's Crystal. I'm returning your call from yesterday."

"Can you hold on a second?" Lena asked.

"Yes." Crystal could hear water running in the background.

"Sorry about that. I was asleep. I went to wash my face," Lena told her.

"I could have called you back."

"No, no. I need to get up anyway. It's funny. Ever since Lange moved out, it's hard for me to wake up. When he was here, I'd get up early to be with him, but now . . . I don't know, it's like my clock is all messed up."

Crystal didn't know what to say. She figured she'd just wait it out and see what was on Lena's mind.

"Would you like to meet me for breakfast?" Lena asked.

This was getting weirder and weirder by the second. It definitely didn't sound like Lena suspected Crystal and Lange of having an affair. Letting her curiosity get the best of her, Crystal agreed to a meeting place.

"See you in an hour," Lena said.

An hour later, Crystal pulled into the parking lot of Clara's Place. She walked through the door and heard Lena call her name. "Crystal, over here."

Lena was already seated. She had on black leggings with boots and a white collared shirt buttoned halfway up with a black bodysuit underneath. Her hair was back in a ponytail. She wore no makeup, just a touch of lip-gloss. Crystal was glad she decided to wear jeans and a wife-beater under her jacket. It took her over twenty minutes to decide, and she figured comfort was the key.

Crystal sat down and forced a smile.

The waitress came over with coffee.

"I'll take tea," Crystal said, looking at the menu in front of her and then at Lena. "Have you ordered?"

"Not yet. I know you're wondering why I called you."

That's an understatement, Crystal thought.

"Well, I'll get straight to the point. I don't know how much Lange has told you, but I'm sure you're aware of the fact we're separated."

Crystal nodded.

"It was mostly my idea."

Crystal didn't respond.

Lena cleared her throat. "Remember the last time you saw me?"

Lena didn't have to refresh her memory.

"Well, he's not the reason. This separation is something that's been in the making for quite some time. I was unhappy and dissatisfied with myself. I was pretending to be something I wasn't, and I finally couldn't take it anymore."

Crystal had to know, "Why are you telling me all this?"

"I don't know. Maybe it's because I need a friend and Lange used to say I should get to know you."

This surprised Crystal. "He would say that?"

"Yes, and well, I know that you two are working on a case together, and obviously if he told you about our little separation, you have some kind of relationship other than business."

Crystal sat up straighter.

"I guess what I'm trying to say is these past couple of weeks have been hell, and I wanted to know if you would talk to Lange about coming back home."

Crystal shifted in her chair. "Why don't you call him up yourself?"

Lena ignored the question. "Did you tell him you saw me out with another man?"

"No."

"I figured as much. I told him about my affair and he took it hard."

Crystal stood up and said, "You know, I feel uncomfortable with this conversation. This was a bad idea."

Lena looked Crystal in the eyes. Crystal felt like Lena was reading her. She turned to walk away, but not before Lena said, "Yeah, maybe it was."

The second Crystal arrived home she called Lange. Once again she left a message. "Call me."

LIFE GOES ON

Over two weeks had passed since Tyson's accident. Everything turned out okay. He was back in school and living with his dad, and Jewell was going by the house every day. King tried to bring up their escapade a number of times, but she would stop him and tell him, "It was a mistake. It never should have happened."

In reality, she wanted it to happen again, though she was still seeing Evan. Sometimes when she was alone, she'd think about it over and over. Next thing she knew, her hands would start roaming. She'd find herself masturbating. A number of times she wanted to pick up the phone, call him and invite him over, but fear of the unknown stopped her.

Thank goodness she had Evan to keep her occupied. He was being very understanding about her spending so much time at King's house. When his friend called him from the hospital to tell him he saw "his black girlfriend hugged up on a black man," he got upset and almost jumped to conclusions. When he didn't hear from her that night, he had to talk himself out of driving to her apartment.

"I'm sorry I had you so worried," she told him when she finally reached him. She went on to tell him about the accident.

He was very sympathetic but felt slighted. "I could have been there for you. I would have liked to have been there for you."

She went on to tell him that she stayed at King's so they could go to the hospital together. Evan didn't understand why she couldn't stay at her own place, but he didn't tell her this. He wanted to ask her if anything happened between the two of them, but he didn't want it to seem like he didn't trust her.

Jewell was thinking about Evan as she and Tyson were sitting in his bedroom.

"You know you don't have to come by so much," Tyson told her.

Jewell's feelings were hurt. "What do you mean I don't have to come over every day?" Don't you miss me?"

"Of course I miss you, but well, I'm not a baby anymore."

King was in the doorway. When he heard this, he started laughing.

"Dad doesn't treat me like a baby. He treats me like a man," Tyson informed her.

"A little man," King said and walked into the room.

Jewell got off the bed, kissed Tyson on the cheek and told him, "I'll try not to baby you so much." Looking at King, she asked, "Walk me to the front door?"

Once in the living room, she asked, "Can you believe him?"

"Yes, I can. He is growing up, you know."

"I know, I know."

"I have a date Thursday. Do you mind coming over and . . . never mind."

"What?" Jewell asked, hoping she heard wrong, hoping she didn't just hear him say he had a date.

"Well, I know how much you miss having Tyson with you, and I was going to get a sitter, but if you want to you can come and watch him. Either that or I'll bring him to you. The choice is yours."

Jewell was still stuck on the fact that he said he had a date. "You're going out on a date on a Thursday? When I agreed to let Tyson come stay with you, I didn't know you'd be leaving him alone on school nights to go on dates." She was jealous and was not hiding it well.

"Look, I don't want to get into an argument over this. Do you want to watch him or should I just get a sitter?"

"No, I'll come over." Jewell turned to leave. She couldn't get out the door quick enough.

SOUL SEARCHING

"Girl, he had the nerve to tell me he was going on a date," Jewell told Elsie.

"Well, what do you expect? You won't give him the time of day unless it relates to Tyson. You can't expect him to be celibate."

"Shit! I don't want him dating."

"Then you have a decision to make."

Elsie was telling Jewell that she had a decision to make, but she was no closer to making one herself. She knew she needed to get real and honest about what she was doing and who she would be doing it with. Her love life was a mess, and it was all her fault. For the past couple of weeks, she had been seeing a lot of Janay. At the same time, she tried to give Summer attention so she wouldn't become suspicious, but it was taking its toll. She knew she couldn't keep this up much longer. What she needed to do was just come clean.

Jewell wanted to get off the subject. "Let's get everyone together and have dinner later."

"I'd like that," Elsie responded.

217

"I'll call everyone."

After they hung up, Jewell called Crystal and told her the plans. Crystal agreed to call Susan. She ended up leaving a message on Susan's cell phone.

Susan was in with her therapist, who had asked her how the habit developed. "Well," Susan told her, "after I graduated from high school, I didn't touch it for some time, but once I started college, I picked it up again."

"Why is that?" Dr. Elliot asked.

"To study, to keep me wide awake. I was popping No-Doz like there was no tomorrow. Eventually they didn't work as well, and I knew several others student were sniffing coke. They seemed to have energy that lasted for days."

"You weren't afraid?"

"Not really, because the couple of times that I did it with Timothy, it made me feel like I could conquer the world. Plus, the way I figured it, I was strong. There was no way I would get addicted."

"When did you figure out that you were?"

Susan looked up. "Just recently. I thought that because I was running a business, paying my bills, still doing all that I've done, that there was no way I was an addict. Then I realized that I couldn't get through my day without at least one hit."

Susan was starting to look forward to her days with Dr. Elliot. She found herself able to open up more with each session. It wasn't easy at all. Some days she craved cocaine like it was the last piece of dessert on earth, but she refused to break down. Timothy helped her get through most days. He'd talk to her or they would do something together. Susan had even joined a gym.

Susan glanced at her watch and said, "I think my hour is up."

Dr. Elliot looked at the clock and said, "You're right."

They stood up and as Susan turned to leave, Dr. Elliot told her, "Susan, you're doing great. I believe that you will overcome this. You just have to believe it as well."

That was just what Susan needed to hear. "Thanks."

When Susan entered the hallway, she turned the ringer back on her cell phone and noticed that she had missed a call. She pressed the button and saw Crystal's number. When she dialed the number, it just rang. *She must be on the other line,* Susan thought.

THE TRUTH COMES OUT

"Lange, there's something I need to tell you." Crystal and Lange were out to lunch. She was tired of holding it in. She needed to tell Lange about the time she'd seen Lena in the mall with another man. She knew some things were better left unsaid, but she was feeling guilty. She also knew that what Lena said about wanting Lange to move back home played a part in this decision.

"What is it?" Lange asked, hearing the seriousness of her tone. "Did you talk to Lena?"

"Yes."

"And?"

"Well, before I tell you what she wanted to talk to me about, I need to tell you this first. I know I should have told you a long time ago, when it first happened, but—"

"Just spit it out, for goodness sake." She was making him nervous.

"I saw Lena with another man a few nights before the office party," she blurted out.

Lange shook his head. "What did you say?"

220

She repeated herself and added, "I know I should have told you when it happened, but I was afraid to. I didn't want you to think I was just telling you because I was attracted to you."

"Well, why are you telling me this now?"

"Because Lena asked me to ask you to move back in."

Lange looked at Crystal like she'd lost her mind. "She did what?"

"She asked me—"

"I heard you, I just don't understand why she would come to you."

"I think she knows about us, or at least suspects something. The way she looked at me, well, it was very uncomfortable."

"You should have told me what you knew, Crystal."

"I know, Lange, and I'm sorry."

"We're supposed to be friends, almost soul mates."

"What do you want me to say?" Crystal reached across the table and held onto his hand.

Standing up, Lange said, "I think I should leave."

"Lange, please don't leave like this."

"Please, Crystal. I just need to think."

Crystal stood up. "About what? Going back home to your wife?"

Lange didn't answer her. He turned toward the door and she turned with him only to see Roger walking in with two men.

They spotted one another at the same time. Roger excused himself from his group and headed toward them. He looked at Lange and back to Crystal.

"What's up, man?" Lange greeted. "I was just leaving."

Roger nodded in response and watched Lange walk out the door. "What was that all about?"

"We were discussing that case I told you about."

"He seemed pretty upset," Roger commented.

"It's not going as well as we expected." Crystal could see that Roger didn't believe a word she was saying.

"Really?" he asked.

Before Crystal could think of another lie, she was saved by the ring of her cell phone. "Hello."

It was Susan. "Where are you? I've been trying to call you."

"Hold on." She placed her hand over the mouthpiece and told Roger it was a client.

"I have to get back to my peeps. I'll let you go."

"All right." Crystal kissed him on the cheek, hoping that would pacify him for the moment.

"Call me later," Roger told her.

"I will."

Crystal walked out the door and placed the phone back to her ear, "I'm back."

"What's up? Where are you?" Susan asked.

"Headed to your house, if you don't mind. I need to talk."

"Sure, come on."

Susan was sitting on the couch sipping a cup of tea when Crystal arrived. "So, what's up?"

"Girl, I've messed up," Crystal said.

"Why, what happened?"

"What do you want to hear about first, my breakfast with Lena this morning, my lunch with Lange when I told him about seeing Lena at the mall with her lover, or about Roger walking in on us and acting suspicious?"

Susan shook her head. "Well, damn."

"I know, right?" Crystal plopped down on the couch. "My life is a mess."

"Girl, please. Your problems are nothing compared to mine."

Crystal told Susan about her breakfast with Lena and her request. "But the way she said it and the way she looked at me, it was like she was taunting me, like she was saying she's the wife and I will never be."

"Don't you think you're reading too much into it?" Susan asked.

Crystal threw her hands up. "I don't know. Maybe I am."

"You never said what's going on with you and Roger."

"He asked me to be his lady."

"And?"

"I'm not ready for that."

"Then you need to tell him, not lead him on."

"I know, girl. I know."

They grew silent, each lost in her own thoughts.

"You know Tina's trial starts next week," Crystal said.

"Are you nervous about seeing Jake?"

"Honestly, I don't know."

On that note, Timothy walked into the house. "Hey, ladies."

Crystal stood up and gave him a hug. "You're looking as handsome as ever."

Timothy rubbed his chin. "Well, you know. What can I say?"

"So, when is the wedding date?" Crystal asked them as she sat back down.

Susan told her the date.

"That's six weeks from now. Is that enough time?"

"Yeah, we want something small and intimate. As a matter of fact, I wanted to ask you to do me a favor."

"What is it? Anything I can do, I will."

"Will you be my maid of honor?"

Crystal smiled and gave Susan a big hug. "Of course. I'd love to. I'd be honored."

Timothy smiled and said, "I'll leave you two alone." He headed up the stairs.

"Enough with my drama. How's your counseling going?"

"It's going well. You should go see her."

Crystal knew Susan was right. She was holding on to so much resentment toward her mother, toward men. She could feel it hindering her, blocking her blessings. She didn't like not talking to her mother, but she just couldn't get past the fact that she was dating Mr. Newton. "You have her card?"

Susan stood up. "Yeah, let me go get it. Oh, before I forget, Elsie called and wanted to know if we wanted to do dinner with her and Jewell tonight."

"I really don't feel like it," Crystal told her.

"That's understandable. I'll just tell her you were busy." On that note, Susan went to get Dr. Elliot's business card.

Crystal visited with Susan a little longer. When she arrived home, there were two messages on her answering service: one from her mother, and the other from Roger. Crystal was hoping Lange had called, but at the same time, she knew she would have to give him more time.

She picked up the phone and dialed her mother's number. She hadn't spoken to her mother since her visit. As stubborn as it might sound, she probably wouldn't be speaking to her now if her mother had not said it was urgent.

THIRTY YEARS YOUNG

It was Jewell's birthday. Not only was she surprised with a bonus check and a raise, but Evan and King both sent bouquets of flowers to the job. When she looked at herself in the mirror, Jewell felt as though she was aging quite well. No wrinkles, no gray hair. One child. Life was good.

Evan was taking her out to dinner and to the theater. They were going to see the play *Chicago*. She'd seen the movie a number of times and was looking forward to seeing it performed live.

Jewell left work a little early so she could go to the mall to buy something special to wear—something sexy yet not too revealing. After all, it was her special night, and this would be the first time she'd made a big deal out of it. Normally, she and Tyson would just have dinner and rent a movie. This year was different. Not only was she living alone, but she received a raise. Therefore, she decided to treat herself to a day of beauty at a local spa. She'd get the works—a body scrub, a massage, facial, manicure and pedicure. She was in the mood to be pampered.

225

When Jewell arrived home five hours later, she was so relaxed from her spa treatment that she just wanted to lay down and luxuriate in the feeling of peace and tranquility it gave. This wasn't possible because she had to get ready for her date. Waiting for her at the door was a package from Evan. She carried it into the house along with the bags she'd brought from the mall.

Like an impatient child, she ripped it open. When Jewell saw what it was, she started jumping up and down. "Oh my God! Oh my God!" Evan bought her a mink coat. Throwing off her leather coat, she let it hit the floor and put on her mink. She ran her hands up and down the front and went to look in the mirror. She looked on the arm and the inside for a price tag, but no such luck. Evan had more taste than that. After prancing in the coat for five minutes, she took it off and draped it on the arm of the chair. She went into her room, laid across the bed and recalled her childhood birthdays. There were no parties, 99-cent gifts, and she was lucky if she got a birthday card.

That was why she vowed that when she got older and had kids, she would go all out for them on their birthdays. She did just that with Tyson, showing him how much he was loved and appreciated. Not that he couldn't tell, but his birthdays were extra special. She didn't want her child growing up feeling like she did-unloved and unimportant. She knew that it played a number on her mind and self-esteem. She wanted Tyson to believe he was a king and he could do all and be all.

Jewell glanced at the clock and saw that she had exactly one hour to prepare for her date with Evan. She went into the bathroom, reached under the cabinet to pull out her chocolate soufflé bath scrub, and turned on the shower. She took off her clothes and was about to step in the shower when she heard the doorbell.

Jewell turned the water off, put on her robe and walked down the hall. "I'm coming, I'm coming," she yelled.

Jewell went to the door and peeked through the peephole. King and Tyson were standing there with what looked like her favorite snack—ice cream cake.

She unlocked and opened the door. She bent over and kissed Tyson on the forehead. "This is a surprise."

Tyson and King started to sing the ghetto version of "Happy Birthday." All the while, King looked her up and down, undressing her with his eyes.

Jewell laughed and told them, "Thank you." She placed the cake in the freezer.

"What? You're not going to cut it now?" King asked.

"I'm going out in less than an hour. I was about to get in the shower."

"Are we still going to dinner tomorrow, Ma?" Tyson asked.

"Of course, sweetie. I wouldn't miss it for the world."

King asked, "So, what are your plans for tonight? Are you going out with your friend?"

The way he said "your friend," Jewell knew he was talking about Evan. "Yes, as a matter of fact I am."

King took Tyson's hand and said, "Well, I guess we better be leaving now."

Before Jewell could respond, King and Tyson were out of the kitchen. Tyson turned around and said, "See you tomorrow Ma!"

Jewell didn't know what to do. She could tell that King was pissed, but shit, he was going on with his life. She saw the hoochie he went out with the week before, so how dare he be upset? *You can't have your cake and eat it too,* Jewell thought. But then again, who was she to say that? If she could have her cake and eat it too, she would.

When Evan arrived, he had a smug look on his face.

"What's with the look?" Jewell asked.

"I have something extra special planned for you tonight."

"Better than the mink?" Jewell asked. She was still in disbelief. She never thought that this girl from the projects would own a real fur. She must have thanked him twenty times.

"It's up there," Evan said.

"Did I tell you I love it?" Jewell asked.

"A number of times."

"It's beautiful."

"For a beautiful person," he responded.

Jewell felt just that way. She had found a Georgio Armani dress on clearance for under two hundred dollars. Normally, she would never spend that much on a piece of clothing, but the color drew her to it. It was a cranberry silk blended with cashmere. It stopped just above her thighs. She wore Barely There stockings by Hanes that matched the color of her skin perfectly. Her 4-inch heels shaped her legs, making her look like a runner, and she had applied her makeup to perfection. That dress, those shoes and the makeup under the mink was perfection.

"Are you ready?" Evan asked.

"Yes." Jewell was ready ever since she woke up.

The musical was excellent. She loved it. The singing and the dancing inspired her so much. When Jewell was a little girl, she had wanted to be a dancer. She could recall standing in front of the mirror, mimicking the girls at the ballet class that she used to sneak into on the way home from school. Sometimes she would get so caught up in the fluidity, the beauty of it all, that she would arrive home late.

"Where the hell have you been?" her mother would yell. "Don't you know that I've been worried sick about you?"

Jewell didn't dare tell her mother where she had been. Once when she asked her mother for dance lessons, the answer was, "No, we can't afford it. You need to concentrate on other things. Plus, that kind of dancing is for white girls."

Jewell begged and pleaded almost every day for two weeks, but the answer stayed the same. Eventually the dream faded. While Jewell sat in the theater, she found the flame being rekindled. Yes, she was thirty now, and to some it might appear late to pursue a childhood dream, but she could at least start taking dance lessons. It would be fun and a form of exercise.

After the show, they were allowed backstage to say hello to the cast members. As it turned out, Evan was related to one of the co-stars. Her name was Lynn.

Jewell didn't think her birthday could get any better.

The night moved along smoothly. They were sipping on champagne when Evan said, "Jewell?"

"Yes?"

"Have you thought about us getting more serious?"

"Well, how much more serious do you want to get?" Jewell asked, a little irritated that he was going there. There was no way she could get serious with him when she'd just discovered her real feelings for King.

"Evan, I'm not ready to be serious. I like how things are between us. My son just moved in with his dad and for the first time, I'm getting to know myself—the real me. Not the mother, not the workhorse, but Jewell. I have free time that I value. I really don't have to answer to anyone, and I'm enjoying this time. I'm not ready to give it up yet."

Evan acted like he didn't even hear her. He reached into his pocket and pulled out a box.

Jewell had to catch her breath. From the shape of the box she could tell that it held a ring. *Please don't let this be happening,* she said to herself over and over. Maybe if she repeated it enough, he'd change his mind.

No such luck. Evan opened the box and pulled out a ring. Jewell couldn't believe her eyes. It was beautiful. She couldn't tell if it was white gold or platinum. What she could tell was that the diamond was over a carat, maybe even two. Jewell glanced around and noticed quite a few people looking their way.

"Jewell, I know we haven't been seeing each other for long, but I can't deny what I feel. I think about you all the time, and I want to be with you. I'm not asking you to say yes. I'm just asking you to think about it, consider it." He placed the ring on the table in front of her.

Although he didn't actually say "marry me," Jewell knew that's what he was thinking. If she didn't still have these feelings for King, she would probably have said yes. She lowered her normal speaking tone so the surrounding parties couldn't hear her and told him, "Evan, I can't accept this ring. Even though you said you don't expect me to say yes, I'd feel like I would be making promises I can't keep."

"You do care for me, don't you?" Evan asked.

"Of course I do," Jewell told him.

"I'm not saying let's do it today, next week or even next month. I'm asking you to consider it, at least."

She didn't want to consider it, so she didn't reply.

"Listen. How about this? How about wearing it on your left hand as a promise ring?"

With people looking their way, Jewell didn't want to embarrass him any more than she felt she already had. She took the ring off the table and said, "Okay."

Evan smiled and relaxed back into his chair.

"But Evan, please understand that this does not mean we're engaged."

When Evan left the next morning, Jewell called Elsie and told her what happened.

"Are you out of your mind?" Elsie asked. "Why are you leading that man on like that?"

"I don't know." Jewell did feel bad. She took the ring off the second he walked out the door.

"What are you going to do when King finds out?"

"Ain't nothing to find out."

"Yeah, okay. I don't know who you think you're fooling," Elsie said, "other than Evan."

They hung up shortly after, and Jewell knew she would have to give the ring back. She glanced over at it, back in the box where she placed it, and thought, *It's a damn shame I have to give that ring up.*

She also knew that by turning Evan down she was making a decision about King. She was ready to give it another try, but it had to be on her terms.

I CAN'T DO THIS

"What was that all about?" Summer asked Elsie when she hung up her cell phone.

"Oh, nothing. Jewell and her man problems."

They were in the grocery store. The week had been a rough one for Elsie. She saw Janay twice and Summer was putting the pressure on more every day about the status of their relationship. Janay had even asked a time or two about them seeing one another exclusively. Elsie wasn't stupid. There was no way she was going to leave Summer for Janay. If she was going to jet, it would be because she was no longer content with where they were in their relationship. She'd finally admitted to herself that she wasn't.

As they were standing in line, Elsie felt a tap on her shoulder. She turned around. Standing behind her was Janay with another woman.

"Well, isn't this a surprise?" Janay said. She looked over at Summer who stared at her like she wanted to whoop her ass.

Elsie started to put the food on the counter.

Janay put her hand out and said, "I'm Janay. And you must be Summer."

Summer shook her hand and nodded. Elsie glanced at her out of the corner of her eyes. She could tell that Summer didn't trust herself to speak. Elsie looked at Janay and rolled her eyes. Janay knowing Summer's name was a dead giveaway that they'd seen one another. Elsie hoped Janay wasn't trying to be funny.

"Hey, Janay. What's up?"

"Nothing. Elsie, this is Jasmine. Jasmine, Elsie and Summer."

Elsie took her in quickly. Actually, she couldn't help but notice how beautiful Jasmine was. She looked like she was biracial, black and perhaps Chinese. She was slim but curvy, and smiled a perfect smile. "Hello."

Elsie was jealous.

"That'll be $79.11," the cashier said.

Glad to be distracted, and uncomfortable with Summer's silence, Elsie said to Janay, "It was nice seeing you." She turned around to push the cart and leave the store as soon as possible.

Janay wasn't letting her get away that easy. "How about we all do lunch or dinner sometimes?"

To this, Summer spoke up. "Not in this lifetime."

Elsie shrugged her shoulders and they were out the door.

Once outside, Summer looked at Elsie with darts in her eyes. "What the hell was that all about?"

"Don't make a scene," Elsie said.

"Don't make a scene? You're actually going to stand there a tell me not to make a scene when it's obvious something is up?"

"What's obvious, Summer? That we know one another, that she introduced herself to you, or that you were rude?"

"I'm not stupid or blind," Summer said.

They walked to the car and rode to Summer's house in silence.

When they pulled up in the driveway, Summer said, "You know we have to talk."

"You're making something out of nothing," Elsie said, not really ready for a confrontation. Shit, every time she turned around, Summer was saying they needed to talk.

They took the bags in the house. Summer went into the kitchen and put the food away while Elsie sat on the couch.

Summer joined Elsie on the couch and asked, "What's going on with you, Elsie? Do you want to break up? Is that it? Are you seeing Janay or thinking about seeing her?"

Elsie huffed.

Summer threw her hands up. "I don't know what to think. You really need to be straight with me and tell me what the hell is going on. Do you want to be with me or not? If not, let me know, so I can move on and you can move on. I haven't been happy, and I can be depressed by myself. I don't need this. I don't have time for games, and I definitely don't want to be led on. So, you need to tell me what's up and not give me the run around."

Elsie was tired of lying. She was tired of the whole charade. She decided at that moment to come clean and suffer the consequences. She turned to face Summer and placed Summer's hands into her own. "I'm not ready to move in."

Summer moved her hands and placed them into her own lap.

Elsie continued. "I think that maybe we need to separate, to take some time apart."

Summer's eyes teared up. "Where is this coming from?"

"I don't know. I just know that we don't feel right anymore. I still love you, but I'm not in love. Summer, please believe me when I tell you it's nothing you did or didn't do. It's me and this emotional roller coaster I've been on."

"Is it Janay?" Summer asked.

Elsie didn't answer her soon enough.

"It's Janay? You're getting back with her?"

"No, no."

Elsie could tell that Summer was trying to read her. "You went out with her?" Summer asked.

"We went on a couple of dates," Elsie answered honestly.

Summer placed her hand over her heart. "You're leaving me for her?"

Elsie was ready for this conversation to end. "No."

"Did you sleep with her?" Summer needed to know.

Elsie lied and denied it.

"Not yet?" Summer asked.

Elsie didn't answer.

Summer stood up. "I think you should leave."

"Don't you want to talk about it some more?"

Summer placed her hands on her hips. "What is there to talk about? You're not in love with me. You don't want to be with me. I'm not going to beg you to stay, Elsie. I have a child now that I need to be concerned about. If you want out, then get out."

The second Elsie stood up, Summer smacked her. Elsie brought her hand up to her face in disbelief.

"Go to hell," Summer said and left the room, knowing Elsie would let herself out.

IT'S FINALLY OVER

Tina's day in court finally arrived. Crystal was a wreck. That morning, any and everything that could go wrong, did. First, she couldn't decide what to wear. When she finally decided on a black suit, she thought it looked too depressing and changed. Then she picked out a red suit and thought that was too showy. As a last resort, she called Susan and asked her opinion. Susan told her to wear blue, because blue meant business.

After she decided on which blue dress to wear, she went out to her truck only to find that she had a flat tire. Crystal felt that at any moment she would have a nervous breakdown. *Why is this happening to me?* she wondered. She didn't want to think that it was a bad omen, but it was hard not to. With no time to wait on AAA, she caught a taxi to the courthouse.

Crystal had to admit to herself that she was more than a little nervous. She and Lange hadn't spoken since she'd told him about seeing Lena out with another man. She wondered if they'd gotten back together, or if he was just that upset with her.

Frazzled, Crystal rushed into the courthouse. She tried not to be disrespectful and do a full out sprint down the hall, but it was a challenge. Going past several people lined up on benches, she could have sworn she heard someone call her name, but there was no way she was stopping. She had to get to Tina. Tina was depending on her.

Crystal took a quick glance at her watch and saw that she was over half an hour late. Thank goodness court never started on time. For this she was grateful but with the luck she was having, it would start promptly today. When Crystal spotted Lange talking to Tina and her mom, she was relieved. She wasn't late after all. She slowed down her pace.

Lange noticed Crystal approaching them. He excused himself and met her halfway. "Let's walk down the hall," he suggested in a low tone.

Crystal took him in with a quickness and noticed that he looked intense in his tailored charcoal gray suit, black shirt, black tie, and black shoes. Crystal wanted to hug him, but knew it would be inappropriate.

"Okay," she told him. "But let me speak to Tina and her mother first."

Crystal went over and gave them each a hug. "Are you both okay?"

Ms. Lord nodded and Tina told her she was glad she was there. "I'm sorry I was late. You would not believe the morning I had."

Ms. Lord looked more nervous than Tina. "How much longer do you think it'll be before we start?"

"Honestly, I can't say, but it shouldn't be much longer. Listen, I'll be right back. There are some things Lange and I need to discuss."

"Anything to do with the case?" Tina asked.

"No," Crystal answered.

"Is everything okay between you two?" Tina wanted to know.

237

Crystal looked at her with raised eyebrows. "Why do you ask me that?"

Tina placed her hands on her hips and said, "I'm not stupid, you know."

"We're just friends, Lange and I." On that note, she left them standing there and went to talk with Lange.

"How are you?" Lange asked.

"I'm fine. What about you? Are you ready?"

"Aren't I always?"

Crystal didn't respond.

"You know his father might be here today. Do you think you will be able to handle that?"

"I have to handle it," she told him while she looked into his eyes. She hoped he would say something about what had transpired between them.

Taking her hand, he told her, "We'll talk about us later."

"You promise?" She couldn't help asking.

"I do," he assured her. "Right now, I just need to concentrate on winning this case."

Before she could respond, Crystal heard, "The Lord case will start in fifteen minutes."

Crystal looked up to see Lange watching her every expression. "Don't worry about me," she told him. "I'm going to be all right."

"You know you don't have to sit there the whole time," Lange told her.

Crystal reached out and took his hand. "I'm okay. Believe me. Excuse me. I have to go to the ladies room."

Once in the ladies' room, Crystal looked in the mirror. She didn't really have to use the bathroom. She just needed to prepare herself. Lange was making her more nervous with his concern, and she just needed a breather.

Crystal felt like she was a victim, not the one there to give support. When a person has to confront her past, she can never know what to expect. When she saw Jake, if he showed, would he say anything? What would she say? How would she react? She hoped she didn't freak out like she did at the club.

After throwing water on her face, she prepared herself for whatever was about to come. When she stepped in the hallway, she saw that Lange, Tina and her mother had entered the courtroom. She opened the door, and the first face she saw was Jake, Sr. Before either of them could think a thought, the bailiff said, "Please stand. Judge Eon is entering the courtroom." She took a deep breath and turned away. It took everything in her power not to glance over in Jake's direction again. Crystal sat behind Lange and Tina, next to Ms. Lord.

Ms. Lord reached over and placed her hand on top of Crystal's. Crystal couldn't help but glance over in Jake's direction. He was staring at her with a look of confusion and shock.

Lange caught this and asked her, "You okay?"

"I am," she told him. "Don't worry about me."

Crystal wanted to get up and walk over to Jake, to get in his face and ask him, "Why? Why did you rape me? How could you have violated me like that? Do you ever think about what you did? Do you regret it or did it mean nothing?" This surprised her, because instead of feeling the fear she thought she would, she just needed to understand why. Answers, more than anything, were what she wanted. She wanted to know how someone could take another by force. How could a man betray someone he knew, someone that had a crush on him? How did he feel now that his son had done the same thing?"

Jake Jr. was on the stand, and the District Attorney was tearing him apart. Jake was coming off as arrogant and ignorant. He didn't stand a chance. Tina handled herself well. She was being strong, brave and her testimony was believable. Crystal felt a sense of pride. They had coached her well. So, it didn't come as a surprise when the verdict came back guilty.

When Crystal first heard those words, she looked over at Jake Sr. and smiled. She felt victorious. Crystal watched along with everyone else as Jake Jr. was led away in handcuffs.

When Tina, Lange, Ms. Lord and Crystal left the courtroom, Jake Sr. was standing in the hallway. Crystal noticed that he was watching them as they said their goodbyes. Crystal and Lange were standing together when he approached them. "Excuse me," he said.

Everyone looked up at him. He addressed Crystal and asked, "May I speak with you for a moment?" Before she could answer, Lange stepped up and told him, "Get the hell away from her."

Crystal touched Lange's arm. "It's okay.

"Are you sure?" Lange asked, looking like he was ready to pounce.

"I'm sure," she told him.

"Well, I'll be right here if you need me."

Crystal took just a few steps away from Lange. She was surprised by how calm she felt. Maybe it was because this win did something for her personally or because she didn't think Jake would try anything here in the courtroom. Then again, she hadn't thougt he would rape her either.

"What is it?" she asked him. "What do you want to say to me?"

Jake cleared his throat and told her, "Um, I don't know how to say this." He glanced out of the corner of his eyes at Lange, who was watching and listening to every word.

"Say what?" Crystal asked, wanting to get this over with.

"I was young and irresponsible. I had a hard head," Jake began. "I thought everyone wanted me, whether they knew it or not."

"Why are you telling me this?"

"I'm trying to apologize for what happened. I'm trying to apologize for what I did to you and for what my son did to that girl."

"You're trying to apologize?" Crystal asked in disbelief.

He nodded.

"And that's supposed to make it okay?" The time had finally come for her to get from him what she always wanted—acknowledgement of what he did to her. Instead of feeling a sense of relief the way she thought she would, she felt angry, like it was a little too late.

"It's not supposed to make it okay, because what I did was inexcusable. I know that. I'm just asking for your forgiveness."

"I can't give that to you Jake . . . not right now anyway."

"I understand. But I hope one day you will be able to." On that note, he walked away, past Lange, who said to him in a threatening tone, "Don't you ever come near her again."

Lange approached Crystal, who by now had tears in her eyes. He wrapped his arms around her.

"He apologized to me," Crystal whispered then broke down.

Lange pulled her to his chest. "It's okay," he told her. "It's okay."

The funny thing was that it was okay, and that was why Crystal was crying. She had been holding onto anger, resentment and hatred for so long. To finally be able to let it go, just a little, was a relief. Forgive him? She wanted to. Heck, she needed to, and figured one day she would. Of course it was easier said than done.

As she wiped her eyes, so many things became clear to Crystal. There were things in her life she needed to change, and she was ready to do just that. It was like all these years she had been holding onto pain and resentment, and she was tired of it. She needed to move on with her life. She needed to get past her past, but most of all she needed her mother. She wanted to talk to her, to move forward.

"Let's go somewhere and eat," Lange suggested. He didn't want her to be alone.

"No, I think I just want to be alone," Crystal told him.

"Well, let me walk you to your car."

"I caught a cab here."

Lange questioned her with his eyes.

"My tire was flat."

"How come you didn't call me? I would have changed it for you."

"I didn't think of it. Plus I have Triple A."

"Well, I'm not going to let you catch a cab home, I'll drive you instead."

Crystal knew Lange wasn't going to allow her to say no, so she agreed. They walked out of the courtroom holding hands.

Once in the car, Lange said, "This has been quite a day, hasn't it?"

"That it has," Crystal replied and looked over at him. "Are you still upset with me about the whole Lena thing?"

"Not really. I just couldn't understand why you didn't tell me that you'd seen Lena with someone else when it happened."

Crystal didn't have an answer, not one that sounded good to her own ears, so she left it alone.

"What's done is done," Lange said. "Crystal, I care about you a great deal. I'm sure you know this. If circumstances were different, I'd try to make you my woman. But they're not. I'm getting separated; you're dating a cop. I don't want to put pressure on you or anything, but once my divorce is final, would you consider dating me? Exclusively."

Crystal's voice was caught in her throat. This was what she had wanted for quite some time. Now that there was a possibility of it happening, she wasn't too sure anymore.

"So, you're not getting back with Lena?"

"No."

"Are you sure about that?"

"Yes, I'm positive."

Crystal looked out the window. "I'm just supposed to let Roger go because you want me to?"

"You care for me, right?" Lange asked.

"More than I want to admit."

"Then let him go," Lange said.

Crystal looked over at him and said, "You say it like it's the easiest thing in the world to do. I can't just let him go like that. He's a good man. I don't want to hurt him." The truth was that Crystal planned on ending it with Roger before this conversation even took place. She just didn't want to answer Lange right away because a part of her knew it was time for her be alone, to get to know herself. She needed to soak in this new sense of freedom she was experiencing. "You don't think that starting a relationship so soon after your divorce is going to look bad?" she asked Lange.

"I don't care how it looks," Lange said. "We're adults."

"Are you sure that a relationship with me wouldn't just be one on the rebound?"

Instead of answering her, Lange said, "I see you need time to think about this."

"Yeah, I do," she told him as he pulled up in front of her house.

"I'll give you that," Lange told her. "You want me to come in?

"No. I think I'm going to go in and call my mother." Lange watched her as she climbed out of the car and walked toward her door.

SECOND TIME AROUND

Jewell and King were at Tyson's first basketball practice. A couple of months had passed since the accident, and they were both relieved to see their little man active again. Jewell wasn't too sure about letting him play this season, but after meeting with the doctors and getting their okay, she decided to give it a try.

Since sitting down, King barely said two words to her. Jewell wondered what that was all about. Shit, she was the one who should have had the attitude. He was on a dating frenzy and it was pissing her off.

The team was on a break when Tyson ran over and gave them each a hug.

"How about we all have dinner together?" Jewell asked.

"I'm staying the night at John's house," Tyson announced.

"Are you asking us or telling us?" King wanted to know.

"I'm asking," Tyson replied as he looked at the ground.

"He's supposed to stay the weekend with you," King told Jewell, "so it's your call."

"It's okay with me," Jewell said. "I'll pick you up tomorrow."

"Thanks, Mom. Thanks, Dad," Tyson said before he ran off.

"Well, does the invitation for dinner still stand or was it just a package deal?" King asked. "I don't have any plans for tonight."

"No hot date?" Jewell asked.

"No."

"Well, it still stands," Jewell said. "Be at my house no later than eight."

King told her he'd bring a bottle of wine.

Later that night, Jewell was taking the steaks out of the oven when the doorbell rang. She glanced at the clock and knew it was King. He was always on time. She placed the steaks on the counter and opened the door.

King sniffed the air. "It smells good in here. I'm starving."

Jewell led the way into the kitchen and while King sat down, Jewell made their plates.

"So, what's up?" King asked.

"Nothing."

"You still seeing the white boy?"

Jewell rolled her eyes. "His name is Evan and yes, I'm still seeing him, but not much longer. I'm thinking about calling it off."

King didn't respond.

Jewell made their plates and sat down. "You've been going out on a lot of dates. What's up with that?"

"I'm single. I can do that."

Jewell didn't want this conversation to become confrontational. What she wanted was a discussion about them. "Are you serious about any of the women you've been dating?"

"Why, Jewell?"

"I just want to know." She wanted to be sure she wasn't setting herself up.

"Maybe. There is one in particular that I'm interested in."

Jewell started to feel queasy. "Let's eat."

As they started to eat, Jewell found herself nibbling. She kept picturing King with a faceless woman, and it was upsetting her more than she cared to admit. Finally unable to handle it, she put her fork down, leaned back into her chair and crossed her arms.

King looked up, fork in midair and said, "What? Why aren't you eating?"

"Because I want to talk," Jewell told him.

"About what?"

"About us."

"Only thing I've wanted to hear in regards to us, is us being a family."

"Maybe I've been thinking about it. Maybe I've been thinking about a whole lot of things, like that night we made love."

King looked annoyed. "Why are you playing with me?"

"Who says I'm playing?"

King stood up. "I'm leaving!"

"I don't want you to leave. I told you I want to talk."

King placed his hands on the table and leaned over. "Jewell, in case you don't remember, I asked you if we could get back together. You basically told me no. We slept together, then we pretended like it never happened. You get upset when I go out on a date—don't think I didn't notice, because I did— yet, you're dating a white man. I'm a little confused here. You say one thing, and now you're trying to change it up. I don't want to be a part of a game."

"What do you mean part of a game?" Jewell asked. "You think I'm playing with you?"

"I don't know what you're doing, but I don't want to be on an emotional roller coaster."

Jewell placed her hand on his arm. "Please don't leave."

King just looked at her.

"When we're done eating we can talk," she told him. "I'll be honest and let you know where I stand, what I want, what I think I can handle, and what I may not be able to handle as far as our future is concerned."

That was what he wanted to hear, so he sat back down.

Jewell turned the radio on a smooth jazz station and they ate in silence. Jewell thought about what she would say, and King wondered what he would hear. Once they were done, Jewell cleared off the table and they went into the living room

"So, let's talk." King sat on the couch.

Jewell sat next to him. She decided to be as honest as possible. "King, I've come to realize that I still love you—that I'm still in love with you."

"Then let's get back together," he interrupted.

"It's not that easy You hurt me."

King interrupted again. "Jewell, we were kids then. Are you saying you don't believe in second chances?"

"I'm not saying that at all. It's just hard to let go. I've loved you since I was a teenager. You were my first boyfriend, my first lover, and you're my son's father. On one hand, I want to be with you. I want for you, Tyson and me to be a family. But on the other hand, I have to ask myself, am I being realistic? What if we're setting ourselves up for failure? That night we made love, I tried to pretend it was just because we were both upset over the accident, but I know that it was so much more than that. I felt a connection. It was one of the heart, and one like I haven't felt since we were together back in the day."

King was growing impatient. "So, what are you saying? Do you want us to be together or not?"

"What I'm saying is let's test it out. Let's not move in together, but be exclusive. I don't want you dating other people, and I won't either. Let's date one another."

"So, you want to be courted?"

"Yes."

"Jewell, that's childish. I love you, you love me. We have a child together. Let's just do this."

"I just don't want to jump into anything," she told him.

"Well, what if I say I don't want to do it that way?"

Jewell was quiet. She just shrugged her shoulders.

"So, you're telling me," King said, "that if I don't agree to your terms, we can't be together."

"What I'm saying is, I'm scared and I want to take it slow."

King was silent.

"Well?"

"Damn, you're making this hard, Jewell. Here a brother is asking you to be his woman, to possibly marry him, and you're talking about let's date. I'm ready to settle down. I'm ready to have more kids. Neither of us are getting any younger."

"I know that, but you—"

"But what? You say you love me."

"And I do."

King took a deep breath. "Fuck it! We'll do this your way. I don't know for how long, but I'll adhere to your plan. Just answer me this—will you stay the night sometimes?"

"Not a good idea. With Tyson there, we don't want to get his hopes up high in case it doesn't work out. But when he's away overnight, of course I will."

King, being the man he was, needed to know, "Well, how are we supposed to make love?"

Jewell laughed. "I'm sure we'll think of a way."

"How about tonight?"

Smiling, she said, "Of course. You're my man now."

"So, this means you're going to dump the white boy?"

"You don't have to say it like that," Jewell said and smiled.

"You just threw the brothers to the wayside," King joked.

Jewell punched him in the arm. "Be quiet."

Together they laughed and looked into looked into each other's eyes. They saw the love and the need that was there. They decided to satisfy that need.

CHANGE IS ON THE WAY

When Crystal arrived home from court, she decided to call her mother, but fear of the unknown kept her from doing it. That night she decided to unplug the phone, turn off her cell, take a bath and chill. She needed to decide what she wanted to do about Lange and Roger and determine how she would go about making up with her mother. Crystal was ready to make changes, to reconcile. Instead of holding onto the past, she wanted to move forward.

The next morning when Crystal woke up, she rolled out of bed, threw on her robe and went downstairs to make a cup of cappuccino. As the milk was steaming, she picked up the phone and dialed her mother's number, a number she knew by heart although she rarely called.

"Good morning," a male voice greeted.

"Um, hi. This is Crystal."

"Hi, Crystal. This is Mr. Newton."

Crystal figured as much, but to hear his voice shocked her. She wanted to hang up and pretend that she never called, but she knew that wouldn't be the answer. She promised herself that she would go with this reconciliation.

"I'd like to speak with my mother."

"She's not here."

"Well, do you know where she's at?"

"The doctor's office," he told her.

"Why? Is she sick?"

Mr. Newton hesitated a second too long.

"Is she?" Crystal couldn't hide the panic in her voice.

"I think maybe she should speak with you. It's not my place to discuss it."

His response irritated Crystal. Her mother was at the doctor's office and he wouldn't tell her why. Obviously, it was something major or else he would have told her. Crystal didn't want to take it here, but she figured maybe guilt would get him to reveal what was going on. "Look, the least you could do after what you've done is tell me what's going on."

He didn't say a word.

"Hello, are you still there?" Crystal said.

"I'm still here and I'm about to hang up. I don't like being disrespected. When you're ready to talk *to* me and not *at* me, call back. Bye."

The phone clicked in her ear and Crystal sat looking at it. "I can't believe he hung up on me." She redialed the number.

He picked up.

"This is Crystal again."

He cut her off. "I don't mean to be rude, but what you said to me was way out of line. Your mother has forgiven me and now that I'm her husband—"

Crystal didn't hear a word after that. She went into shock. "I'll call back," she said and hung up. Crystal sat down, ignoring her drink. She kept repeating the word "husband" over and over. She couldn't believe her mother had gotten married.

251

Damn, were they that estranged? Crystal made a decision. She looked at her schedule, saw that she didn't have any court dates for another two weeks, and immediately called her travel agent. She was going to Charlotte to find out what the hell was going on.

A NEW START

Susan and Timothy were in the middle of dinner. They were celebrating Susan's first thirty days of being drug free.

"How do you feel?" Timothy wanted to know. "Or do I need to ask?"

Susan smiled because she knew he was trying to get her to open up more to him about the whole experience. He still didn't understand why she wouldn't attend the NA meetings with him. He thought the support of a group was more productive than the support of an individual.

"Not that I think you going to counseling is a bad thing. I just thought we could attend meetings together."

Once again, she told him no, it wasn't open for discussion. She had to do this her way. Finally, he let go and let God.

"How do I feel?" Susan repeated his question. "Well, I have days when all I think about is a hit. Sometimes I think that I could handle it now, that I won't go overboard. The craving is definitely still there, and I know it'll probably be a while before it goes away, but I'm dealing with it."

Timothy took her hand in his and ran his fingers across the engagement ring. "You know I'm proud of you, right?"

"I know. You know what's funny? I didn't realize how difficult this would be. I depended on that stuff just to get me through the day, and now it's all on me."

"You know I'm curious about what you and your counselor talk about."

Susan moved her hand and took a sip of her water. "But you also know that's between her and me."

"I know. I just thought I'd give it a try."

As Susan laughed, her cell phone rang.

"Don't answer it," Timothy told her. "This is our night out."

Susan let it ring. It stopped, but two seconds later, it started ringing again. She looked at Timothy, who was frowning. "It must be important," she said.

"Go ahead. Answer it."

She did. "Hello."

It was Crystal. "Susan, are you busy?"

"I'm out with Timothy."

"I won't be in the office for the next few days. I'm flying out to Charlotte to see my mother. I think something may be wrong." She went on to tell Susan about the phone call.

Susan looked up to see Timothy giving her the "hurry up off the phone" look. "Listen, sweetie. Do what you have to do and know you have my support. I'm going to call you when I get home, all right?"

That night after Susan and Timothy made love, he dozed off and she picked up the phone to return Crystal's call. Crystal sounded so disturbed, like she really needed to talk.

"You're just going to pop up, just like that?" Susan asked Crystal.

"Yes. I need to know what the hell is going on."

Susan had to let Crystal have it. "You know you were wrong, don't you?"

"What are you talking about?"

"What you said to him. After what you did to me," Susan mimicked Crystal.

Crystal knew that Susan was right. Here she was talking about change and letting go, yet she was throwing the past up in someone else's face. "If he would have just told me why my mother was at the doctor's, I wouldn't have said it. He was acting all mysterious and serious and shit. What was I supposed to do?"

"It might not even be anything serious. You know you could be working yourself up for nothing." Susan tried making her feel better.

"I know my mother, Susan. She's never been sick a day in her life, at least that I can remember. So for her to go to a doctor, well, it scares me. Not only that, but we need to talk. I mean really talk. I'm ready to develop a better relationship with her."

"Damn, change must be in the air. You're making big strides, and I've made them. Are we growing up after thirty?" Susan asked.

Crystal laughed. "So, are you ready for your big day?"

"A little. Do you know who you're bringing to the wedding? Lange or Roger?"

Crystal rolled her eyes. "Ha, ha. Real funny."

LIFE BEGINS NOW

The next morning before leaving for the airport, Crystal called Roger and told him about the phone call to her mother's house.

"Well, when are you coming back?" he wanted to know.

"I'm not sure. Maybe in a few days, maybe a week. It depends on what's going on when I get there. Something about that call just didn't feel right."

"Will you call me while you're away?"

"I'll try, Roger, but I can't make any promises."

She called Lange next, and was relieved when his answering service picked up. She left a message telling him she would be out of town for a few days. "I'll call you when I return."

Crystal glanced at the clock and noticed that she had less than four hours until her flight. She still needed to shower and drop Billie off at the dog kennel. Time was flying, so she knew she had to get a move on.

Two hours later, dressed in a Roc-a-Wear sweat suit, Crystal sat at the airport reading and waiting for her flight to be called. Not a world-class traveler, she was a bit nervous about flying. Whenever Crystal flew, it had to be first class and it was imperative that she sit by the window. Looking at the clouds allowed her to stay calm and relaxed. It made her feel like she was that much closer to God. She said a short prayer asking God to please allow the plane to take off and land safely.

Once she was on the plane, she took her seat, put on her seatbelt, and requested a glass of wine. Before she knew it, she was so relaxed from the wine that she dozed off. Three hours later the plane was landing.

Was she ready for this? She asked herself as she searched for the rental car company. Was she ready to make up with her mother and see her new husband, the man she chose to hate for so long? After paying for the car, Crystal drove as slowly as she could to her mother's house. She had no idea what she would say or how she would say it. She asked God for guidance in what to say. In light of the trial and her making the decision to put the past behind her, Crystal knew this was the right thing to do.

When Crystal turned the corner and spotted her mother's house, she noticed someone pulling into the driveway. She pulled up behind the car and saw her mother step out. She blew the horn. When her mother turned around, Crystal opened her door, stepped out of the car and said, "Hi, Ma!"

Mrs. Gem dropped her clutch purse and met Crystal halfway up the driveway. There were tears in her eyes. Crystal opened her arms, allowing her tears to flow as well.

"Oh my! What are you doing here? When did you get in? How come you didn't call me and let me know you were coming?" Mrs. Gem couldn't get her words out fast enough.

"I wanted to surprise you," Crystal told her.

"Well, you've definitely done that."

Together they walked toward the house. When they got to the porch, Mr. Newton opened the door. He had been watching the whole scene through the curtains.

"Crystal," he said with a nod.

Mrs. Gem stood back, afraid of what Crystal's reaction would be. Crystal decided to be an adult and not be rude. "Trevor." She knew she was wrong for calling him by his first name, but it was her way of letting him know that she was an adult now.

"Let me take your bags," he said, reaching out. After their brief conversation, he had a gut feeling that she would visit. He wasn't surprised by her sudden appearance.

Crystal nodded her greeting and handed him her bags. She followed her mother into the living room.

"Are you hungry? Do you need anything to eat?" her mother asked.

"No. I just want to get settled, then we need to talk. All of us."

"Is everything okay?" Mrs. Gem placed her hands on Crystal's lower back. She yearned for contact.

"That's what I'm here to find out."

"Your room is upstairs. Go get settled. I'm going to make you something to eat anyway, and when you're ready, come on down."

Crystal turned to leave the living room, but stopped and took another look at her mother. She had to admit, she was glad she came.

While Crystal was upstairs, Mrs. Gem and Trevor were in the kitchen talking quietly.

"I wonder what she's doing here," Mrs. Gem said. Crystal had never just popped up before.

Trevor hadn't told her about the phone call. He didn't want to upset her, but knew it was time to 'fess up. "Well, she called yesterday when you were at the doctor's. I told her where you were and she got really upset, started asking me all sorts of questions. I told her it was best that she spoke to you. I guess she decided to do it in person." He didn't tell her how rude

Crystal was to him. It was irrelevant, and it was something he and Crystal needed to handle on their own. "I also told her we were married."

"You did what?" Mrs. Gem wanted to give Crystal the news herself, but standing there she had to admit that she was a little relieved that Trevor did it for her. Mrs. Gem knew the time would come. She just wanted to be a bit more prepared for it.

Well, now she knew the explanation for the sudden appearance of her daughter. She'd recently left a message on Crystal's answering machine, but Crystal never called her back. She figured she hadn't gotten over the last visit. She was calling to let Crystal know she'd gotten married, but also to let her know that she'd been diagnosed with cancer.

"So, are you going to tell her?" Trevor asked.

Mrs. Gem knew he was talking about the cancer. "I don't know. First I need to find out why she's here, if it's because she's concerned about me or if it's something else," Mrs. Gem answered.

"I think that no matter what it is, you have to tell her. She has a right to know."

Mrs. Gem knew that her husband was right.

Just then, Crystal appeared in the kitchen. "Tell me what?"

Wanting to handle this a different way, Mrs. Gem chose to ignore the question. "Did you get settled in?"

"Yes." Crystal knew her mother was trying to ignore her question.

"I made you a salad."

"I told you I wasn't hungry, Ma."

"I know, but it'll make me feel better to know that you have something in your stomach."

Looking her mother straight in the eye, Crystal asked, "What is it you have to tell me?"

"How long are you here for?" her mother asked.

"It depends on what it is you're not telling me." Crystal was getting nervous. She knew whatever it was wouldn't be something to celebrate.

"Oh, it's nothing," Mrs. Gem lied. Trevor shot her a look that Crystal caught.

"I already know you two are married. What else could there be? Are you having a baby or something?" Crystal certainly hoped not, but stranger things had happened.

"Let's talk about it later. Tell me what you've been up to."

Frustrated, Crystal said, "Just tell me, Ma. I didn't come all the way down here for nothing. Something is going on and I need to know what it is."

"She's an adult. Just tell her," Trevor said.

Mrs. Gem moved over to the table and sat down. She motioned for Crystal to do the same. "I have cancer," she blurted out.

Crystal looked from Trevor to her mother and back to Trevor, who said, "I'll leave you two alone."

Once he left the room, Crystal said, "Did you just say you have cancer?" She hoped she heard wrong.

"Yes," Mrs. Gem replied.

For the second time that day, Crystal felt her eyes welling up. "How long have you known? Why are you just telling me now? Where is it? Has it spread? Is it life threatening?"

Crystal wanted answers, and she wanted them now. She called Trevor into the room. The second he returned, Crystal attacked him. "How come you didn't tell me over the phone? I have a right to know. This is my mother, for God's sake."

"I didn't feel it was my place," he told her.

"Don't blame him, Crystal," Mrs. Gem said. "I called you and left a message. I said it was an emergency, and you never called back."

"I did call you back." Crystal was in hysterics. "I just didn't leave a message on the answering machine."

"I'm supposed to know that?"

260

Crystal couldn't say anything. She just hung her head and shed tears. It hurt to think she'd been holding a grudge this long and her mother was ill. She felt like a fool. She stood up, then Mrs. Gem stood up. "Ma, Trevor, I owe you both an apology."

Mrs. Gem spread her arms for a hug, and Crystal fell into them. She stepped from her mother's embrace, looked at Trevor and said, "I've been holding onto my anger and hatred for quite some time now. I resented what you did by paying my mother off, and I resented that she allowed it. I have to be honest and say I still don't understand, but I know that I have to let it go. I want to forgive you both. I won't forget, but I will forgive."

Trevor started to say something, but Crystal put her hand up to cut him off. "Please, let me finish. You've been there for my mother. I know that she can't help it, and I have no control over who she falls in love with. Hell, everybody deserves to have someone to love, and it's obvious that she's forgiven you. I can't sit here and tell you I'm going to be the best daughter-in-law in the world, because there are still some issues I have to resolve. But I'm sure in time, we'll learn to appreciate one another. At least I'll learn to appreciate what my mother appreciates and loves in you." Crystal looked over at her mother and held her hands. "I want to make a doctor's appointment, and I want us all to go together. I need to hear from the doctor how serious this is."

"Okay," Mrs. Gem told her, "but eat your salad first."

The following day, they went to the doctor's office. Her mother had breast cancer and would need treatment. It was too late to have her breast removed. Chemotherapy would have to start as soon as possible. Crystal was devastated, but tried not to show it. She found herself wanting to do everything for her mother. She waited on her hand and foot, to the point that her mother told her to take it down a notch. She tried to talk her mother into moving back up north so they could be closer.

"Who's going to cook for you, clean for you, do the laundry?" Crystal wanted to know.

"I'm not an invalid," her mother would tell her. "I've been doing things on my own for this long. Plus, I have Trevor with me."

Crystal had to admit this made her just a little jealous. She wanted to be the one to take care of her mother. She didn't want to return to her home or her business, but when she talked about it, Mrs. Gem wouldn't hear it. "You have your own life. You cannot put it on hold to take care of me. I won't allow it."

A few days before it was time for her to leave, Crystal and Trevor sat down and had a long discussion. They talked about the past.

"I was just trying to look out for my family or for what I believed to be my family," he told Crystal. "I was raised to handle things no matter what the situation or the cost."

Crystal told him about Jake Jr., and he just shook his head. "The apple doesn't fall far from the tree, huh?"

He did admit to Crystal that his heart ached just a bit. After he divorced Jake's mother, they stayed in contact because, even though he wasn't Jake's biological father, he had raised him. Once Jake grew up, they lost contact. Less of an effort was made to maintain a relationship.

Crystal finally admitted to herself that Trevor was not the monster she made him out to be.

While she was in Charlotte for ten days, the only people she spoke to were Roger and Susan, letting them know about her mother's condition. Susan told her that clients were calling and Lange called a number of times, asking for the number to reach her. Roger offered to come down and keep her company. Of course she told him no, but not because she didn't want his company. She just wanted to be with her mother without any distractions. With just a few days left before it was time to leave, she knew that once she got home, she would be rearranging her schedule to travel back and forth.

The day finally arrived for Crystal to go home. She, her mother and Trevor were at the airport. Crystal and her mother were holding hands. "I'll be back as soon as possible," she told her mother.

"Aw, sweetie, you don't have to change your schedule up because of me."

"I want to, Mom. Please let me do this." Crystal looked over at Trevor and said, "You continue taking care of my mother. Okay?"

"I will," he assured her.

The announcer was calling her flight.

"I have to go," Crystal said. She kissed them both on the cheek, shocking not only herself but her mother and Trevor, as well.

Four hours later when she arrived home, she found a card and flowers on her doorstep. *Welcome back.* The card was from Lange. She wondered how he knew she would be coming home. It didn't matter. On the flight home, she'd made a few decisions.

TIME TO MOVE ON

Jewell had no idea what she would say to Evan, but she knew it was time to stop ducking him and making up excuses for not seeing him. After all, Evan wasn't a stupid man. He was decent, and deserved to be with someone who didn't have doubts about their relationship. Jewell decided to break up with Evan in a public place. That way she could say what needed to be said and walk away without causing a scene. She'd spent all day thinking about what she would say and how she would say it. The conclusion was there wouldn't be an easy way. His feelings were bound to be hurt.

The one thing she was certain of was that she wouldn't tell him she was getting back with King. He didn't need to know. Her plan was to tell him that she needed space, that she decided she wasn't ready for a relationship—at least not the kind he wanted—and she thought it was best for him to move on. She was going to tell him that he was a good man who deserved someone who was ready to accept what he was willing to give.

She'd convinced herself that by placing the blame on herself, it wouldn't make him feel like he failed. She just wanted her family to be together. The time she'd been

264

spending with King and Tyson made her realize this even more.

She and King hadn't told Tyson about reuniting, at least not yet. King wanted to, but Jewell felt they should give it time. Little did she know, Tyson knew that something was up.

One evening as they lay across her bed watching a movie, he asked, "Ma, what's up with you and Dad?"

"What do you mean, what's up with us?"

"I don't know. You two have been acting really funny, whispering and stuff. It's like you're being extra nice to each other."

Laughing, Jewell asked, "Are you saying we were mean to each other before?"

"No, but you act almost like boyfriend and girlfriend."

Jewell was tickled pink. "What do you know about girlfriends and boyfriends?" Teasing him, she asked, "Do you have a girlfriend?"

Tyson started to blush. "For real, Mom. You and Dad are always touching each other and stuff. Are you two getting married or something?"

"No. No. We just . . . um. We just . . ." She didn't know what to tell him. "Ask your father," she said, thinking that would get him off her case.

"I did. He told me to ask you."

Jewell smiled. She should have known better.

"Well, your father and I are dating one another."

"Does this mean we're going to be a family again?"

"We're already a family, sweetheart," Jewell told him, hoping he would drop the subject.

No such luck. "But are we going to be a family together in the same house?"

All Jewell could say was, "I don't know yet."

Later that night when King arrived to pick up Tyson, Jewell asked, "Why didn't you let me know Tyson was asking questions?"

"The way I figured it," King said, "is that he'd ask you also."

Jewell told him he was right, and she repeated the conversation verbatim.

"So, did you break up with the white boy yet?" That was all King wanted to know.

"Not yet."

King walked out of the house and slammed the door behind him.

Jewell walked over to the phone, called King's house and left a message on his answering machine, "Please don't be angry. I'm going to do it this weekend."

That was why she was at TGI Friday's now, heading Evan's way. He'd already taken a seat and was looking through the menu. He looked up and smiled when he saw her. When she arrived at the table, he stood up and pulled her seat out. "I've missed you." He tried to place a kiss on her lips, but she turned her head and the kiss landed on her cheek.

"So, what's up?" Evan asked as he sat down.

On edge, Jewell said, "Nothing. Why?"

"I haven't seen you in over a week, and when I do, I try to kiss you and you turn your head."

Jewell didn't realize that she'd done that. "I'm sorry. My mind is just preoccupied."

"With what?"

"Just stuff at work," she lied.

The waitress came over and asked, "Would you like something to drink?"

Jewell ordered a Margarita on the rocks with extra tequila. She figured she'd need the extra courage. Evan ordered a rum and Coke. The waitress left their menus. Evan just sat staring at Jewell while she tried to pretend that she didn't notice.

"Jewell?"

She looked up.

"Why don't you be honest with me and tell me what's up?"

Jewell decided not to put it off any longer. She opened her purse, pulled out the ring Evan had given to her and put it on the table in front of them. Jewell knew when he first gave it to her she should have given it back. But as they say, diamonds are a girl's best friend.

Evan glanced at the ring and asked, "What's this? Why are you putting the ring on the table?"

"I've decided to give it back to you. I can't accept it," Jewell told him.

"Why not?"

"I've decided that what you want and what I want are two different things. We're moving in two different directions, and I don't want to pretend anymore."

"You don't want to pretend? Jewell, what are you talking about?"

"You know what I'm talking about, Evan. Please don't make this any harder than it has to be. I'm not ready for a commitment. I can't pretend that I am, and I don't want to lead you on."

The waitress came back over. "Are you ready to order?"

"No, we need some more time," Evan answered without taking his eyes off Jewell. He noticed that Jewell wasn't returning his gaze. Instead, she looked surprised by whatever was behind him. Evan turned around to see what she was looking at.

King had just entered the restaurant with a friend. "Isn't this a coincidence? You're dumping me, and in walks your son's father. Wouldn't he love to be a part of this?"

Little did Evan know, he was. At that exact moment, Jewell saw Trey pointing in their direction. King and Trey were friends during their youth, and Jewell never liked him. He was always a troublemaker, and it appeared that he hadn't changed.

King looked in Jewell's face and frowned. He started walking in their direction.

"Damn." Jewell wanted this night to be drama free. Evan looked at her and smirked. King was soon standing in front of them.

"Well, well, well. What do we have here?" He spotted the ring on the table. "Or should I ask what do we have there?"

Evan put his hand out, and King surprisingly shook it.

Being sarcastic, King asked, "Are we getting engaged?"

Jewell didn't know what to say.

"Actually," Evan volunteered, "you'll be happy to know she's giving me the ring back and—"

Jewell shot Evan a look that he understood to mean this was between them.

"Can I see you for a second?" King asked Jewell.

"No." Jewell was not in the mood.

"I'll only take up a minute of your time." Looking at Evan, he asked, "You don't mind, do you?"

"Go ahead and take care of your business," Evan said.

Trey was standing off to the side, amused. "I'm going to sit down, man."

Jewell stood up and followed King to the back of the restaurant. She asked him where Tyson was. It was just something to say.

"With Trey's girl and son."

"Oh."

"So, what's up with you and Evan out on a date?"

"It's not a date. I came to break up with him. Didn't you get my message?"

"Yeah, I got it. What? You couldn't break up over the phone?"

"I could have, but I chose not to," Jewell said.

"Have you told him?" King wanted to know.

"I was doing that when you walked over."

"Oh. I'll let you go back and handle your business then."

Jewell turned to walk back over to Evan.

"Hey!" King called out.

Turning around, Jewell asked, "What now?"

"Can I have a kiss?"

Jewell rolled her eyes and turned away. When she reached the table, Evan was standing up.

"Where are you going?"

"I can tell when I'm not wanted," Evan told her.

"Please, Evan, let's talk about this."

"There's nothing to talk about. I love you, but you don't love me. I want to be with you, but you don't want to be with me. What more is there to say?"

Jewell didn't have a reply.

Evan shook his head and said, "I didn't think so."

He walked away, leaving her standing there.

King watched Evan leave the restaurant then approached Jewell. "You want some company tonight?"

Jewell just looked at him.

"Well?"

"No, King. I think I just need to be alone." She turned to leave the restaurant, but King grabbed her by the waist and pulled her to him.

She hoped Evan had left and wasn't in the parking lot witnessing this.

"I love you," King told her.

"Yeah, I know," she responded.

That night when Jewell arrived home, she tried calling Elsie, but there no answer at her house and she wasn't picking up her cell phone.

MOVING ON

Elsie was over at Janay's house. She decided the time had come to end the affair they were having. The shit was not only draining her, but she found herself missing Summer as well. The other night, she almost picked up the telephone and called Summer, but decided it was best to leave well enough alone. Plus, she didn't want to play head games or mess with Summer's feelings. She knew it was too soon to ask if they could just be friends or even to suggest occasional sex. When she thought about it, she knew she messed up. Don't get it twisted. She still didn't want to move in with Summer and take it to the level Summer wanted to, but she didn't want Summer completely out of her life either.

"So, are you going away with me this weekend?" Janay asked Elsie, bringing her back to the here and now.

"No, Janay, I've decided not to go."

Janay looked at Elsie expectantly, as if she were waiting for an explanation. Elsie offered none.

"Why not?" Janay wanted to know. She knew Elsie and Summer were no longer together, although it wasn't because Elsie had told her. She heard it through the grapevine, which was very short in the gay community. Janay planned on making Elsie hers once again. The plan was to wine, dine and charm her on a cruise. It was an annual event given by the African-American gay community.

"I just don't think it's a good idea." Elsie was trying to break the news in an easy way, unlike how she did it with Summer.

"Why not? Do you have other plans?" Janay had on a long, black satin nightgown, almost sheer. She looked sexy as hell. Her plan was to seduce Elsie, have her stay the night, get up and cook breakfast. She could tell now that this wasn't going to go as planned. She looked down at Elsie's hands and noticed they were crossed, as though she were nervous.

"After some serious thought, I've decided that it would be best for us to just be friends."

Janay snapped her head up. She was caught off guard. "What? What do you mean just friends?" She wasn't trying to hear it. She placed her hand in Elsie's hair and moved her fingers down the nape of her neck.

Elsie grabbed Janay's hand and asked, "Didn't you just hear what I said?"

"I think you need to rethink it. How about we go upstairs and make love? After we're done, we can discuss our relationship."

"Janay, why do you always think lovemaking is the answer? This time it's not. And why are you trying to make this harder than it needs to be?"

"We just got back together, and already you're talking about breaking up."

Elsie stood up. "We haven't gotten back together. We were just seeing one another. We started this whole thing off wrong anyway. I cheated on Summer with you, and we both know that was wrong."

"Well, you weren't happy with her anyway, so what difference does it make?"

"It just does. Listen, I'm sorry if I led you on, but how was I to know you were making this out to be so much more than it was?"

"What, you thought I was just wasting my time?"

"I don't know what I thought. What I know is I've decided I don't want to be in any kind of relationship. I've never really had a chance to be by myself. I've never done that before. I've always gone from one relationship to another, and somewhere down the line, I lost myself."

Pissed off, Janay said, "So, you came over here to tell me this bullshit? You could have told me this over the phone."

"I could have, and maybe I should have, but I didn't. I thought you would understand." Elsie grabbed her purse and walked toward the door.

"You know this is it. You'll never have another chance with me," Janay stated, placing her hands on her hips.

Elsie didn't feel a need to respond. She just walked out the door and closed another chapter of her life.

END OF AFFAIRS

Roger and Crystal were lying in the bed. They'd just finished making love and were basking in the afterglow. Crystal was feeling good about her decision to start life over, her way, alcohol-free. She wanted to have a clear head and be of sound mind and body when she went to visit her mom.

She decided to end a relationship—the one she had with Lange. It wasn't easy, because she still lusted after him, but lust and love were two different things, and she needed something more substantial. To her surprise, when she broke the news to him, he understood. He wished her the best and told her it didn't mean they couldn't hang out sometimes.

She'd thought of telling Roger the same thing, and was all set to do so when he came over. It didn't go as planned.

Earlier that day, Roger called and said he wanted to see her. Not having any plans for the day, she told him to come on over. She could use the company. She figured Roger would be a nice distraction. Crystal couldn't stop thinking about her mother. She was consumed with making plans to go see her again as soon as possible.

When Roger arrived, his first question was, "How's your mom?"

They were sitting on the couch in the living room. Crystal had spoken to her earlier, and she sounded fine. "That's   good to hear. Do you know when you're going to see her again?"

"In about two weeks," Crystal responded. Two weeks seemed so far away, but she had a case she needed to wrap up, and it was stressing the hell out of her.

Roger noticed her tenseness and told her, "Listen, you need to relax. Everything is going to work out. You're going to be there by your mother's side, and with prayer and patience, it'll work out."

Crystal looked at Roger and asked him, "How can you be so sure?"

"It's called faith, sweetie."

"Easier said than done," Crystal told him.

Roger stood up and walked behind the couch. He placed his hands on Crystal's shoulders and started massaging them. "With your traveling back and forth to North Carolina, who's going to take care of Billie?" Billie had finally gotten used to Roger and no longer growled at him.

Crystal relaxed under Roger's touch. "I placed an ad in the paper, and three people are coming to look at him today."

"So, you're going to sell him to a stranger?"

"I don't have much of a choice," Crystal said.

"How about I take Billie?"

"Stop playing." Crystal turned to face Roger, to see if he was serious.

"I'm not playing. I'm serious. I've been thinking about getting a pet, and why not have one I'm familiar with? Plus, this way you won't be giving him to a stranger. You'll still get to see him."

Crystal wanted so badly to say yes, but she didn't want to feel obligated to Roger because of a dog.

"Don't worry," Roger said, reading her expression. "It won't hold you to me."

"I wasn't thinking that," she told him.

"Yes, you were. It was written all over your face."

Crystal smirked.

"I'll tell you what," Roger told her. "Meet with the people, and if you don't find one you like, I'll be more than happy to take him home with me."

"Okay, that's a plan," she told him.

Roger ended up spending the whole day at Crystal's and meeting with the potential owners alongside her. As it turned out, she didn't like anyone.

After the third person left, Roger laughed and asked her, "You don't think you're being too picky?"

"I probably am," she confessed.

She knew that she would end up taking Roger up on his offer. Exhausted and in need of a nap, Crystal yawned.

"Want me to give you a massage before you turn in?" Roger offered.

Not one to turn down such an offer, Crystal said, "Yes. I'd like that very much."

So upstairs they went. Once in the bedroom, Crystal asked Roger, "You want me to undress?"

"Yes." There was a huskiness in his voice.

"A massage only, right?"

"Unless you want more."

Crystal figured he would say that, and she chose not to answer him, because one never knows . . .

After undressing down to her boy-cut panties, she lay on her stomach and closed her eyes. The massage oil lay near the bed, and she relaxed under Roger's slow, even strokes.

"What's on your mind?" he asked, thinking it was her mother.

"Us," she told him.

"What about us?"

"You want the truth?" Crystal asked.

Roger stopped massaging and braced himself.

Crystal turned over and sat up in the bed. "Before you arrived today, I was thinking about telling you I thought it best if we don't see one another anymore. But after spending the whole day with you and feeling your love for me, I've come to realize it's what I want. I enjoy what you give me. I enjoy feeling like you have my back, like you have my best interests at heart."

Roger sat on the bed next to her. "So, what are you telling me?"

"That I'm ready to be your girl."

Roger responded by leaning over and placing his lips on hers. "Do you know how long I've waited to hear those words?"

Crystal started unbuttoning Roger's shirt and told him, "Make love to me, Roger. Make love to me like it's our first time together."

As Roger stood up to undress, Crystal's phone started to ring.

"Don't answer it," Roger said.

"I have to. I'm expecting my mother to call. I promise I won't forget where we left off." Crystal leaned over and picked up the phone. It was Susan.

"I'm just calling to remind you about tomorrow. Please be here early. I'm going to need the support of my best friend."

Crystal smiled. Susan and Timothy's wedding date was one day away, and it was a pleasure knowing they were starting a new drug-free life together.

"I won't forget," she reassured Susan, "Remember, you are not alone in this."

When Crystal hung up, she was smiling. Roger asked, "What are you smiling about?"

How could Crystal explain to him all the changes that the women in the office made over the past six months? Would he understand the significance of it? She decided not to try.

It was best kept between sister girls.

PLEASE EMAIL THE AUTHOR AT
<u>msangelhunter@aol.com</u>
AND CHECK OUT HER WEBSITE AT
<u>WWW.MSANGELHUNTER.COM</u>